Hannah Emery



frag...

events...

my family, ... Saturday

going out for ch... and having cosy weekends

away. I live in Black... husband and our little girl.

Find out more at hannahcemery.wordpress.com and follow me on Twitter @hannahcemery.

# *The Secrets of Castle du Rêve*

HANNAH EMERY

A division of HarperCollins*Publishers*
www.harpercollins.co.uk

Harper*Impulse* an imprint of
HarperCollins*Publishers*
1 London Bridge Street
London SE1 9GF

www.harpercollins.co.uk

A Paperback Original 2016

First published in Great Britain in ebook format by Harper*Impulse* 2016



A catalogue record for this book
is available from the British Library

ISBN: 9780008171872



Set in Minion by Palimpsest Book Production Ltd, Falkirk, Stirlingshire

Printed and bound in Great Britain

*For Jessica and Isobel*

# *The Castle of Dreams*

*Look around you. Look at the golden stone of the walls, glistening with history and secrets. Look at the elegant, arched windows that shine with the rich colours of the past. You stand in what was once the dining room of the enchanting Castle du Rêve. Some say that if you listen closely enough, you will be able to hear the distant music of a grand medieval banquet in the main hall, the trotting of noble horses across the courtyard, the whispering of voices long dead.*

*Castle du Rêve was built for Edward du Rêve following the Norman Conquest. For hundreds of years, the castle was known by all of Silenshore for lavish banquets, indulgence and pleasure. Some of the castle has been replaced since those strange medieval times, but its legacy remains ensnared in the walls that stand around you.*

*During World War II, Castle du Rêve became the home to evacuee children from London, who were hosted by Robert and Catherine du Rêve. The children were astonished to begin their strange new lives in the castle, for the ways of the du Rêves were so very different from the ones they had left behind. The du Rêves continued, in spite of the gloom that pervaded the country, to throw opulent parties and serve mysteriously copious amounts of butter, and dance as though everything was wonderful. Children were seen running through the lush green gardens, playing in the courtyard and riding well-groomed ponies across the cobbles.*

*It was after the war that the castle became blanketed in mystery. For in spite of the du Rêves' generosity, their fortune appeared to run out suddenly. One night they vanished from the castle without a trace and within a few weeks, Silenshore University opened. The warm glow of glittering lights faded from within and became replaced with piles of books and the shouts of students. The life of the castle as a private home, and as Castle du Rêve, was over.*

*The du Rêves have not been seen by anybody since they left the castle. Some say that their wealth was in land only: that they drowned in rising taxes and repairs needed on the castle, and sold it to the University before the grand estate crumbled into a tragic ruin. After all, castles do not glitter without some gold behind them.*

*Others say that the du Rêves were always rich, but that a scandal forced them to pack their shimmering finery and shoot off into the frozen twilight, never to be seen again.*

*It is possible that the du Rêves returned to France after hundreds of years in England. Some say they left something here, more than the memory of sparkling jewels and charming smiles and balls. They whisper that one or more of the du Rêves are amongst us, living a life so different from the one of wealth and plenty that they had. Perhaps this is so. Perhaps there is a du Rêve beside you, or behind you. Perhaps you are a du Rêve yourself. Perhaps you will never know.*

**V. Lace, 1964**
**Silenshore University**

# PART ONE

# CHAPTER 1

## *Isobel 2010*

*My Queen,*

*I'm writing to you because I don't quite know what else to do.*

*You told me that you were going with Sally to take care of her aunt, but I saw Sally working in Clover's today. I asked how her aunt was, and she said that she doesn't have an aunt.*

*If it hadn't been for Sally's name badge then I would perhaps have doubted myself. But I know it was her, and so I know that what you told me wasn't the truth.*

*I want to see you. Where are you? Why are you hiding from me? Please, stop running from me and, if you get this, write back to me. Tell me.*

*Yours,*
*H.*

Isobel sits watching strands of her brittle auburn hair float to the ground like autumn leaves.

Today is a day for change.

As she stares at herself in the vast mirror, Isobel thinks of Tom and watches her lips curve into a small, excited smile. She hasn't had her hair cut since she met him. But Tom seems to be the type of man who will notice a shorter, blunter cut. He'll notice, and he'll like it.

The hairdresser is intrigued by the developments in Isobel's love life since her last haircut. She asks forthright questions about Tom as she snips into ribbons of Isobel's hair. Isobel answers each question precisely, her words singing along with the hum of hairdryers and the clicking of straighteners. She could talk about him all day long if she had to.

*They've been together for about a month.*

*He was married, but he's been divorced for ages.*

*He's a chef at an Italian restaurant in Ashwood.*

*He lives in a flat at the promenade end of Silenshore.*

*He's older than Isobel, but that doesn't matter for now.*

It's just as there's a lull in conversation, as she sits in the swivelling leather chair with only her own gigantic reflection to look at, that Isobel feels a colossal wave of nausea rising through her body.

'Fringe?' the hairdresser asks, her scissors poised at Isobel's pale forehead.

Isobel nods, not because she wants a fringe, but because the sickness is so all-consuming that she can't speak and she can't think.

This is the third time this has happened in the past week.

Isobel brings her hand up to her mouth, the black cape that the hairdresser put on her spreading like a raven's wing and spilling her hair ends out onto the floor. She closes her eyes, tries to forget how potent the toxic smells of bleach and shampoo are. She takes a breath, and then another, and wonders for a moment if it's passed. But then, like a momentarily still wave, the nausea roars up again, spilling from Isobel in a humiliating fountain of vomit. It spills out from her hands, through her fingers, splashing out onto the tiled floor.

The hairdresser steps back and Isobel wipes her mouth with her sleeve, then immediately regrets it.

'I am so, so sorry,' she says quietly, her mouth vile with acid.

'Don't worry about it. I'll grab the mop,' the hairdresser says, clattering the scissors down next to a pile of glossy magazines.

After the hairdresser has mopped the floor and Isobel has given her the revolting cape in a crumpled, ruined ball, and she has taken off her favourite polka-dot top, sitting in her denim jacket over her bra in silent horror while the hairdresser quickly finishes the cut and talks about sickness bugs, Isobel pays and leaves the salon. She climbs the ascending cobbles shakily, looking up to where Silenshore Castle High School sprawls. It's a grey afternoon and the golden stone of the castle is blackened by the dark sky. Isobel can see her classroom in the left turret, shrouded in half-term stillness. She's taught English at the castle for four years now. She can't imagine doing anything else.

Tearing her gaze away from the school, Isobel focuses on the line of shops at her side. A flash of panic sears through her as she marches into Boots, picks up what she needs and pays. When she reaches her flat, she hears her flatmate Iris calling hello, and asking what her haircut's like. Without answering, Isobel stumbles to the bathroom, pulling the box from the Boots carrier and tearing into the packaging. Iris calls her again, but Isobel can't shout anything back. Hot fear melts her insides as she stares at the two lines slowly appearing on the white stick in her hands.

She hears a wail and it's only when the bathroom door opens and sees Iris's eyes wide with panic that Isobel realises it was her own wail, and that she's still wailing now.

'Isobel! What's happened?' Iris asks. Then her eyes drop from Isobel's face to the test she's holding. 'Oh God.' She comes closer, peels the test from Isobel's fingers and stares at it.

'I'm going to go to Tom's. I'll tell him he doesn't have to be involved. He won't want to keep it. It's too soon. It won't work.' Isobel says, her voice high and shaking.

'You're in shock,' Iris says. She gives the test back to Isobel and squeezes her shoulder. 'Come out when you're ready. I'll get the kettle on.'

When Isobel comes out of the bathroom, Iris is standing in their tiny kitchen, stirring two steaming mugs. She hands one to Isobel.

'Sit down, breathe, and have this before you do anything or go anywhere.'

Isobel stays standing and takes a gulp. It's way too hot. Scalding pain sears through her. She spits it out into the cluttered kitchen sink, but it's too late: the inside of her mouth feels burnt and raw. She slams the cup down on the worktop, the boiling liquid sloshing over the rim onto her hand, making an ugly red patch on her skin.

'I'm going to see Tom,' she says. She pulls off her denim jacket and grabs a t-shirt from where it's been drying on the radiator near the front door. It's one of Iris's, one that she sleeps in. But her own polka dot top is still stuffed in her bag, covered in vomit. She should take it out of her bag, get changed into something that at least belongs to her and wait for her tea to cool down. She should phone Tom to check that he's in and she should sit down and think about how to deal with this logically. But she can't.

She swings open the door, yells goodbye to Iris and is gone.

It starts to rain almost as soon as Isobel steps out onto the street. The rain in Silenshore always tastes of salt: bitter and sharp. It runs down her face, into her mouth as she rushes forwards.

'This can't be happening', she says to herself. A passerby looks at her cautiously from the other side of the road, because it obviously isn't normal to talk to yourself and Isobel usually knows this and manages to stop herself doing it. But not today.

'No, no, no.' Her words are lost as she walks closer to the crashing sea. She looks out to the beach and sees sand and rocks darkened by the black skies. Her head throbs. It's too cold to just be wearing a t-shirt and the wind bites at her skin. How can it be almost winter already? When Isobel first met Tom just over a month ago, it was a cloudless September day, bright with the heat of late summer. Silenshore Castle High School was hosting the first-ever summer fair in its own grounds. Isobel was in charge of a second-hand bookstall, her shoulders burning fluorescent pink in the sun. The day smelt of dry, hot paperbacks and coins dampened by moist hands; of barbecued beef burgers and sausages that were being served to the meandering crowds by the school chef. It was as Isobel was rearranging the curling books on her stall that she felt a shadow descend on her. A customer, she thought idly, or a colleague. But then she lifted her eyes and saw Tom.

'Any recommendations?' he asked, gesturing towards the pile of titles that was spread across the foldout table.

His cool green eyes were almost translucent in the sun and his smile was wide and white. His face was exquisite. Isobel suddenly felt dizzy. She clutched the edge of the table, hoping he wouldn't notice the effect he was having on her.

'What kind of thing are you looking for?'

The man put his hand up to mask his face from the sun as he spoke. 'Something a bit different, I think.'

'Well, there's a good pile of mysteries here. A book of fairy tales, though that's probably not your style. Or there's this one, a crime thriller? That might be the most manly of the bunch.'

'I'm gratified that you think that's what would suit me,' the man said, his arm still poised crookedly over his head. His hair was dark, flecked at the sides with the kind of grey that made a man more distinguished and attractive. He was older than Isobel, but not too old. Definitely not too old.

'I'll tell you what,' Isobel said, bending and taking out a paper bag from the pile under the table. 'If you promise not to tell anyone, I'll give it to you for free.'

She felt a thrill run through her at the flirtation she heard in her voice. Freebies because the customer was a gorgeous older man had not been something they'd talked about in the endless staff meetings about the fair. She imagined telling Iris, both of them hooting with laughter.

'Okay,' the man said after a minute. 'How about this? I'll take it as a review copy. And then once I've read it, I'll take you out for dinner and tell you what I thought.'

Isobel scribbled her number down on the inside cover, her hands trembling slightly, and then handed him the book in a blue paper bag.

'I'm Tom,' he said, holding out his hand for her to shake. His was cool, in spite of the roaring heat. As she gazed at his face, she wondered for a frightening moment if he might be the father of one of her pupils. She did some quick calculations. Could be possible.

'I'm Isobel Blythe. I teach English. Do you know one of the pupils here, or…' her words drifted off as Tom shook his head.

'No. I don't know the school at all. I just find the castle fascinating. I've always wanted to visit and have a look around, but never had the opportunity. I saw a poster advertising the fair today and thought I'd wander up.'

'I'm glad you did,' Isobel smiled, relieved.

'Me too,' said Tom. And as Isobel watched him wrap the bag tightly around the book and place it in his back pocket, her world shifted. The day was simple and incredible, bright with heat and possibility.

And now, it is almost winter and everything is different.

She stands on Tom's doorstep, blinking back rain and tears and takes a deep, shaking breath. Perhaps he's not in. Perhaps she'll need to go to Ashwood and see if he's working, because she can't remember if he said he was. She turns away from the door to his flat, but then he's there with her, taking her hands in his and asking what's wrong, asking her why she's crying.

She says the words but she can't tell if he's taken them in, because he stands still and stares at her and doesn't seem to respond.

'I'm pregnant, Tom,' she says again. Panic shoots through her, erupting like a firework in the pit of her stomach.

He pales, swallows. 'Come in.'

## CHAPTER 2

# *Evelyn: 1939*

The day of the evacuees it was as though Evelyn was in a snow globe and somebody had picked it up and shaken it roughly, so that she and everything that was familiar to her came loose and floated about.

There were fifteen evacuees in total, and they were sent to Castle du Rêve because their homes and schools in London weren't safe any more. Evelyn didn't know much about the war, because whenever her parents talked about it, they spoke in whispers that hung in the air like cobwebs, too high for Evelyn to reach and untangle. But she had gathered that the southeast coast, places dotted around Hastings, like Silenshore, were much safer than London, and that this was the reason for other children coming, rather suddenly, to live with them.

On the day that they were due to arrive, Evelyn waited impatiently at her bedroom window. She was frenzied with excitement, her fingers tapping on the sill restlessly. She had told herself she shouldn't move from this spot, because she didn't want to miss the first glimpse of the other children. She didn't want to miss anything. Evelyn's bedroom was in one of the turrets of the Castle du Rêve, with rounded walls and an arched window that rose so high it almost touched the ceiling. Through her window, beyond the shining leaves of the trees outside, Evelyn could see the silver sea and a boat bobbing in the distance. She wondered how the evacuees would arrive.

A year ago, Richard the chauffeur would perhaps have brought some of the children back in his long black car. But he'd gone to war now, his face red with excitement about what Evelyn thought might be a more thrilling life. She wondered if Richard might be back soon, when the war was all done with. She'd heard whispers of their daily, Elizabeth, leaving them too, her father hissing that she'd simply have to stay, that they couldn't do without her, and her mother sighing, and then her father saying they'd just have to see what happened. If Elizabeth was going, nobody had told Evelyn, but then again, nobody ever really told Evelyn anything, even though she was almost eleven.

When Evelyn had been sitting at her window for what seemed like a whole year, an ugly red bus swung into the drive. She watched, her stomach flipping with excitement as children jumped down from the doors of the bus, each holding a suitcase. How on earth would Evelyn pack if she were to leave the castle suddenly? She'd want to take all sorts of things: the hairbrush that her mother had given to her on her birthday, her books, her paints, her special cup that she drank her milk from. Had these children left behind all of their favourite things? She wanted to ask them, to know everything about them this minute. She jumped to her feet and ran along the corridor outside her bedroom, past golden-framed paintings of her grand ancestors, down the wide staircase that swept down the centre of the castle. She reached the front door as it was being pulled open by Elizabeth. The smell hit Evelyn moments later: a strange, potent mix of unbathed flesh, urine and what she could only imagine was the city and its rats and smoky grey houses.

The children looked younger than Evelyn, except for one girl with long legs who was much taller than all the others. They were louder than she'd expected them to be, some chatting, some coughing, others simply making noise by shuffling their feet and banging their brown cases down. They all wore labels around their necks and Evelyn squinted to see what was written on them, but couldn't make out anything except for blurs of numbers and letters.

As she crept closer towards them, some of them noticed her. A boy smiled, revealing crooked teeth with a gap in the very middle. When the tall girl smiled and said hello to Evelyn, she revealed the very same teeth. *Brother and sister*, Evelyn realised as she stared and stared. Some of the children didn't smile at all. Some held onto one another's hands and looked away from her, up at the wooden-panelled ceiling. Others looked down at the polished floor. One boy ran his dirty shoe along it, as though he was testing out ice for skating on.

Evelyn's mother and father appeared at the door behind the children within a few moments. Her father nodded at the group, and her mother touched a few on the shoulder gently as she passed them to enter the castle. Evelyn thought about the children's own mothers and how they might feel about all this. What would it be like to say goodbye to your family? Quite exciting, she supposed.

'Welcome to Castle du Rêve,' Evelyn's mother said, her voice tinkling in the big hallway. 'I'm Catherine du Rêve and this is my husband Robert. We hope you'll all be comfortable here.'

Some of the children laughed and Evelyn felt herself turn red as she wondered what was funny. But her mother didn't seem to notice.

'Elizabeth, our daily, has made up plenty of beds in our spare rooms. If you'd like to get settled, then perhaps have a look round before teatime at five that would be fine. There are some rooms we'd rather you left alone, if you'd be so kind. Elizabeth will show you around and tell you which places must be avoided. I'm very sure we will all live quite peacefully together.'

Evelyn joined in with the line of children as they stormed up the stairs of the castle, their cases banging, their voices high and loud. She felt like one of them, like she *belonged* with them.

*This*, she thought happily, *will change everything.*

The tall girl was called Mary and she was thirteen. The little boy with the matching gapped front teeth was her brother, Sid, and was ten, the same age as Evelyn. Sid was rather loud and ran everywhere instead of walking. Evelyn liked them the most. The other boys seemed to have less energy than Sid. There was a little fat boy with a coat that was too small for him and he was called Derek. He said very little and stared up at everything as though he had no idea where he was. When eggs were served for breakfast the day after they all arrived, he poked at the slimy yolk, his freckled nose wrinkled.

'What is it?' Evelyn saw him whisper to Rita, who was eleven, and had long ginger hair in a tatty plait down her back. Rita shrugged and sliced hers, then popped a piece into her mouth. 'Don't know,' she said as she chewed. 'But it tastes strange.'

Most of the children talked non-stop. It was as though they had all been best friends forever, but, as Mary told Evelyn, most of them had never met before coming to the castle.

'I'm lucky because I've got Sid here with me,' Mary said, before taking an enormous bite of toast. She chewed for a while before carrying on. 'Your parents didn't want to take him at first. They'd got enough of us, I reckon. But I said I wouldn't get on that bus unless he did too. So here he is. But we didn't know any of the others before yesterday, and I don't think any of them knew each other.' Mary swallowed and smiled, and Evelyn saw that the crooked teeth were a pale shade of mustard. Mary didn't seem to care and smiled broadly as she talked, which made her look pretty all the same. 'Perhaps,' she continued, 'we'll see more of our friends who we know from home when we go to school. We're going to the school on the High Street. Do you go there too?'

Evelyn shook her head. She'd seen the school before when she'd walked with Miss Silver to the promenade: a tall building that was surrounded by what looked like marshy fields. She'd never been inside, but imagined it to be loud and full of strong smells like ink and cabbage and boys. 'No,' she replied quietly. 'I have a governess, so I do my lessons here in the castle.'

'At home? That must be a bit lonely. I can't say I fancy staying at home all day every day.'

'It's boring,' Evelyn said. 'That's why it's good that you're here.' She wished that she could have breakfast with Mary every morning. It was only because Evelyn's father had gone out early that day that Evelyn had been allowed to sit in the kitchen with them, instead of in the dining room.

'I'm not sure it should be a regular habit,' Mrs du Rêve had said that morning. 'Your father won't like it. But perhaps, as they've just arrived, one day won't hurt.' She'd stroked Evelyn's hair and smiled her beautiful smile.

'Your castle is wonderful. But I don't know if I'd much like not having any school friends. You're missing out a bit,' Mary said now, as she cut into her egg decisively.

'Yes,' Evelyn said, pushing her own breakfast around her plate. Food tasted different in the kitchen, as though it had been soured by all the smells of cooking and boiling of copper pans and people. 'I am.'

'Was London frightening?' Evelyn asked Mary one day after the children had been at the castle for about a week. They had been running around the castle grounds with the other children, playing hide and seek, but the game had come to an end now and Evelyn and Mary were in the bedroom that the evacuees were sharing. It was the first time Evelyn had ever been in this room: she'd never had a need to before. The unpleasant smell that she had noticed when the evacuees first arrived lingered in here, attached to the socks and teddy bears and slippers and handkerchiefs that the children had brought with them.

Mary shrugged. 'No, it wasn't that frightening. There was nothing really happening. The war will all be over soon anyway. I can't wait until it is.'

'Is that yours?' Evelyn asked, as she noticed a doll lying on the floor.

'Yes,' Mary said. 'I know I'm a bit old for dolls, really. But she reminds me of home, and so I couldn't help bring her. I didn't know where on earth I would end up, so I wanted something of mine with me other than a flannel and a coat.'

'She's so beautiful,' Evelyn said. She'd had doll after doll, and still received the occasional one at Christmas or on birthdays. But this one was nicer, somehow, than all of Evelyn's. Although she'd obviously been played with over and over again, and her paint was chipping, her black hair was threaded with strands of sparkle, and her dress was embroidered with glimmering thread.

'Here,' Mary said, handing Evelyn the doll. 'Have a proper look.'

'I like things that sparkle,' Evelyn said, stroking the doll's hair. 'There's something special about such beautiful things, don't you think?'

Mary laughed. 'I suppose there is. You're lucky. There's enough sparkle in this castle to last you a lifetime,'

Evelyn shrugged. 'I don't feel as though there is. I'm dying to explore other places. It's been more fun in the castle with you here, though. I'll be lonely when you all go back home.'

'I won't have chance to be lonely,' Mary said with a huff. 'I'll be going straight to work after I've finished school. And then I'll just have to hope someone marries me. You're lucky, Evelyn. You're beautiful. I'll be lucky to even get an offer.'

'That's not true,' said Evelyn. 'You're beautiful too. And strong and brave, and kind.'

Mary gave a snort of laughter. 'Boys don't want strength and bravery from a girl, Evelyn. They want golden hair and big blue eyes, like yours. You know,' Mary said, staring down at the doll on the bed, 'your beauty could get you to all sorts of places.'

'I hope so. I want to be in films. I want to live in Hollywood and be famous,' Evelyn said, her heart fluttering at just the thought.

'You could be. You could do anything. Especially now. The war's going to change everything, Evelyn. And when it does, you should be ready.'

That night, Evelyn's parents threw one of their parties at the castle. Evelyn and the children weren't allowed downstairs, of course. But after the most elaborate furniture in the castle had been dragged around from room to room, and Elizabeth had scurried up and down the staircase a hundred times, and the kitchen seemed to glow with the preparation of all the food that would be given to the guests; when the first chords of music began to echo through the castle, Evelyn beckoned for the children to follow her upstairs to her bedroom. They threw themselves up the staircase breathlessly, falling into Evelyn's room all at once.

'We can have our own party in here,' Evelyn said, her eyes shining. 'I always pretend I'm having a party of my own, and tonight it will be the best ever, because you're all here too!'

She took Mary's hand, which was cool in hers, and they danced together, giggling as Mary's feet tangled around Evelyn's. The other children danced too, laughing as they bumped into one another. When they couldn't dance any more for laughing, they collapsed on the floor of Evelyn's bedroom, out of breath.

'Are you all hungry?' Evelyn asked, and as the children nodded, she pulled out from under her bed a tray of rich buttery food that she had sneaked out of the kitchen earlier on. They sat and ate cakes and biscuits, the smells of the party from downstairs floating up around them: a mixture of sweet perfumes and sugar and wine.

'This is the best party I've ever been to,' said Derek, a smear of cream on his lip.

'Me too,' said Mary.

Sid shrugged. 'It's okay. But we could make it even more exciting. Let's play a game of dares.'

Derek sat up straighter. 'Dares in a castle!' he said, his eyes wide. 'Yes, let's!'

And so they played. Sid dared Derek to run downstairs and take a sip of somebody's champagne. He was gone for a while, and when he came back, he hiccupped loudly. 'Champagne's horrible,' he said.

Mary stood up. 'I'll do the same dare. I want to taste champagne.' She darted from the room, but a few minutes later she was back, clutching her sides and laughing. 'They saw me before I could get a sip! I told them I'd got lost and they showed me back up here.'

'Well that's the end of that,' said Sid. 'They'll be looking out for us now. We need some new dares. Evelyn, it's your turn. What shall we make her do?' he asked the group.

'Well, going downstairs is no good for Evelyn. She lives here, so there's not much that's daring about that,' Sid said, frowning with the effort needed to think of a good dare.

'What about if you go somewhere in the castle you're not allowed to go?' Derek said. 'That would be a proper dare.'

'I could go in my parents' room. I'm not really allowed in there.'

'Yes!' Sid shouted, his eyes wide with the excitement of the game. 'Do that and bring something for us to see from their room. Something we won't have seen before.'

Evelyn stumbled to her feet and thought for a minute. Then she grinned.

'Wait here.'

She knew exactly where the mirror was. She remembered the first time she'd ever seen it, when her mother was looking into it and didn't know Evelyn was there. It was the most beautiful thing Evelyn had ever seen, covered in what looked like shimmering blue diamonds.

'Can I have a look?' she'd asked. Her mother had spun around.

'Evelyn! I didn't know you were in here. You can look. But do not touch. This mirror has been in my family for generations. It's very valuable.'

Evelyn had stared down into the glass, her round face and golden hair framed by the sparkling stones.

'Don't ever touch it,' her mother had said, sliding the mirror into her dressing table drawer and closing it firmly. 'Promise me, Evelyn?'

'Yes,' Evelyn had said, with her fingers crossed behind her back.

Now, Evelyn raced to her parents' room, her heart thumping in time with the music that floated up from the party. She glanced around to check that nobody could see her before she flung the drawer open and took out the mirror. Holding it took her breath away: it was heavy and sharp, the stones pricking her skin as she clutched it and ran back to her own bedroom.

'I've got this,' she announced breathlessly as she returned to the other children. 'My mother told me that I wasn't allowed to have it, or even touch it.' Her face burned: she was thrilled and frightened all at once. Her heart thumped and thumped in her chest as Mary gasped over the mirror and Sid fingered the glass. But there was no need to be scared, Evelyn reminded herself.

It was just a mirror, and she would put it back soon.

Nobody would ever know.

# CHAPTER 3

# *Isobel 2010*

*My Queen,*
*It's fortunate that I know where you live, because if I couldn't write to you, I would most probably expire: a brutal, red death. I only hope that these letters will be passed onto you, and that you will write back to me and tell me where you are. I have visited Lace Antiques seven times this week. I have had to buy a painting of a rather ugly dog and a chipped crystal vase to keep your father happy. I wanted neither. I only want you.*

*Please, tell me my dear. Where have you gone?*

*H*

Seconds pass, and Tom still doesn't speak. Isobel stands in the doorway to his lounge, staring at the television, where cars tear around a black track that's glossy with rain. The whirring of the engines makes her want to scream. She sees the remote on the arm of the sofa, seizes it, mutes the cars and then tosses it back down. But then there is silence, which is somehow even worse. She squeezes her eyes shut and tries to take a steady breath, but panic still roars inside her.

'Tom,' she says, her eyes still closed. As she speaks, she feels his arms closing around her. She clutches onto him.

'When?' he asks eventually.

She hasn't even thought about this. She counts now, losing track once and having to start again. Isobel doesn't understand her body like other women seem to. She can't say for definite when she missed a period because they come and go with no warning. 'June, I think.' Her thoughts flit against each other and tears spill out again, her head throbbing. 'Yes, end of June. It's too soon. We can't do it. You don't have to—'. She opens her eyes, sees Tom through her tears: his ashen shock, his wide eyes.

'I should go,' she says next, turning from him so abruptly that the room spins. 'I'll leave you to it for a bit. You don't need me here, in a mess like this.'

'Isobel.' Tom's voice is sharp but kind, his grip on her arm firm but gentle. 'Come on. Sit down.' He goes to the tiny kitchen and roots around in the fridge, taking out a can of Coke and handing it to her. 'Here.'

She's sitting on the couch when he comes and sits so close to her that it almost feels like they are one person. He watches her swig from the icy can, waits for her to swallow and take a few deep breaths so that she can listen to what he has to say.

'This is our issue. We'll be shocked together, and we'll sort it out together. You're going nowhere.'

It's as if Tom has clicked a switch inside Isobel. She takes a wobbly breath and another gulp of her drink. Her trembling hands begin to still and her banging heart quietens.

'I'm stunned,' Tom continues, his hand resting on her knee, his other hand rubbing his face. 'But I love you, Isobel. And I want us to really think about this. I want us to think about whether it's something we can do. For what it's worth, I think it probably is.'

Isobel stares at him. 'You do?'

His eyes fix on something that Isobel can't see. They are soft green, crinkled slightly around the edges by life. His lashes are thick, dark and straight. 'Yes. I really do.'

She thinks for a minute. June. Next summer, a pram, a tiny little pink person. Tom, holding the baby, shushing it and rocking it gently. 'Maybe,' she says, the word making her lighter somehow. Anxiety still claws at her and shock ripples through her body. But the raw terror has cleared. She leans her head against Tom's shoulder, inhaling his warm scent of mint, herbs, an earthy aftershave she doesn't know the name of. He turns and kisses her gently, and for a split second she feels as though there's nothing wrong at all.

'I don't know how it'll work,' she says as she nestles back into Tom and puts her feet up beside her. 'But I trust you.' She takes the remote from where she threw it down on the sofa just after she arrived and turns the TV back on. The racing has stopped. The winner is being interviewed, beaming through his helmet.

They watch for a while, curled together like cats. Isobel's mind whirs steadily through hundreds of thoughts. She gazes around Tom's flat and thinks of her own. They are both so small.

But they have until June. She closes her eyes again, presses her body against Tom's.

The first day back after half term is one of those days that never gets light. November darkness lingers in Isobel's classroom: even with the lights on, it's dingy. The English department is based in one of the round turrets at the top, with an arched window that rises so high it almost touches the ceiling. Isobel taps out emails on her laptop as the pupils work, glancing now and again around the room and out of the huge windows at the side of her desk.

The sky outside is a brooding purple-grey. Seagulls swoop past, cawing like rooks. The trees along the entrance to the school are almost skeletal now that winter is coming, their branches clawing in the wind. Between the trees, the grey sea churns in the distance. Isobel loves the view, loves this classroom. She can sense the past here, seeping from the huge stone bricks. When she can, Isobel weaves into her lessons stories about the castle and its past. She makes the younger classes write stories about the ghosts that might be trapped in the walls, about the horses and soldiers that might have trotted across the courtyard and the grand people who lived here when it was first built hundreds of years ago. She tells them about the enigmatic Edward du Rêve, whom the castle was built for, and how his family stayed here for generations. She tells them about how later, the chateau-style castle was used as Silenshore University for over forty years.

Isobel remembers her mother telling her stories about the strange disappearance of the du Rêves. She tries to recall the details now, as she watches silver raindrops begin to gather on the windowpanes. She sees scenes from a long time ago in her mind: images of sitting up in bed, her hair in a plait so that it would be crimped in the morning, her mother sitting on the pale-pink chair in the corner of the room with her long, thin legs crossed as she told Isobel stories to send her to sleep. Words come back to Isobel now, shrouded in her mother's voice: *they just vanished!* But Isobel can't remember the details. There are so many fragments of conversations with her mother that lie in Isobel's mind like bits of broken china. If she thinks about them too closely, or tries to touch them, their sharp edges sting her.

She clears her throat and a few of the more restless pupils look up from their biro scrawls, eyes round with hope that the lesson is over. When Isobel announces that it is, there's a sigh of contentment and a final rustle of papers. She clicks her laptop shut and collects the answers in, the thought of what she needs to do now that her working day is over looming in her mind.

When she reaches the bottom of the main staircase, Isobel turns away from the double doors that lead into the main hall and reception area, and instead pulls open the side door and steps into the wet afternoon. Impressive as it is, Silenshore Castle has too many secret exits to be a high school: teachers and children escape all too often. Isobel should stay and do her marking, and normally she would. But today, she can't concentrate until she has seen her father.

Blythe Finances is about halfway down Castle Street, between the Co-op and Wheels chippy. Isobel regrets not bringing her car as the raindrops hammer down on her like needles. She has an umbrella, but the hostile wind whips it out of shape. By the time she arrives at the shop, rain has seeped through her pumps, her feet squelching unpleasantly as she pulls open the door.

Isobel's dad sits at his usual desk, surrounded by files and Post-its. He looks away from his screen briefly and smiles as he sees Isobel.

'Izzie! What brings you here?'

She shrugs. 'Thought we needed a catch-up. Got time?'

Graham clicks his mouse a few times and glances at his watch. 'Jon's finished, so there's only me here. I've just got a few phone calls to make, but then I've got a bit of time.'

'I can wait,' Isobel says. 'I'll go up to the flat, shall I?'

'Go on, then,' her dad says. 'I'll be up as soon as I'm done.'

Isobel surveys the lounge as she reaches the flat. A dining table that used to be the family one, on which she knows her clandestine initials are carved somewhere, sags with junk in the corner. There are no dining chairs: they've somehow all disappeared over time. The whole room seems wrong: the lampshade isn't straight, the clock is four hours fast. A curling rug lies in the centre of the small room, fuzzy with cat hair. The perpetrator of the fuzz, Duke, licks his paws dolefully next to Isobel. The curtains are drawn, as they always are. She can see a crack of her father's bedroom through the open door. His bed is unmade, his room littered with books and clothes.

Isobel shakes her head and pulls out her phone. She has a message from Tom.

*Hope it goes okay. Can't wait to see you later. T xxx*

She taps out a reply as she waits for her dad to come up. He might be a while. He's more and more involved in the business lately, and less inclined to spend time with Isobel. It's fine, she tells herself, because he's busy and he's okay and that's the main thing. But it's not like it used to be.

After fifteen minutes of flicking through her phone, Isobel stands up, restless. Just as she reaches for the door, it opens, and her dad hurries in.

'Sorry, sorry,' he says. 'I just needed to get those phone calls made.'

Isobel sits down on the old brown sofa and gestures for her dad to do the same.

'That's okay. Are you done for the day now?'

'No. I'll go back down for a bit, I think. Plenty to be getting on with, as usual. So, what's new?' he asks.

'Well,' she begins.

Her father pats his knee for Duke to join him. The cat springs up and curls on his lap. 'Yes. We're listening.'

'I've met someone. A man. It's going brilliantly.'

'I'm so pleased. That's great. And?'

'Why does there have to be more?'

'With a man, there's always more.'

Isobel shakes her head and laughs. Then there's a silence until Duke begins purring loudly, the glottal sounds filling the room.

'I'm pregnant, Dad.'

As she blurts the words out, Isobel remembers all the other things she has blurted out to her father over the years. *I'm doing teacher training, I've got a job at Silenshore Castle High School, I'm going to rent a flat with Iris*. Her mother always spoke softly, prepped them carefully, built a platform for whatever she was going to say. Isobel has never been like that. She can't ever think of words other than those that are on her mind. The words she wants to say blink, fluorescent and blinding. No others can be seen. She tries to look at her father but his eyes are lowered.

'Dad?'

'Are you happy?' he asks eventually, looking up at her.

'I'm really happy. I panicked at first,' she admits. 'I'm still kind of scared, I suppose.'

'Oh, everyone's always scared of something, Izzie. So if that's all you have to contend with, then things aren't so bad.'

They chat for a few minutes. Graham asks when the baby will arrive, and they speculate on if it might be a girl or boy. Isobel tells her father trivial things about Tom: his shifts at the restaurant in Ashwood, his good dress sense, his flat. She makes some tea and quickly wipes the kitchen worktop while she waits for the kettle to boil. There are breadcrumbs, hard pellets of rice and shiny slivers of cheese stuck to her cloth when she's finished. The tang of fish lingers in the air of the small kitchen, which mixes with the scent of tea and makes Isobel gag behind her sleeve.

For once, her father doesn't snap or take offence that she has cleaned a surface and tried to make his flat more inhabitable. But after they have drunk their tea, Graham stands up.

'I'd better get back down to the office.'

Isobel looks up at him as he stands, preoccupied, waiting for her to let him go back to bury his head in his paperwork. It's been the same for over two years now, since that slow, inevitable morning when her mother died. Isobel's dad always worked hard when Isobel was a child, but he usually made sure he finished in time to help her with her homework or watch Blue Peter together or eat pizza on a Friday night. Now, it's as though his family mode has been switched off, and Isobel can't find how to turn it back on, to tune him back into her.

'Come on, then. I'm going to Tom's anyway,' she says. As they clatter down the uncarpeted stairs, a sweet, warm scent blooms in the air and overpowers the smell of frying fish and chips and vinegar from next door.

'I can smell the bread again,' Isobel says. The office downstairs used to be her grandparents' bakery. Even though bread hasn't been baked here for over thirty years, every now and again the overbearing aromas of yeast and flour, sugar and butter waft through the air.

'It's trapped in the walls. They don't want us to ever forget it,' Graham says. He says it every time they smell the bread. Even though Isobel has heard it so many times, it still makes her feel uneasy, as though the spirits of her grandparents are watching them from somewhere, their faces dusted white with flour and death.

They reach the bottom and she gives her father a brief hug. He looks down at her, at her stomach.

'Doesn't look like there's much in there yet,' he observes.

'No, I know. I suppose it's only a matter of time, though.'

He lifts a hand and places it gently on her belly, his unexpected touch warm and heavy. They stand for a moment, not speaking, until he moves his hand away. Isobel smiles at him, surprised and glad.

'I think you'll be just fine,' he says.

When Tom swings open the door to his flat later that night, the sugary smell of cooked apples swirls in the air. He's wearing a grey t-shirt, and to see him uncharacteristically casual makes Isobel smile and reach up to kiss him. He lingers, his hands around her waist. 'I've been thinking about you all day. How are you feeling?'

'Okay,' Isobel says, feeling a broad grin spread over her face. 'I'm feeling good today, actually. And something in here smells fantastic. It's making me hungry.'

'That's because I'm doing one of my specialities. You're going to love it.'

'I'm loving the t-shirt too,' she says, touching the soft grey cotton. 'I usually like a man in a suit,' she says with a wink. 'But you really pull off casual.'

Tom laughs. 'Well, that's a relief. How did it go with your dad?'

'He was fine with it. Calmer than I was. I think I expected him to freak out. But I'm not sure why. Maybe it's because I freaked out.'

'Maybe it's because you're his little girl. That's a bit of a cliché, though, I suppose.'

Isobel shakes her head. 'I'm not sure. To be honest, since Mum died, I feel like we're not that close. It felt a bit weird even telling him about you. I don't speak to him that much about real life these days. He's always distracted by work. But today was good, I suppose, because I had to talk to him properly, and I suppose he had to listen.'

'I'm glad,' Tom says. 'I felt a bit nervous, actually. Dads can be funny about who their daughters end up with, can't they?'

Isobel smiles. 'I think he could see how happy you make me. That helped.'

The words are luminous and dance around them. Tom's face brightens and he leans down to kiss Isobel. After her long day, Isobel wants to melt into him, into his scent of herbs and wine. She pulls him closer and they linger over their kiss until Tom pulls away reluctantly.

'Dinner calls,' he says apologetically, going over to the hob.

'Isn't this like being at work?' Isobel asks. 'I'd have thought you'd be sick of cooking for other people. I was expecting a microwave meal. Or a takeaway.'

'A man in a suit and a microwave meal?' Tom laughs. 'You had some strange expectations, Isobel Blythe.'

Isobel laughed. 'Well, all I can say is that you've exceeded my expectations anyway, as always. I can't wait to taste your cooking. What are we having?' She sits down at the small glass table.

Tom clears his throat and whips a white tea towel over his shoulder. '*Filet mignon de porc Normande*,' he says with an uncharacteristically dramatic flourish of the hands. 'Normandy Pork.'

'It smells amazing. Is this a throwback from your time in

France?' Isobel remembers Tom mentioning that he spent a year or so living in France when they first met.

'Yes, I suppose it is. I tried this dish for the first time there, although I never cooked it. I didn't cook much when I lived in France. I mostly existed on bread and cheese. Have you been to France?'

'No. But I know a lot about Paris because Iris really wants to go. She's obsessed.'

'She's got good taste. It's not a bad place to be obsessed with.' Tom says as he stirs the pot on his sleek black hob. 'What about you? Where's your number-one destination?'

'Vienna,' Isobel replies quickly. 'I've always wanted to go to Vienna.'

Tom smiles and comes to sit at the table. 'The city of dreams?'

Isobel nods. 'I even love that it's called that.'

'I've never been. But I'd definitely go. We'll add it to our list.'

'Our list?'

'Yeah. You know: have a baby, then go to France and then do Vienna.'

Isobel laughs. 'That's a pretty short list.'

'Well, we need to keep it manageable.' Tom scores a match and lights some tea lights on the table, and then goes back to the kitchen.

'Actually,' Isobel says, standing up and following Tom. 'I kind of have a thing agreed with Iris. She promised to go to Vienna with me. My mum lived there when she was young, and she used to talk about it a lot. She made it sound like something out of a fairy tale: all castles and balls and music. When she died, I suggested to my dad that we should go. He got upset with me, said it was a terrible idea to go there without her, and I haven't brought it up with him since. We had a bit of a falling out about it, which kind of made me even more determined to go.'

Iris had promised Isobel she'd go with her to Vienna on one condition: that they could go to Paris together too. She'd dug out a battered Paris brochure from her bedside drawer and printed out a webpage on Vienna for Isobel. Then she'd taken a shoebox from her wardrobe, tipped out the shoes onto her bed, and put the papers together in there instead. 'This can be our box of dreams,' she'd said.

They had laughed at the drama in Iris's voice, at the clichéd title she had given the box. But they had kept it and filled it with more leaflets and printouts until the sides bulged.

Tom nods. 'I know what you mean. My mum can sometimes be funny about remembering my dad, and things they did when they were young. It's like it just hurts too much to think about the past.'

'I can understand that. But losing her also taught me that life's short. So I try to make the most of it. Obviously, it hurts to think about her sometimes because I miss her so much. But I do want to try and keep her with us, by doing things that she liked. I think that's what she would have wanted me to do. But my dad doesn't seem to think like that.'

'Well, he might come round. But I'm with you. I think Vienna sounds brilliant. And it doesn't matter who you go with, it can still be on the list.'

'Thanks, Tom. That means a lot.'

Tom grins and winks suggestively. 'You can show me exactly how much after dinner. I mean, *Filet mignon de porc Normande.*'

Isobel laughs and sits at the table. 'It's gorgeous,' she says as she bites into a tender piece of pork. The flavours of cider and sweet apples have seeped into the meat and the taste is comforting.

'No nausea?' Tom asks.

'Nope. None at all.' In fact, Isobel's stomach growls as she begins eating. She has another mouthful and takes a piece of warm bread from the basket that Tom has put between them on the table.

'So, do you get to cook much French stuff at work?' she asks when she has finished chewing.

'Not really. It's mostly quite thoughtless Italian food. Pizza and pasta. I don't get to choose the menu, which is a bit frustrating. But this is actually another item for our list,' adds Tom as he slices neatly into his meat. 'I really want to open a French restaurant at some point. I would've done it already, but starting up a business isn't cheap, so I'm having to save up and be patient. It'll happen one day, I'm sure.'

'Where would you open your restaurant?' The restaurant Tom works at now is in the centre of Ashwood, which is a grey and uninspiring town that was mainly built in the 1960s – all concrete estates and uniform buildings and towers of flats. It's impossible to imagine a French restaurant there.

'I'd open it in Silenshore. This place needs to be famous for something other than people going missing and never coming back.'

Isobel thinks of the stories she's heard over the years: of the strange disappearing du Rêve family, of the man who was found dead at the castle in the 1960s, of the girl who was taken away one Valentine's day and was never seen again. 'I think all the mystery makes Silenshore more special,' she says. 'There's something almost mystical about the castle and all its secrets. Plus, if you hadn't been so drawn to the castle, we would never have met.'

'I know. I owe the castle a lot. Like I said when we first talked at the school fair, something has always pulled me to it, although I couldn't tell you exactly what it was.'

'I like to think it's because you somehow knew I was there. That's why you felt you wanted to go through the gates,' Isobel blurts out, then laughs at her own openness.

'You're probably right. At least that's one mystery solved.' Tom says, reaching out for Isobel's hand across the plates and lacing his fingers through hers.

## CHAPTER 4

# *Victoria: 1964*

Victoria would never have even met Harry if it weren't for the rain.

He didn't have any interest in antiques, she realised later, and he certainly didn't need to buy any that afternoon. He only ducked into Lace Antiques because of the fat drops of salty rain that began to drum down on him without any kind of forewarning.

Victoria was sitting behind the counter, staring into a mirror that she'd found that morning. Her father always told her not to touch his things, that he'd box her ears if he found out that she'd been rooting and touching potential money-makers. But the morning had been so very *long*, and the customers who had come into the shop had been frustratingly indifferent to what was out on display. So Victoria had decided to move some of the objects around a little, and then, before she knew it, she was on her hands and knees in the corner, where some stock she'd never seen before was tossed into an old brown suitcase.

Once she had fiddled with the brittle clasp on the case and opened it up, Victoria had found a strange old doll with shimmering black hair and a cracked red smile. There were some discoloured white beads too, which Victoria hung around her neck, the thick, salty fragrance of the case clinging to them and permeating her dress. It was no wonder these things weren't on the shelves. She leant further into the case, almost pulled in by its intoxicating scent. Something silver glinted in the corner and she reached for it.

*You're like a magpie*, her mother had said once, a long time ago. *All that glitters is not gold, darling. You'll end in trouble if you go for everything that sparkles.*

As Victoria tugged the cool, metallic object out of the cavernous case, she saw that it was a beautiful hand mirror, its back encrusted with deep-blue sapphires. She sat back on her heels and turned the mirror over in her hands to see her reflection, then over again to see the glittering dark case, then over again to stare at herself: her pale skin, opaque with youth, her black hair and heavy fringe that sat above her eyes like the brim of a hat.

It was moments after Victoria stared at her unblinking reflection, as a thunder cloud trawled through the sky like a pirate ship, that the shop door swung open, and Victoria fell in love.

Frederick, the shop cat, showed an instant affinity to the man at the door, purring and wheedling around his legs. Victoria, gazing down at Frederick in a moment of panic that he would cover the man's trousers in unappealing grey cat fuzz, noticed that the man was wearing beautiful brown suede shoes, which the rain had threatened to ruin.

*You can tell everything about a man by his shoes*, Victoria had heard somebody say once, though she couldn't remember who. *Everything.*

Victoria looked at the shoes and tried to work out the Everything that had been promised. But when all she could see was the tightly wound laces, the faint pattern of rain on the sides of the shoe, the water that was seeping up from the heel, she moved her gaze upwards, where it was drawn, all at once, to the man's exquisite face.

'Can I help you?' she asked, moving forwards and scooping Frederick up in her arms.

'I was just wanting a little shelter, I'm afraid. I wasn't expecting such an onslaught of rain.'

*An onslaught.* What a wonderful expression to use.

Frederick yowled and attempted to wriggle from Victoria's grasp. Not wanting to seem intimidated by a small grey cat, she grasped him with all her might. But Frederick, his sights set firmly on freedom, unleashed his claws as he scrambled out of her arms and over her shoulder. She yelped as his claw ripped through her yellow dress and into her white, soft skin beneath.

The man took a step forward immediately, his face all the more attractive for its air of perfect concern.

'You're bleeding,' he said.

Victoria sniffed. 'It doesn't hurt,' she said, only just managing to ignore the bolt of pain that was coursing through her. 'It'll soon stop.'

The man pulled out the chair from behind the counter. 'Here. At least have a little sit down.'

Victoria smiled as she took the offered seat. 'Are you really sure there's nothing you need to buy?'

The man shook his head. 'I feel quite guilty now, coming in here and upsetting your day. I have an important meeting today, and I didn't want to arrive looking like something washed ashore, so I thought I would just nip in here to stay dry.'

'Where do you work?'

'I'm a lecturer of English Literature at the University. We have an author coming in later to discuss some talks we want him to give to some of our prospective students. I admire him, so I wanted to make a good impression.'

'Who's the author?'

'It's Robert Bell. Do you know him?'

Victoria stood up, forgetting her wounded shoulder and her

weakness from moments before. 'Robert Bell! He's one of my favourites!'

'You read Robert Bell books? Well, you really aren't what you seem, are you?'

Victoria grinned. 'I like mysteries. I read them all the time.' She rushed over to the counter and retrieved a tattered copy of *The Blue Door* from its place underneath a pile of receipts.

The man grinned: a wide, wonderful grin that showed off a broad set of teeth, his left canine slightly crooked, the rest in perfect white rows. 'You know, I don't think there'd be a problem with you coming along to one of the talks if you wanted to. I think you'd enjoy it. I could arrange for you to attend as a visitor, if you'd like?'

'I'd love to!' Victoria said, wondering if she would sit with the man, wondering if he might offer to take her for a cup of tea afterwards, wondering if her father would let her say yes if he did. He wouldn't, she knew it. She would have to keep it to herself, somehow.

'Well, as soon as the talks are arranged, I'll come back here and tell you when they'll be.'

Victoria nodded, knowing that her life as she knew it was gone, and in its place was one where all she thought of, dreamt of, was this man who stood before her with his white teeth and his rained-on suede brown shoes.

'Forgive me,' the man said, holding out his hand and offering to shake Victoria's. His hand was firm, strong, warm around hers. She wanted to hold it forever. 'I didn't tell you my name. It's Harry.'

'I'm Victoria.'

'Ah. Like the Queen,' Harry smiled.

Victoria smiled back. 'Yes. Just like the Queen,' she said, pleased with her tone of voice and aware, somehow, that it was a different tone to any she had ever used before.

'Well,' Harry said after a few seconds, 'I'd best be going. But it really has been excellent to meet you.' He looked up out of the front window of the shop. Through the clocks, the candelabras, the stacked picture frames, the glass case of twinkling brooches, the sun could be seen glowing through the clouds. 'It's dried up as quickly as it arrived,' he added.

Victoria, suddenly remembering her injured shoulder again, touched it and winced. Harry winced with her.

'Get that seen to,' he said kindly as he opened the door. The hum of the crowds on the promenade beyond, the shouts of excited children on their holidays, the screams of seagulls merged with the monotonous ticking of clocks in the shop for a moment.

Then the door swung shut and he was gone.

Lace Antiques was a small, narrow shop with a sloping floor and walls that were crawling with paintings, clocks and bowed shelves. A fine layer of velvet dust lay over the top of almost everything in the shop. Victoria didn't like cleaning, her father was too busy at auctions to clean, and her mother was always too tired to clean. And so the layer of dust remained.

Behind the counter, which was piled high with yellowed pamphlets about Silenshore, more clocks (really, it sometimes seemed as if clocks were *all* Victoria's father bought) and a small cracked bowl of garnets that her mother placed there to bring the business success, was a white door. The white door led to the stairs up to Victoria's parents' flat, which, like the shop, was veiled in dust, tangled belongings and a brooding quiet that threatened to build into a sudden storm at any minute.

It was an hour after Harry left the shop, leaving a chest-tightening scent of cigarettes and rain behind him, that Victoria heard the white door behind her edge open. It wouldn't be her father behind the door because he was at an auction, probably bidding for some useless clock at that very moment. That left only her mother.

Victoria didn't turn around, but continued staring in the

mirror she had found before Harry arrived. She was trying to work out what he might have seen when he looked at her. How strange that the image seen through Harry's eyes could have been so very different to what Victoria saw in the mirror before her. She wondered if he'd seen the faint scar on the bridge of her nose from when she'd tumbled downstairs as a baby, or the way her black hair flicked up ever so slightly on the left side of her temple, or the green flecks in her bright-blue eyes. She wondered if he had thought she was beautiful. The way he'd looked at her when he was in the shop made her sure that he did. But now that he'd gone, that certainty had vanished with him.

Victoria raised an eyebrow and inspected the impact the movement had on her features. If she saw Harry again, she would remember to raise an eyebrow. It looked quite good.

'Victoria!'

The shout was unexpected, so unexpected that Victoria swivelled around in panic, almost dropping the mirror. It slipped slightly from her grasp and the jagged sapphires on the back scraped across her fingers. She tightened her grip around it and looked up at her mother, who was staring at Victoria in horror.

'What are you doing with that mirror? Where did you get it from?'

Victoria hesitated. She'd had the story all planned for her father. *A customer opened the case and got the mirror out. I was just about to put it back.* But her mother was different. She hadn't expected her mother to even come into the shop, and she certainly hadn't thought her mother would notice the mirror, because her mother never really noticed anything.

'I found it in the suitcase. I like it.' Victoria said.

But her mother wasn't listening. She was trying to take the mirror, trying to unpeel Victoria's fingers from its rough, glittering handle.

'You mustn't play with that, darling. It's not safe.'

Victoria thought of Harry, remembered how she could

somehow smell his skin, remembered the way he shook her hand. He did think she was beautiful, she was suddenly sure of it again. And the mirror, the whole morning, was now a part of Victoria's time with Harry. She didn't want it to end, any of it. She didn't want it snatched from her hands, treated like a childish game and nothing more. She wasn't a child: she was sixteen, and if she was going to be trapped in this shop all day every day for the rest of her life then she should be able to touch whatever she wanted to.

'Victoria!' her mother shouted again, giving up on wrestling with Victoria's tight grasp. 'You cannot play with that mirror!' Her hands crept up to her face, and Victoria watched as her mother suddenly seemed to wilt. The fight in her had gone as suddenly as it had arrived. 'Just promise me you will put it away and leave it alone,' she finished quietly. She turned and disappeared behind the white door again, as smoothly as a ghost, leaving the mirror behind.

Sleep was out of reach for Victoria that night. Her mind was bright with the image of Harry, and she tossed from one position to the next, wondering when he might return to the shop. She replayed their conversation over and over again in her mind until the black night had turned into a blue dawn. He hadn't said he would be back the next day, or even soon. It all depended on Robert Bell, the author, and when he arranged to give the talks that Harry would invite Victoria to.

*Robert Bell*, thought Victoria as she heard the clatter of the milkman's bottles break through the silent morning, *please, please arrange to do your talks soon.*

And as the milkman clinked his way down the winding hill of Silenshore, and the birds began to sing, and the blue dawn turned into a pale-yellow morning, Victoria finally fell asleep.

Since they had left school last month, Sally Winters had come into the antique shop every Tuesday to see Victoria. Sally worked at Clover's Tea Rooms at the other end of Silenshore, near the promenade, and Tuesday was her day off. Normally, when the door swung open with Sally's rather forceful push, Victoria would do a quick mental run-through of all the things she wanted to talk to Sally about, all the things she wanted to ask Sally about the week that had just passed. But this Tuesday, the day after Harry, Victoria yelped and jumped up as soon as she saw Sally through the glass, scurrying over to the door and ushering her in.

Sally's silver-blue eyes widened in wonder at the tale of Harry. She sighed when Victoria had finished talking, her slim face drawn down in disappointment that she wasn't at the centre of this thrilling new romance.

'Is he handsome?' she asked without waiting for a response. 'I wish I could meet someone handsome. I hate working at Clover's. Do you think Harry has any nice friends who would like to meet me?'

'I'll ask him,' Victoria said. She turned to the mirror, which she had brought downstairs with her when she had opened up the shop. 'Do you think,' she said quickly, 'that I should start wearing my hair up more often? Do you think it makes me look older?' Victoria tore off her red headband and gathered her black hair in her hands.

'A little, perhaps.' Sally frowned. 'How old is Harry?'

Victoria shrugged. 'I'm not sure, exactly. In his twenties, I think.'

'Twenties? Wow, Victoria. I bet he's nothing like the boys from school.'

Victoria grinned. 'You're right. He's nothing like them at all. I have a special feeling about him. I feel so excited all of the time.' She poured two cups of tea from the teapot that she'd also brought downstairs. Every Tuesday when she visited Lace Antiques, Sally always stayed for a cup of tea served in one of the beautifully fragile china cups that had been collected by the shop over the years. Victoria had bought an orange sponge cake from Blythe's Bakery across the road yesterday and had already sliced a piece each for Sally and herself.

They sat chatting about Harry for a while, the cake and cups between them on the counter, the sweet tang of orange in the air, until Sally stood up from her stool and brushed down her striped dress, yawning as though everything was a terrible bore. 'I suppose I'd better be going. Mum's given me so many jobs to do at home that Tuesday rarely feels like a day off lately.'

When she'd waved Sally off down the street, Victoria poured herself another cup of tea. She had chosen the blue cup, the one with the very fine crack around the base, finer than a hair. Using the blue cup took a certain amount of bravery; it could split and break at any moment. But today felt like a day where it wouldn't split. And feelings were everything. Whenever Victoria felt something, it was usually right. And that is why, when Harry didn't come through the door of Lace Antiques that day, or the next day, or the day after that, Victoria couldn't quite believe it.

*Surely the Robert Bell talks have been arranged by now*, Victoria thought on Friday. Her mother had been in bed all week, and her father rarely bothered to work in the shop, so Victoria had spent three days waiting for the door to open and Harry to saunter in. She couldn't remember if he was the sauntering kind, but she thought that he might be.

'Where is he?' she asked Frederick the cat. 'Do you think he'll ever return here?'

Frederick glanced at her regally, then began licking his pristine grey coat. Victoria touched her shoulder where Frederick's claws had dug into her when Harry had been there. The mark had gone, she had seen that morning as she had dressed; the final speck of dried blood had been brushed away to reveal brand-new skin. It was, quite simply, as though nothing had ever happened.

Suddenly alive with frustration, Victoria took one final look at the unmoving front door, burst out of the back of the shop and flew up the narrow stairs and along the landing to her mother's bedroom. She swung the door open, stagnant air rushing from the room in a bid to escape.

'Are you getting up today, Mum? I need to leave the shop. I need to go out somewhere.'

There was a murmur from the bed, from beneath the mound of knotted blankets and pillows.

'Mum?'

It was quite normal for Victoria's mother to spend days, sometimes weeks, in bed. Mrs Lace did not *live*, she slept. Sometimes, she would get dressed and float down to the shop, stinking of perfume, long strings of pearls rattling around her slender neck. But then Victoria's father would storm home and shout something, or worse, smoulder silently and then push past them both. Silence meant the worst, because silence was normally followed by a storm. Storms were followed by the pearls being hung up in an upstairs cupboard, the perfume fading, and Victoria's mother returning to her bed for a week or so.

'I heard you, darling. I'll be down later, perhaps.'

Victoria stood in the doorway of the bedroom. The air was heavy with sleep, with heavy breaths and dreams and sweat. Her mother's bony body was motionless in the middle of the bed somewhere. Victoria gazed at the dressing table to her right, from which makeup and jewellery spilled. She wandered over and touched a lipstick. Her mother still did not move. Victoria picked the lipstick up, twisting the base to reveal a shock of pointed red wax. She stared at the lipstick for a moment before twisting it back down and replacing the lid with a quiet click. Clutching it, she turned around.

'Be careful with that,' she heard her mother murmur as Victoria left the room.

By the time Victoria had applied the lipstick and wiped away the smear that bled out from her top lip onto her pale skin, and put on her favourite yellow shoes, and transferred the small amount of money in the till to the locked cabinet in the kitchen, as she did every night, it was almost three o'clock. Victoria's father was normally back home at around seven, after drinking in The Smuggler's Ship.

Four hours was plenty.

She locked the shop door quietly, just in case the sound did make her mother get up out of bed. As she left Lace Antiques and stepped out onto Castle Street, Victoria stole a brief glance at her mother's bedroom window upstairs. Her jittering heart stilled when greeted with unmoving curtains, behind which a sleepy darkness was promised.

From the rocky beach at the bottom end, Silenshore rose upwards in an uneven hill, to where the silvery-grey spires of the University rose into the clouds. Victoria could remember being tugged along by her mother on rare occasions when she was very small, up Castle Street, and perhaps into the butcher's and the bakery and Boots the chemist. But every time they got near the top of the hill, where the fragrance of salt and sand faded and was replaced by the damp, dark scent of the old castle towering above them, her mother would grip Victoria's hand so tightly that Victoria could feel their bones clicking against each other, and they would turn around to walk home in a mysterious silence. So Victoria had never, ever gone further than a third of the way up the hill, past the colourful, exotic window of Harper's Dresses.

Until now.

The spring air was warm and as she walked briskly upwards, Victoria felt her clothes become damp with perspiration. She stopped for a moment and sat on a bench outside Harper's. Fumbling with her handbag, she took out a mint and placed it on her tongue. She hadn't been nervous before she'd left the shop, so where had the sudden shaking fingers, the shallow breaths come from?

She crunched down on the mint, and stood up, swallowing

the glassy fragments as she neared the wide expanse of shadows cast down by the sprawling university. Now that she was getting closer to the imposing stone building, the looming, ghostly turrets that Victoria had gazed at so many times throughout her childhood were somehow less intimidating, and more elegant than Victoria had ever noticed. Arched windows glittered beneath them, the golden stone carved with intricate detail to frame the leaded glass.

Victoria followed the signs for the English department and, with short breaths and the image of Harry firmly before her eyes, picked up pace along the cobbles. Although the term was probably over, he might still be busy speaking to students or other lecturers. But as soon as he saw that Victoria was outside his office, he might dismiss them. They would pass her, whispering the rumours they had heard about Harry's new love who had the name of a queen, who had raven-black hair and porcelain skin, that this must be her, that she was just like the girl everyone was talking about.

The English department was in a squat building that lacked the drama of the rest of the castle. That was a shame, Victoria thought as she stepped through the green swinging door. It would have been quite nice to have her romance begin in the mystical, shining castle, rather than a dreary hut that reminded her of her old school. When she reached the office with Harry's name on the door, Victoria glanced behind her to check that nobody was watching, and pressed her fist quietly against the bright teak.

Nothing.

She leaned her head against the wood and listened hard. The faint rustling of papers came from within. He *was* in there, then. She knocked again, more of a rap this time: the knock of somebody who meant business. The sound of rustling was quickly replaced by the creak of a chair and two light footsteps. Then the door swung open.

His face was squarer than Victoria had remembered, but no

less exquisite for it. His hair, which she had taken for black, was actually the dark brown of cocoa. He ran his hand through it and ruffled it slightly.

'Victoria! What a nice surprise to see you here!'

'I'm sorry to come uninvited.'

Harry frowned. 'Not at all.'

'It's just that I was thinking about the Robert Bell talk. I wondered if you'd managed to get it arranged yet.'

Harry gazed at Victoria for a few more seconds. He ran his hand through his hair again, looked behind him into the untidy, square office that lay beyond the door, and then nodded.

'Forgive me if I appear distracted. Seeing you just…I was very much in my own world before you came. But I have arranged the talk by Robert Bell,' Harry continued. 'It's next week. I was going to come to the shop this weekend and tell you.'

Victoria looked back up at him. 'Really?'

He smiled then, a generous, wide smile that took her back to the dream she'd had last night. It wasn't so much a dream, more of an image that had endured in her mind for the whole night, of Harry taking her hand and smiling at her, again and again as she tossed around underneath her tangle of blankets.

'Yes. I was looking forward to seeing you again. The talk is on Monday at four. If you get here a bit earlier, you'll get a good seat.'

'Then I will be here at half past three,' Victoria said, feeling a strange excitement crackling in the air around them.

'I'll look forward to it.' Harry looked for a few moments as though he wanted to say more, but then somebody came down the corridor, and Harry smiled once more, then disappeared back into his office, closing his door gently behind him.

On Monday night, Victoria's father was travelling to London and staying overnight so that he could attend an auction in London on Tuesday. Normally, when he visited auctions, the time he was gone was filled with a crisp, brittle tension. If he was what he called *winning* at the auction, then a couple of days later he would return home drunk, buoyant, red-faced with alcoholic cheer. If he wasn't winning, if some other sod had bought up the collection he wanted, the one that would make Lace Antiques get through another blasted winter, then he would crash home drunk, pale and angry. Sometimes, if she was up to it, Mrs Lace went with her husband to the auctions. She had her uses, being so beautiful. She could sometimes make the auctioneer overlook a nod or a tap on the opposite side of the room.

Tuesday's auction in London was an important one, and Victoria's mother found enough spirit in her to get out of bed, hang some beads around her neck that she said were lucky, pack her small, mint-green suitcase and disappear off with Victoria's father.

'We'll see you tomorrow, darling,' she said, disappearing through the shop's front door in a cloud of Chanel No 5.

Victoria had already made the sign that she would put on the shop door whilst she was gone. She had sat crossed-legged on the floor in her bedroom when her parents had gone to bed the night before, writing in large black letters on a piece of card:

TAKEN ILL. PLEASE COME BACK TOMORROW.

She had been sick, she would tell her parents if they somehow found out the shop had been left closed this afternoon. She had suddenly been as sick as a dog, gone to bed for a few hours, but was much better now. Who could argue with that?

Now, she taped the sign to the glass on the front door, her fingers trembling a little with thrill at the thought of seeing Harry again.

The walk to the University was longer than Victoria had remembered, and her limbs were tight with anticipation by the time she arrived at the majestic iron gates. With a judder of nerves, she remembered that Harry hadn't told her which room the talk was being held in. She looked at her watch. Ten past three. She was a little early, but Harry had told her to get a good seat and she simply couldn't have waited any longer. She walked down the tree-lined driveway and looked around her, gazing at the high stone buildings and the squat little place where Harry's office was, searching for some kind of clue as to where she should be. Perhaps Harry expected her to meet him in his office?

A group of girls went past, swinging their satchels from their shoulders confidently and chatting loudly about the dancing they had done the night before.

'Excuse me?' Victoria said. 'Are you here for the Robert Bell talk?'

They continued on as though she hadn't spoken, bags swinging, heels clicking. Apart from them, there was nobody else around.

Well, if nobody was going to speak to her, she had no choice but to just find Harry. The door to the English block clanged shut behind her as she peered down the corridor and saw that his office door was open this time. Quickening her pace, she reached Harry just as he was leaving his office and locking the door. He spun around, the white grin that melted Victoria's insides broad on his face.

'Victoria! I was just wondering if you'd arrive soon. You're early, that's good. You can come over with me and meet Robert, if you like.'

It was at this moment, a moment which should have been a pure beam of elation, that Victoria realised with a jolt that she'd forgotten her copy of *The Blue Door*. She could see it in her mind, lying under some papers on the counter at Lace Antiques. In fact, she hadn't even picked up the book since the day that Harry had come in. How had she been so silly? She should have finished reading it and brought it with her for Robert Bell to sign. Now Harry would think that she didn't appreciate meeting Robert. She looked up at Harry's face, which was bright in expectation.

'I've forgotten my copy of *The Blue Door*,' Victoria blurted out.

Harry turned back to his door and rattled his key back into the lock. He emerged seconds later and held out a worn edition of the book.

'Here you go. Have my copy. I wasn't going to get it signed, so you might as well.'

Victoria took the book from Harry, aware that their fingers were going to meet, aware that tonight's sleep would again be a blur of Harry's face, his voice, his scent.

'Thank you, Harry. I haven't had a chance to finish it, but I—'

'Oh, don't worry about that. Mr Bell won't mind at all, as long as you're enjoying it?'

They were walking now, out of the low building and into the warm, green air of summer. The castle spread out before them, its pale-gold stone gleaming in the sun.

'Oh, I am. At least, I was. I haven't read for a while. I've not been able to concentrate,' Victoria said. It was as though Harry pulled her thoughts from her like a magnet. She shouldn't have told him that, should she? Sally always said that you should make boys work for you. You shouldn't let on that you liked them quite as much as you did.

But as she glanced at Harry, his strides long, his emerald-green tie blowing slightly in the pleasant breeze, his jaw strong, his countenance confident of exactly where he was going, Victoria realised that what Sally said about boys bore absolutely no relation to Harry, because Harry was a man, and what was more, he was the man who Victoria was going to marry.

'Ah,' Harry said. 'So who do you think has the missing girl?'

Victoria forced her mind to return from her daydreams and gathered her thoughts back to when she had last read some of *The Blue Door*. 'I don't know yet. I feel as though we're meant to think the girl's teacher has kidnapped her. But I don't think that he has a house with blue doors in it. He lives in a small flat, doesn't he? And the ransom note said that she was behind a blue door. The man who plays music on the street is rather strange, but I think he's too much of an obvious choice.'

'What do you make of the detective?'

'Oh, I like him. He's not very confident in himself, but I think he should be. I'm sure he'll crack the mystery.'

'Well, you try and beat him to it. I'm positive that you will. You're clever enough,' Harry said, as he pushed open a set of heavy double doors.

The room where the talk was to take place was not so much a room but a theatre. The worn red chairs ascended up from the wide expanse of stage and were all empty. Victoria imagined what it would be like to sit in the theatre and listen to lectures about books, writing and poetry. Why had it never occurred to her before that there was a life outside Lace Antiques? Sitting in these red chairs and listening to lectures about books would be nothing like the monotony of school. It would be a whole new exciting world.

'He's not here yet,' Harry said. 'Why don't we sit down? He won't be long.'

'Did you always know you wanted to work here?' Victoria asked him, settling into a red seat that was harder and less inviting than it looked.

'Yes. I did, actually. I used to live at the top of the hill and look up at the spires of the castle from my bedroom window and wonder how I'd cope if I didn't one day have something to do with it. It's beautiful, isn't it?'

Victoria nodded vigorously. 'It's very beautiful. I've always wanted to come here and my mother never let me. But whenever I'm walking up Castle Street and I see the castle it seems to want to pull me in somehow.'

Harry nodded. 'I agree. I always felt rather the same. But the funny thing is, even though I got what I wanted, and I work here, I'm stuck in the ugliest block of the lot. No spires, no turrets, no nothing.'

Victoria laughed. 'I'd noticed that. You should ask to be moved to the very top of the highest turret.'

'I might!' Harry laughed too, and Victoria fought the urge to touch him somehow, satisfying herself slightly by shuffling a little further towards him.

'Have you worked here long?' she asked.

'Eight years. I studied English here and then a few years later I started as an assistant lecturer.'

'Your dream came true,' Victoria pointed out.

Harry gazed at Victoria for a few moments, something flickering across his features. 'I suppose it did. Well, one of them did, at least.'

Victoria stared back at him, until they heard the heavy door of the lecture theatre swing open and the air in the room shifted with the presence of another person.

'Ah. Here's Robert,' Harry said, touching Victoria's hand and then standing up. 'Let's get started.'

Robert Bell was much shorter than Victoria had imagined him to be, with tufts of grey hair and a rather round belly. He smiled at Victoria and held out his hand to shake it. She took it, the new thrill of shaking hands with authors and sitting in lecture theatres flickering inside her like a candle.

'Robert, this is Victoria Lace, one of your biggest fans,' Harry said to Robert.

'I'm reading *The Blue Door* at the moment,' Victoria said, handing Harry's copy of the book to Robert. 'I haven't finished it, I'm afraid, although I'm very much enjoying it. I was wondering if you'd sign it for me?'

'Of course,' said Robert, taking a pen from his breast pocket.

*To Miss Lace*

*May your life be filled with dreams come true and blue doors opened.*

*Best wishes,*

*Robert Bell*

Victoria read it and smiled at Robert. She thought of the sudden new feelings she had since she'd met Harry, the empty shop, the TAKEN ILL sign, her absent parents.

'Thank you, Mr Bell. I hope so too.'

The lecture theatre began to fill up soon after Robert had signed Victoria's book. Robert spoke quietly and the audience strained to hear his words. He talked about how he never, ever planned his books, how he wrote every day in his shed (even in the winter, he said) and how the characters became as important to him as his friends (some girls at the back sniggered at this).

'You have to write about what you know,' Robert said towards the end of his talk. 'Or at least start with that. Write about the kind of people, places and feelings you know, and the rest will follow.'

Victoria gazed at Robert as he spoke. What did she know? The shop, her favourite novels, her sleeping mother and her angry father. That wasn't enough. Her eyes drifted over to Harry and lingered on him for a while. What would it be like to know him: to know him *properly*? What would it be like to know how his skin smelt when he first woke up, and how his hair felt beneath her fingertips, and how his voice changed when he was frustrated, or excited, or sad? Her blood fizzed and tingled beneath her skin as she watched him. A daydream began to cloud her mind, where she lived with Harry and could touch him and talk to him whenever she wanted. The daydream flickered before her eyes, beautiful and inspiring, gently lulling her along to the dulcet melody of Robert Bell's voice.

When the talk had finished, and Robert had answered a smattering of questions, the theatre slowly emptied, the prospective students numb and silent after an hour of being talked at. Robert spoke briefly to Harry and appearing to be relieved to take up his notes, waved at Victoria and left the room.

The theatre was now empty except for Victoria and Harry. They were back where they had started.

'Thank you for letting me have your book signed,' Victoria said as she stood and wandered over to the stage. 'Perhaps I could bring you my copy instead? And then it'll have been a straight swap.'

'I'd like that. So, what did you think of Robert Bell?'

'I thought he was wonderful. I want to be a writer too.'

'What do you want to write?'

'I want to write mysteries, like he does. Nobody would expect me to write mysteries. I'd like to surprise everyone.'

'Well, remember where you started, won't you. When you're a famous mystery author, remember who introduced you to your muse.'

Victoria nodded and stared up at Harry so hard, so intently, that she ached.

'I'm quite sorry that the talk is over. It feels so very flat going back home after that,' she admitted.

Harry looked at his watch. 'Would you like to get a drink?' he asked after a few seconds. 'I'd quite like some fresh air and a walk, if you'd like to join me.'

## CHAPTER 5

# *Isobel: 2010*

*My Queen Victoria,*
*Sarah and I had a silly disagreement today, which culminated in her throwing an omelette at me, just like you did on that wonderful day that feels like so long ago. I should have been angry at Sarah, or at the least, shamed. Instead it made me think of you: your sweet, sweet kisses and your terrible cooking. I would rather eat a raw omelette every day than be without you.*

*Write to me.*

*H*

On Friday, Isobel stays in her classroom for a while after the last class has gone. She marks practice exams, ticking and crossing deftly, until the pile on her desk is finished. She stands up and grabs her coat from the back of the chair, shivering as the cool air from the room snakes around her. As she glances out of the window, she sees something that makes her move closer to the glass. Tom's Volkswagen Polo is parked outside and if she squints Isobel can see Tom sitting in the driver's seat. He must be waiting for her, although they haven't planned anything: Tom said he was working tonight and Isobel has plans for a night in with Iris.

Isobel takes her bag from the desk and rushes from her classroom and down the staircase. The side entrance is locked, so she flies through the main doors and round to where Tom waits.

'What's the matter?' she says breathlessly as she pulls the passenger door open.

Tom leans over and grins. 'It's a good job Iris warned me you'd come out late, otherwise I might have thought you'd succumbed to the curse of the vanishing people of Silenshore!'

'But what are you doing here? I thought you were working tonight.'

'Nope. Get in.'

Iris throws her bag into the foot well and climbs into the car, still catching her breath. 'When did you speak to Iris?'

'When she was helping me plan this weekend. She told me what to pack for you. I didn't have a clue.'

'Pack? For what?'

'Oh, I'm taking you away for a night. It's been a crazy few weeks, what with our shock and everything. I think we need a treat. We're driving to London tonight. It'll be late when we get there but we'll stay over, then spend the day there tomorrow. If you want to, that is.'

Isobel feels her heart rush at Tom, the way he's packed the car – she sees her floral weekend bag squashed onto the backseat – the way he's spoken to Iris and planned a surprise. 'Nobody's ever done anything like this for me before,' she says.

'Well, I'm glad to be the one to do it, then,' Tom says as he starts the car. He leans across and kisses her softly on the cheek. 'Ready?'

'You really have all my stuff?' Isobel asks, incredulous.

'Yep. Straighteners, shampoo and conditioner, your facewash in the green bottle, some blue dress that Iris picked, phone charger, makeup bag, toothbrush…I think that's it, isn't it?'

'Pyjamas?'

Tom wiggles his eyebrows comically. 'Not needed.'

Isobel laughs, excitement fizzing up inside her and spilling out. 'Then let's go!'

The next morning, after lying under the crisp, tight hotel sheets and sitting in a warm bath filled with chalky complimentary bath salts, Isobel kneels on the floor in front of a brightly lit mirror and puts on her makeup. Her skin has always been clear and pale, but pregnancy is doing strange things to her, sending chemicals soaring through her blood and out of her pores. Her face is rounder now, too. She brushes some translucent powder over her pink cheeks and sits back.

'So are you still not going to tell me what we're doing today?' she asks Tom, who is lying on the bed reading the free newspaper.

He puts the paper down on the bed and sits forward. After staring at her own face in the mirror, Isobel feels a surge of pleasure from looking at Tom's. His features are defined, but not sharp. His teeth are straight and white. She went out with a man before Tom whose teeth you couldn't see because he never really smiled, so that every time she wasn't with him, she couldn't remember what his teeth looked like. With Tom, she can always picture his smile perfectly.

'No, I'm not telling you anything yet' he says. 'You'll find out where we're going when we get there.'

'Are you driving us there?'

'No, we'll leave the car parked here.'

'Well, then, I'll know what we're doing when we get off the Tube.'

'We're not getting the Tube,' Tom says, moving from the bed and sitting on the floor next to Isobel amongst lipstick and powder, eyeliner and blusher brushes.

'Well, then I'll know when you tell the cab driver.'

Tom shakes his head and laughs. 'Smart arse.'

When they climb into the juddering black Hackney cab that

smells of the cabbie's leather jacket and yesterday's cigarettes, Tom hands him a note that Isobel saw him scribble in the hotel reception just before they left. The driver rolls his eyes, gives a brief nod, then swings the cab out of the hotel's grounds and onto the road carelessly.

When the taxi stops, Tom turns to Isobel and raises a dark eyebrow.

'Portobello Road!' she gasps.

'Yeah. You've mentioned that you like vintage things a lot, so I thought we should do this kind of thing before our shopping consists only of Mothercare trips.'

Isobel squeals, and sees the taxi driver rolls his eyes again through the smeared rearview mirror. She takes out her bright-purple purse and pushes some money through the partition, waving away Tom's money.

'Can I have the note, please?' she asks. The driver twists around, confusion blurring his unpleasantly roguish features. 'The one that my partner gave you when we set off,' she says, looking at him expectantly.

It's pushed back through the glass, along with her change, creased and dented by pound coins. She looks down at the piece of paper as the cab rattles off down the road. Tom's writing is block-like, square.

*Please take us to Portobello Market, but don't tell her – it's a surprise!*

Tom takes her hand. 'What did you ask him to give you that for?'

Isobel clutches it to her chest. 'I want to keep it. Today is perfect and I want to always remember it.'

It's still early and the morning air is crisp and cold. They meander through the endless antiques, Isobel stopping at the brightly coloured jewellery stalls and gazing out over the amber brooches, mint-green bracelets, glittering black-stone rings.

'Are you going to get something?' Tom asks.

'Yes. Definitely.'

They stop at a stall crammed with stock: elegant teapots, jewellery, gold-rimmed saucers, china animals, staring Victorian dolls.

'Look! We could get the baby something,' Isobel says, reaching for a small doll with china lips and stiff black curls.

Tom grimaces and backs away slightly. 'I don't know. Something about old things like that freaks me out. Especially dolls.'

Isobel nestles the doll back amongst the others. 'I love them. But we can leave it if you want. It might even be a boy. If it's a girl, we can get her a vintage doll when she's a bit older. Look at this, though.' She pulls a ring with a ruby-coloured stone from the mass of items. 'It's beautiful.'

'Taking it, love?' the female seller asks, not missing a beat. 'Ruby is the stone of love and energy. It keeps you safe and makes you powerful. Warns you of danger too.'

Her voice is monotone: it's as though the woman is reading from a prompt card for the hundredth time that week, and the stone in the ring obviously isn't a real ruby, but there's something about the words that Isobel likes. She slides the cool ring onto her middle finger and moves her head, watching the red stone twinkle in the weak light. 'Yes. I will,' she says. She picks up a turquoise compact mirror in the shape of a rose. 'I'll take this, too.'

'You'll be safe now,' the woman says as she stuffs Isobel's notes into her till.

A couple of weeks after their London trip, Isobel lies in Tom's bed, staring up at his cracked grey ceiling. He always wakes later than her. Every time she's stayed over here, she has woken early and listened to Tom's easy breaths and the sound of the thrashing sea.

It is Sunday. Exactly two months to the day that Isobel and Tom first met.

Isobel turns over onto her side, stares out of the curtainless window at the blank grey sky, and waits for Tom to wake up.

'Happy anniversary,' she says when he does. She leans across him, into the warmth of his sleep and kisses his forehead.

'Anniversary? How long have I been asleep?' Tom asks lazily, draping an arm over Isobel.

'Oh, a hundred years.'

'Then our baby is a hundred years old now?'

Isobel laughs and kisses Tom again. 'It's our two-month anniversary. I was just thinking, it's two months since we met in September.'

'Wow. It seems longer. I can't imagine not knowing you.'

'I know. I can't imagine things any different, now. The baby, us.'

'Let's celebrate. I'm off today, so let's go out for lunch somewhere, and then look for some things for the baby.'

Isobel imagines a shop full of married couples and bright toys and muted newborn clothes: lemon and white and beige. She feels the tug of excitement that has been bubbling inside her for the past few weeks, even stronger now.

'Okay. Let's do it.'

After lunch in Mayor's, the high street's biggest café, they drive to a nursery shop just outside Silenshore in a grey retail park with huge square chain stores lined with car parks and trolleys. The shop smells sweet, like talcum powder and fresh cotton. Isobel stares at the prams and cots and car seats. Tom leans over them, checking the straps and the mattresses, muttering things about regulations and price.

'It's bad luck to buy a pram before the baby's born. We can't get a pram today,' Isobel says as she sees Tom checking the price dangling from a tight black hood.

'I'm just looking,' he murmurs, before wandering over to the cribs.

Isobel pushes one gently and it rocks. She moves along the

aisle, through wooden and white cribs, until she reaches the last one. It's mahogany: a dark, luscious colour that reminds Isobel of another place and time.

'I like this one,' she calls to Tom. He puts down a yellow blanket and walks over to her.

'It's very nice,' he says as Isobel runs her fingers along the glossy wooden sides. 'Do you prefer that to white?'

Isobel nods emphatically. 'Yes, definitely. Why, do you prefer white?'

Tom laughs and puts his hands up in mock defense. 'No, no. I was just checking that you were happy with your choice.'

'Shall we go back to mine once we've paid for it?' he asks. 'I'll put the crib together, and we can see how it looks. If we know we're happy with it then we can take it down again and store it until the baby arrives.'

'Okay.' Isobel feels doubt niggling at her, but pushes it away impatiently. 'Sounds great.'

Once Tom has carried the box up the stairs to his flat, and Isobel has made them a cup of tea each, and they have sat and sipped it, listening to the patter of the rain that soon turns into pelting shards of water against the glass and into the sea outside, Tom opens the box and peers inside.

About twenty minutes later the crib is made. Tom works methodically, taking the instructions seriously, frowning at the paper and the letter-coded parts and the minute screws that scatter from his hands and roll across the uneven floor.

Isobel knows as soon as he makes the frame. She knew it in the shop, really, but refused to succumb to the doubt. Now, there's no avoiding it, no pushing it aside.

The crib is too big.

It won't fit in the bedroom. It only just fits in the lounge, in front of the television, with the coffee table pushed up against the window.

They stare at it, their eyes glazing over. As soon as one of them says it, it's real.

'There's no room for it, is there?' Isobel says eventually.

Tom shrugs, but his face is ever so slightly pink with the stress of the tiny screws and the letters, and now the dimensions that mean all his efforts are wasted. 'I'll carry it to my bedroom, and we'll see if there's any way it'll fit in there.'

Isobel follows him, watching as he sets the crib down at the door, watching as he shuffles it further into the room, until it won't go in any more.

'It won't fit,' he says eventually. 'I'm not sure what we can do, other than perhaps get a smaller bed. Or a smaller crib. But the others were pretty much the same size, as far as I can remember.'

Isobel stares at the mahogany bars that are wedged between Tom's bed and the door. If the crib is left there, she'll have to vault over it to get to bed.

'What about your flat?' Tom asks.

'My bedroom isn't much bigger than yours. And anyway, that website I was looking at last night said that the baby will only be in our room for six months max. What will we do after that?'

Last night, when Isobel was reading an article on newborn sleep, six months had seemed like a lifetime. Now, it seems like an impossibly short time to adjust to another person with a mahogany crib and a need for a bedroom of its own.

Tom drops onto the bed. 'I'm not sure,' he says. 'Did you find out how long you're contracted to stay in your flat?'

'Yes. Only another few months.'

Tom nods. 'Okay. I suppose it's irrelevant, really, because I have to pay rent for here for almost another year. I can't afford more rent on top of that.'

'And I won't be able to afford much more once I'm on maternity pay,' Isobel says. Her temples ache and she rubs them. 'What are we going to do?'

Tom thinks, is silent. The wind cracks against the windows

outside, whipping the sea and the sand up and slamming them against the panes. Eventually, he looks at Isobel and takes a deep breath.

'I have an idea. But I'm not sure you'll like it.'

Isobel nods. 'Go on.'

## CHAPTER 6

# *Evelyn: 1947*

Evelyn dropped one more pair of stockings into the case that lay open on her bed. It was quite full, but then it was very difficult to know what to pack, and so she'd thrown in quite a lot. She stood up, excitement flooding through her as she looked out of her tall bedroom window at Silenshore.

Today was the day.

Today, from her position at the end of the elegant castle, Evelyn felt like she was on the very edge of the world, in control of everything. She was eighteen now, and she had waited, year after year, for her life to jolt into action, to somehow be catapulted into Hollywood as she'd planned. She'd read in her mother's magazines about stars like Carole Lombard, who had been spotted by film directors in the street and offered film roles that changed everything. She imagined it happening to her: a frantic packing of her mother's best suitcase, a tangle of necklaces being thrown in along with lipsticks and perfumes and furs, a tearful goodbye as Evelyn left for a sudden new life. But it hadn't happened yet, because Evelyn barely left the castle. There was nowhere to *go* in Silenshore. There was nothing to do and nobody to meet. Years ago, Evelyn might have met someone useful at one of her parents' parties. But since the war, there weren't as many parties as Evelyn would have liked. In fact, there were hardly any.

Poor Mary, the evacuee, had been right when she'd said the war would change everything: it had. But it hadn't changed enough for Evelyn. She would have to do that herself. And she couldn't wait for life to come and claim her any longer. She needed to go and claim her life.

Throwing open the huge dark oak doors of her wardrobe, Evelyn was greeted by her own scent, as a stranger might be. It smelt of spring flowers and sugar. That would change. A new life had to have a new, more mature, scent. She reached into the wardrobe and pulled out a yellow crepe dress. Yellow was the perfect colour. There was, she was sure, a pair of yellow shoes at the back of her wardrobe that she hadn't worn since last summer. She fell down to her hands and knees, and scrambled amongst her things until she found one of the shoes. The other was further back; she could see its heel sticking out from a mound of bags. As she pulled the bags out of the way, her fingers fell onto something cool and sharp: the mirror. She yanked it from the tangle of straps, and ran her hands over the cool glass.

She'd put the mirror back in her mother's drawer all those years ago, after the game of dares with the evacuees. She'd never had a real reason to take it again: there were certainly no more games of dares after the children had returned to their homes in London a few months after they'd arrived. But still, Evelyn hadn't been able to stop thinking about it. It was as though, childish as it sounded when she thought about it now, the mirror wanted Evelyn to have it. She'd creep into her mother's room to just touch it, to glance in it, to stare down at the beautiful blue sapphires that framed the glass. In the end, she'd hidden it in her own room, and if her mother had noticed it missing then she hadn't said anything.

Her mother.

At the thought of Mrs du Rêve, Evelyn felt an immediate rush of guilt. It had been so easy for Evelyn to tell her the white lie: that she was going to stay with Mary in London for a while. Evelyn and Mary had scribbled out letter after letter to each other all through the war. Strong, brave Mary. Evelyn would have given anything for that to be true. But as bombs fell down on London like raindrops, Mary's letters stopped. She'd written to Mary again and again but the lack of reply told her more than she needed to know. Evelyn's mother didn't know that Mary had stopped writing, didn't know that Evelyn was actually rushing into London by herself, to claim the glittering life that belonged to her. Evelyn had expected Mrs du Rêve to scoff at the idea of going to stay with a common girl in the East End. But she hadn't, which had made Evelyn feel even more guilty. But if she'd told her mother the truth, she wouldn't have agreed to it. So there had simply been no choice.

Evelyn blinked at her reflection, then laid the mirror in her case, between the folds of a skirt. There was no way she could leave the castle without it.

The castle gardens smelt of ripe fruit and September sunshine and flowers: the perfect scent for such a glorious day. Evelyn hurried down Castle Street with her suitcase, drawn by the sea that glinted as though it was filled with jagged diamonds. She wanted to throw herself into the cool, silver waves, to plunge into the silence of the water, to rise up again and thrash her arms and legs around, and then lie on craggy rocks under the sun. Her legs propelled her further and further forwards, until she saw something that made her stop and stand still, her heart pounding, her mouth wide open to draw in huge lungfuls of salty air.

It was a shop, but it looked more like a cavern or a witch's den full of twinkling beauty. Evelyn looked at her watch. It was ten to twelve, so if she hurried, she had time to go into the shop before the train to London arrived in fifteen minutes.

As Evelyn stepped inside, she stared around at the gems and

pearls and gold and silver that spilt out from every cabinet and shelf. The man behind the counter smiled at her, his eyes tracing her young, curving figure and she blushed with the exotic pleasure of a man's gaze. He was handsome: broad, masculine and dark, like a king of a faraway country.

The man stared at Evelyn for what seemed like a long time. Then he smiled and his whole face changed. 'Can I help you?' he asked.

Evelyn grinned at him. 'I couldn't help but come into your shop. I've lived in the castle all my life, but I've never noticed it before.'

The man smiled back. 'I've just opened. Only been in Silenshore a few weeks. But it looks like we have bad timing. Have I moved here just as you're leaving?'

Evelyn felt an unexpected prickle of disappointment about her plans. 'Yes, I suppose we have. I'm off to London. My train's in fifteen minutes.'

'Oh, well, if you're going to London then I'll let you off. It's one of the best places you can go to. Which part?'

Evelyn remembered the address Mary used to write from. She didn't know many places in London, so that would have to do. 'Bethnal Green,' she said. 'But I probably won't stay there long,' she hurried on. 'I want to see all the different parts of the city.'

'Have you got someone to show you round?

Evelyn looked down at a table that glinted with a rainbow of colour and fingered some green glass beads. She wanted to tell this man the truth, all about how she was going to arrive in London and try to get a job, to start all over again and take some classes in acting. But if her mother were to ask around…

'Yes. I'm going to stay with a friend,' she said reluctantly.

'That's good. Can't have a beautiful lady like you wandering the streets of London alone.'

Something inside Evelyn bloomed at his words, as though he'd unlocked needs she hadn't even known were there. She looked around: there were clocks everywhere, swinging pendulums and ticking hands that reminded her how close her train was getting.

'Do you know London well?' she asked the man, her hands lingering around the beads.

'It's where I'm from. I go back all the time to the auctions. I know a lot of people there. If there's anything you want from London, I can get it for you.'

Evelyn thought for a minute. 'Do you know any actors? Anybody to do with the theatres?'

The man smiled. 'Oh, I know plenty of theatre people. So that's what you're up to? You want to be famous?'

If anybody else had seen into Evelyn's soul so easily, past her yellow dress and carefully brushed hair and her mother's red lipstick, she would have been quite embarrassed. But there was something about the man that made her feel quite at ease.

'Yes,' she said, hearing the glitter of excitement in her voice. 'I do want to be famous.'

'I'm going to London in a few weeks. We can meet up, if you like. I'll introduce you to my friends. There's no way they could turn down a beauty like you. Let me know the address of your friend's house and I'll come for you, if she won't mind. I'm Jack, by the way.'

Jack held out his hand for her to shake and Evelyn took it. His touch was warm, his hands as she had always imagined a real man's hands to feel: slightly worn, strong. Evelyn smiled, but her words faltered. 'I'm not sure of her exact address.'

Jack stared at her. 'I hope this friend's real. Because if she's not, London won't be much fun alone.'

Evelyn felt herself blush and she laughed. 'Am I that bad a liar?'

'It was a white lie,' Jack said, grinning. 'You best get working on it, though, if I'm going to make you into a famous actress.'

'Oh, you can't make me famous,' Evelyn said, although her flipping stomach betrayed her words.

Jack shrugged. 'I think I can. I know the right people. And you've got the looks. But you know best. Off you go to London and I'll just have to hope that I find you when I next go. You can always write to me and let me know where you end up. Take those with you, if you like,' he said, gesturing to the glass beads that Evelyn had picked up.

'Oh, I…' Evelyn found herself reaching for her purse, but Jack put a hand on hers and stopped her. He took the beads from their place on the table before them and held them up to Evelyn's neck, fastening them deftly, his fingers brushing against the bare skin on her collarbone. She could smell his breath on her skin when he came close to her, smoky and dark and like nothing else she'd ever smelt.

'Like them?' he asked.

Evelyn nodded, knowing that her life as she knew it was gone, and in its place was one where all she thought of, dreamt of, was this man who stood before her with eyes the colour of chocolate and broad, strong shoulders. 'I love them.'

'You can think of me when you wear them in London,' Jack said. 'That's if you're still going. You could always wait a few weeks and we could go together, make a day of it and meet up with my friends. Or, you could go and catch your train right now.'

As he spoke, a clock above him chimed twelve.

'I think,' said Evelyn, 'I'm already a little too late.'

## CHAPTER 7

# *Isobel: 2010*

*My Queen,*

*I miss you. My days are long. How, when one year ago I did not know you existed, can I find it so impossible to live without you now? It makes no sense.*

*I can still only thank all the stars in the world that it rained that day when we first met.*

*I want to find you. I wondered if I should question your father the last time I visited the shop, but his expression told me to leave well alone. What has happened? Find me. Tell me.*

*H*

Isobel watches Tom as he pauses before speaking again. His face is tense and she tries to skip ahead, to guess his solution to having no space in either of their flats for the baby, or its new crib. But she can't think of what he might be about to say. He has no other properties, no money. He's just told her that. So how can he have a plan?

'My mum always offers for me to move in with her,' Tom says after a minute, breaking into Isobel's thoughts. 'She has a big house on West Street, and she lives on her own.'

Isobel frowns and gazes at Tom, at his broad shoulders and perfect face, his wide hands that make him seem strong and protective. He looks like a man who knows what he's doing, who has life all planned out. He doesn't look like someone who would suggest moving in with anybody's parents, especially his own.

'I don't know. I don't think I can,' Isobel says, then immediately feels guilty. Tom's trying to help, to work things out. 'I'm sorry,' she says quietly. 'I just can't imagine it.'

'I know it wouldn't be ideal. I've always point blank refused to live with her, because I'll admit that she can be a bit difficult sometimes. But now, for the first time, staying with her for a time seems to almost make sense. Think about it: we could save up our wages and then get somewhere together in a year or two. She could help us with the baby too.'

'Do you get on with her?'

'Pretty much. Like I said, she has her moments.'

'That doesn't sound great,' Isobel says.

Tom sighs. 'Well, what about your dad? Would you feel better staying with him for a while?'

Isobel closes her eyes and pictures her dad's flat. Even if it wasn't a mess, it would be way too small. 'No. No way.'

Tom is quiet for a moment. 'Shall I ring her, then?' he asks eventually, his words even and calm. 'I won't say anything about moving in yet. I'll just arrange for us to go round, so that you can meet her. She got back from her holiday last night, actually, so I was thinking we could visit her anyway. Then, once you've met each other, we can decide.'

Isobel touches her slightly rounded abdomen and stares at the crushed bed and crib, and thinks of the person inside her who is growing a little bigger, a little more human, every minute.

'Yes, okay. Ring her.'

On Wednesday morning, Isobel wakes up disoriented, a buzzing sound filling her mind and forcing her away from her dreams.

She opens her eyes and takes a moment to realise that she's at her own flat, not Tom's. The buzzing noise is Iris's hairdryer, which Isobel normally sleeps through. How quickly she has become used to quiet.

She closes her eyes again and thinks of the day ahead. Muted sounds from Iris's bedroom next door resonate through the wall. When Isobel hears Iris's door open, she swings her legs out of bed and pads out of the room. Iris grins when she sees Isobel. She's ready for work and is wearing a short skirt with black tights and gold shoes covered in tiny sparkling stones.

'Morning,' she says. 'I was just going, but I've got time for a quick coffee if you want one?'

'I'd love one,' Isobel says. The novelty of being home at the flat with Iris is strange after almost a week of being at Tom's. Isobel would never have got up just to see Iris before. She would have stayed in bed for an extra half an hour, oblivious to hair-dryers and coffees and Iris leaving for work. They would have caught up later. But she can't do that today.

'Are you back at Tom's later instead of here?' Iris asks. It's as though she can read Isobel's mind. Sometimes they joke that she can: they've been friends for so long that they can usually guess each other's thoughts.

Isobel's blurred memories of the first days of primary school, the warm milk and the teachers towering above her and the home corner with its naked dolls and battered pram, are tangled with memories of Iris. Everybody thought they were sisters, because they both had red hair. It was a lazy assumption: Iris's hair was bright and thin, and Isobel's was a heavy auburn mass. Their faces, even at four, gave clues to how different they would grow to be: Iris's was wide, her eyes green. Isobel's eyes were dark brown. Iris had a peppering of freckles on her cheeks and shoulders; Isobel had none. But the differences didn't seem to be as important as their one similarity. Their names were spoken together by teachers and parents, binding them together as one.

Now, over twenty years later, they are still as close as they were then. They love living together. And because of Isobel, it's going to change.

'Yes. I'm meeting Tom's mum for the first time today. We're going to hers straight after I finish work.'

'Wow.' Iris perches on one of their breakfast bar stools and crosses her slim legs. 'Things really are getting serious now. It's exciting!'

Isobel is quiet for a moment. Then she takes a deep breath. 'Tom's suggested that we move in with her.'

Iris's eyes widen. 'Isobel! That's huge!'

'I know. I wasn't sure at first.'

'I wouldn't mind a baby in our flat, you know,' Iris says.

'Thanks, Iris. I feel guilty for leaving here. I thought we'd live together for ages.'

Iris waves away Isobel's apologies. 'Oh, one of us was bound to get swept off our feet and carried off to somewhere else at some point.'

'Ha, to his mother's? I'm not sure it'll be quite like you make it sound!' Isobel laughs. 'It's pretty good with him, though. So I'm hoping it'll work out.'

'I'm sure that she'll be fine. Does Tom say much about her?'

Isobel shakes her head and sips her coffee. It's caffeinated and tastes better than any coffee she has drunk in weeks. 'Not much. Actually, I can tell he doesn't love the idea of living with her. He's just so logical.'

Iris nods. 'Well, perhaps it's time to give logical a try. And if it doesn't work, then I'm always going to be here.' She looks at her watch. 'Well, figuratively speaking anyway. I actually should go to the gallery, really. I said I'd get in a bit early today.' She jumps down from her stool and gives Isobel a brief, tight hug. 'Good luck. She'll love you.'

Tom meets Isobel at the school gates when she's finished work for the day, his head bowed against the darkening wind, his eyes darting as he looks out for Isobel amongst the swathes of teenagers.

'Ready?' he asks as she links her arm into his.

She nods. 'Ready.'

They walk a little way down Castle Street, the streetlights casting yellow down on them as the daylight fades into a purple darkness. As they pass shops, Tom looks at them, craning his neck to see inside.

'I love the buildings up here,' he explains. 'I'm always imagining my French restaurant in one of these.'

Isobel looks up. The Victorian terraces near to the castle are bigger and grander than those near the promenade, as though the style of the castle floods through them. The turrets on the end buildings, the high arched windows and intricately carved stone pillars between shops are beaten by weather and time, but still beautiful.

'That's a great idea. A restaurant would be just right up here. I'd help you set it up. You know, I'm actually related to a long line of Silenshore foodies,' Isobel says. 'My grandparents owned a bakery and their parents before them opened it. It was where my dad's office is now.'

'Really? That's impressive! But you don't cook, do you?'

Isobel laughs. 'I make nice toast.'

'Oh, so you're sticking with the bread theme, then.'

'Yes, I suppose I am. I've never been much of a cook. I definitely don't feel like I have baking talents in my blood.'

'And presumably your dad doesn't either?'

'No. There was a big family row about it, actually. His parents expected him to carry on the baking tradition. But he just wasn't into it. He was the oldest child, so the shop was passed to him, even though he was adamant that he didn't want it. He wanted his younger brother to have it, but he was about ten years younger than Dad, and not really old enough to take on the bakery at the time. Dad ran it for about a year, but hated it. Then he met my mum. She worked in the shop with him and ran it while he did his finance courses. Then he opened his office. If it hadn't been for Mum, Dad would have been a miserable baker all his life, and wouldn't have ever done what he wanted to do. But I suppose now he misses her so much that it doesn't make much difference. He doesn't seem happy any more. I sometimes wonder if he will ever be happy again.'

'I don't know,' says Tom. 'It's the age-old question, I suppose. Isn't it better to have had something great and then lose it, than to never have had it at all?'

Isobel thinks, her mind whirling with images of her mother and the baby and Tom. 'I think it must be,' she says. She turns her head and stares back at the houses near the castle. They look majestic and fairy-tale like, their flaking paint and cracking facades invisible from a distance.

As they walk on, Isobel tastes the bitterness of salt from the sea and sand crunches beneath them on the pavement. Tom is quiet, his grip on her hand firm and warm. They carry on further down the hill before turning right about halfway down, onto West Street.

'Mum lives in one of the houses up there. It's not much further.'

The houses on the street are spacious cottages that all bear an individual style. Isobel can see that they were probably built in the sixties: they are lower and wider than the rest of the houses in Silenshore and don't seem to belong. Isobel can see a park at the end of the road. It looks deserted and eerie in the winter darkness. A swing creaks backwards and forwards in the wind and Isobel averts her gaze, focusing on the front door that Tom pulls her towards, and then pushes open.

The hall is empty when Tom and Isobel walk in. A strong, shiny scent of lavender and polish wafts through the air. Photographs line the cream walls: Tom at school, Tom at university, Tom on holiday before a grey backdrop of dramatic mountains.

'Mum?' Tom shouts as they peer into the empty sitting room on the right.

A voice echoes from further on in the house: a small hum rather than a word. Tom leads Isobel along the hall and gestures for her to step into the room on the right. Isobel looks down at the floor, which is a cool grey slate.

Tom's mother is standing at an Aga that seems too old for the house. She's a tall woman, stooped in apology.

'Tom,' she says with a small smile. Her voice is delicate.

'Hi Mum. Good trip?'

'Oh, as far as they go.' She replies with a wave of her slim hand. She looks at Isobel. 'I went on a walking holiday.' She bends down to stroke the head of the chocolate Lab that has padded into the kitchen.

Isobel nods enthusiastically. 'I've never been on that kind of holiday. But I've heard they're really good.'

Tom's mother nods vaguely and then turns back to her stirring for a moment. 'So you're both well?'

Isobel looks up at Tom. He is more agitated than usual, his features tight with tension. 'Yes. This is Isobel, Mum.'

She looks at them both and gives a strange snorting laugh. 'I guessed. And I'm Daphne, as I'm sure you've gathered. He's told me a little about you, Isobel. Do you like casserole?'

'Yes,' Isobel says. When was the last time she ate a casserole? Probably in the eighties with her parents. 'Tom's very good at cooking. He's been making me some of his French dishes.'

Daphne nods and stirs some more. Tom gestures for Isobel to sit down at the worn pine table that sprawls out in the corner of the large room.

'It's a nice spacious house,' Isobel says. Words rattle out of her about the house and Silenshore and Tom, and Daphne responds to them quietly and calmly. Tom makes some tea and tells them about some customers who left the restaurant without paying this afternoon.

After they have eaten the enormous red pan of chicken casserole that Daphne places on the table and had another cup of tea each, Tom clears his throat. The food that Isobel has eaten for fear of appearing rude suddenly feels like dough in her stomach, rising and swelling and making her feel frightened and sick. *Don't tell her yet*, she says with a glance at Tom. He gives an almost imperceptible nod and tells Daphne that Isobel works at Silenshore Castle High School.

'Ah. Do you like it? I imagine it's hard work.' Daphne says as she stands and clears the table.

'I do like it. I love teaching English, and obviously it's quite special to be able to work in the castle. It's a beautiful building, and I love all its mystery and secrets. It makes it a cool place to work.'

Daphne busies herself with the dishes, clanking cutlery and scraping grey chicken bones into the burnt casserole dish. 'I've never heard of any secrets to do with the castle. I think they're all myths.'

Isobel thinks of the gothic turrets and the cool, dark corridors. It was built for secrets. 'I suppose I just think of it as secretive because of the people who've gone missing from there.'

Daphne sweeps the dishes from the table. 'I'll get us all some apple cake' she says as she crashes the dishes into the sink.

Isobel stares down at the slice of cake that Daphne places down in front of her, trying to block the strong smell of cinnamon and sugar from her mind.

'Mum?' Tom says, after setting aside the tiny cake fork that Daphne laid on the plate, and eating a crumbling slice with his fingers. 'We've actually got some news.'

Isobel wants to moan. Perhaps she does. She feels somehow dissociated from herself, as though she's not really there. Her insides feel hot and melting. It's as though she's regressed to how she felt when she first took the pregnancy test. Or maybe she's never moved on from those first fearful moments. Maybe she's just made herself think she has.

Daphne looks up from her cake, her own fork poised over it. 'Oh?'

'Isobel's pregnant.'

Daphne puts her fork back down on her plate. Isobel tenses, waiting for a storm of words or an excited shriek, waiting for something that shakes her and makes her feel relieved or worried or anything other than nervous and taut with anticipation.

But there is very little discernable response on Daphne's face. Her steel-grey eyebrows raise, but her eyes and mouth betray nothing.

'We know it's very soon. It wasn't planned,' Isobel says, feeling the heat from her body rise to her face. 'I'm very lucky that Tom is so pleased, though, and we're so happy together, so I – we, I should say, feel as though we will be okay. We're really excited.'

Daphne nods and looks at Tom. 'You're a grown man, Tom. It's certainly a shock, but I've no doubt you'll rise to the occasion.'

Her words are clipped, cool. Isobel steals a glance at Tom. Is Daphne furious, or is she always like this?

Tom bites into his cake again. 'We both will. Already, the shock is starting to sink in a bit. We're trying to focus on practical things now.'

Isobel nods and pushes her untouched cake along the pine table. 'I'm sorry, I can't eat that. I feel a bit sick.'

Daphne reaches out for Isobel's hand and squeezes it. Her fingers are rough and dry, her skin cold. 'I can imagine you're frightened. But honestly, this is a gift for you both.'

The sentiment of the words are all Isobel could have hoped for. The way Daphne grips her hand should make Isobel feel supported and safe. Tom grins when he sees them holding hands across the table, as though everything is as it should be, as though he couldn't have wanted better. Obviously, he's used to Daphne's strange mannerisms.

'When are you due?' Daphne asks, retracting her cool hand as suddenly as she offered it.

'I haven't had my first scan yet. But I think it'll be June.'

Daphne is quiet for a moment, then eyes Tom. Something seems to be exchanged between them, between their glances. Then Daphne clears her throat.

'Tom's probably told you that I've often been on at him to move in here. I know he likes his flat, but it's not big enough to raise a baby in, as I'm sure you both realise. I'd be more than happy to have you here, you know. Just until you've found your feet.'

Tom nods. 'Thanks, Mum. We appreciate that. It's a big decision for us, though, to give up our homes. Are we okay to get back to you on it?'

Daphne dips her cake into the neat pool of cream on the side of her plate and eats it delicately. 'Of course you are. Take all the time you need.'

# CHAPTER 8

## *Victoria: 1964*

After the Robert Bell talk, Victoria and Harry walked off campus and down the hill, past Clover's, past the crooked rows of shops, through the sloping park towards the bottom of the hill and then meandered through the narrow cobbled road that led to West Street.

'What are they digging for?' Victoria asked as they walked away from the bustle of Silenshore's main street. The spare ground ahead of them that had always been boggy and overgrown, hilly and neglected, was now being bulldozed into grey, flat land. Aggressive vehicles vibrated and roared around them, making Harry lean closer to Victoria when he replied so that she would hear him.

'They're building houses,' he said, the air around her electric as he came closer.

Victoria gazed at the juddering machines, the shouting men, the foundations of what would be people's homes, and suddenly she felt very strange. Something inside her sank and her legs trembled. Without thinking, she clutched Harry's hand. His fingers entwined with hers.

'I feel like I need to sit down,' she said, turning away from the digging and grinding and grey dust that clouded the air ahead of them.

'Of course. Are you alright?' Harry asked, frowning in concern.

Victoria nodded, the odd feeling of weakness vanishing as suddenly as it had appeared. As she clutched Harry's hand, her legs regained their strength. 'I'm fine now. Let's keep walking.'

They wandered past an ice-cream van and Harry bought them ice creams. Victoria breathed in the salty, golden air. The hot afternoon was beginning to give way to a cool, gentle evening that was the colour of honey.

'I'll be quite sad to return home after today,' she said as they edged their way down to the beach. The sand at Silenshore wasn't smooth and never-ending like a real beach, but grey and uneven with pebbles. The tide crashed in the distance, dark and frothing like witch's brew. People were scattered across the sand, eating fish and chips from Wheels' Fisheries, throwing balls that blew sideways in the wind. Their scents of sweet perfumes saved for their holiday and sharp vinegar floated in the air, mingling with the salty fragrances of the sea and shells that crunched beneath their feet.

Harry licked his ice cream. 'I feel the same. I'm glad you enjoyed the talk. I've never met anyone who enjoys mystery books as much as I do. I'm so glad to have met you that day, Victoria.'

'I'm glad too.' Victoria looked at her ice cream and suddenly felt quite sick.

*Lovesick*, she heard Sally say in her head. Was she? Was there such a thing? Staring at the insurmountable vanilla hump in her hand, it seemed there was.

Harry stopped walking and turned to her. He had finished his ice cream, and there was a hint of pale cream on his top lip.

'Victoria, I'm sorry that I didn't come to visit you at the shop like I said I would. I wanted to, more than anything. I knew straight away that you were special.'

Harry stopped and Victoria waited. Sometimes, people had plenty more to say, even if they had stopped talking. *Especially* if they had stopped talking.

'I wanted to see more of you,' Harry continued eventually, 'but I'm a little older than you, and I—'

'That doesn't matter at all,' Victoria interrupted. 'My father is much older than my mother.'

She didn't add that her father was a vile bully, because that wasn't to do with his age. Jack could be precisely the same age as his wife and he would still beat her and boss her and make her weep and sleep for days on end. Victoria pushed her parents out of her mind.

'I don't want to get you involved in something that's no good for you,' Harry was saying, 'But if I'm honest, there's something about you I can't shake off.'

'I don't care whether you're good for me or not. I can't shake you off either,' Victoria said, Harry's words sweet in her mouth.

Harry had moved closer to Victoria and as she finished her speech she moved her foot and slipped on an uneven rock. Harry's arms flew out to steady her and she held on to them tightly, because even though she knew she wouldn't fall without them, it was nice to have them there just in case. His arms were strong and hard. Victoria had danced with a boy called Peter Cooper at Sally's birthday party last year, and his arms had been floppy and thin.

'Victoria. I'm twenty-eight, and you—'

'No, Harry, listen. I'm eighteen,' Victoria said, even though she wasn't, even though she was only just sixteen, because she never wanted to dance with Peter Cooper or anybody like him ever again, because she only ever wanted to dance with Harry and she could see him teetering on the brink of her life, about to be lost forever. 'I'm eighteen, and you don't need to worry about what's good for me, because I know what I want and what I need, and it's not to be left standing alone on this beach. Please, don't say anything else, otherwise today will be ruined in my mind.'

She wanted to kiss him then, but even though she was in love with him, kissing him seemed too frightening, so she fell into him instead, flopping against him, her head against his broad chest. She felt his arm close in around her and she breathed in his scent of books and Harry, and she thanked the universe for making it rain last Monday.

After their little outbursts, they picked their way across the beach, then when it seemed like the tide was closing in, turned back and returned up the slope, onto the promenade. The shops along the promenade were beginning to close. People wandered back to their hotels for teatime, sandals swinging in their hands, faces pink with freedom and sun and happy memories. For the first time that day, there was a little chill in the air that worked its way through Victoria's white cardigan and onto her skin.

'My parents are away today. They've gone to London,' she said. 'You can come to the shop, if you like.' Would Harry like whisky? There was a bottle under the sink that Victoria wasn't meant to know about, and up until now had never been altogether interested in.

Harry looked at his watch and nodded. 'I'd love to.'

Lace Antiques was towards the middle of Castle Street, a few minutes' walk from the promenade. When they reached the shop, Victoria remembered the sign that was in the window and blushed as Harry read it, his features scrunched in confusion.

'Fallen ill?'

'Oh, my father wouldn't have let me come to the University if I'd asked him. So I made my own mind up. He'll never know.'

Harry raised an eyebrow as Victoria unlocked the door and swung it open for the musty scent of other people's old possessions to greet them. 'You really are intriguing, Victoria Lace,' he said.

Victoria locked the door behind them and tore down the sign. She crumpled it into a ball and tossed it into an open chest filled with antique dolls and bears. 'The shop is officially closed now, anyway. And it's been such a sunny day that nobody would have wanted to come in a musty old shop anyway. I'll bet nobody even saw it.'

'Something tells me you're not too interested in whether they did or not,' Harry said with a smile.

'I'm not. Today has made it clear to me. I don't want to work in my parents' shop selling dead people's things,' she said, motioning around the dingy shop. 'I want to be a writer. I want to write mysteries like Robert Bell. Listening to him today and meeting you has made me realise that I want to be a writer, and that I need to go to university to be any good at it.'

'University?'

'Yes. I want to study English Literature. Robert Bell said to write about what you know, but I don't feel like I know anything, or anyone. So I don't think what I've written must be any good.'

'I didn't know you'd already written some pieces. I'd love to read them, if you'd let me.'

Victoria thought of her box of writing upstairs in her bedroom. She'd never imagined that anybody would actually read any of it. She'd never imagined she'd meet anybody who wanted to.

'Maybe,' Victoria said, wandering behind the counter and sifting through some receipts.

'I will help you, Victoria, if you're serious about coming to read English. How did you do in your exams? And have you just been working here since?'

'I did quite well in my O levels,' Victoria said, her cheeks turning crimson. She *thought* she'd done well. She hadn't had her results yet, though, but if she told Harry that then he wouldn't think she was eighteen any more, and he wouldn't continue leaning towards her over the counter, his breath on her skin, his eyes burning into hers.

'And you've done your A levels, have you?'

Victoria looked down, said nothing.

'You haven't got A levels?'

'Well, I've been working here since I left school. My father doesn't agree with university.'

Harry laughed. 'I'm often stuck for what to say when I hear

people don't agree with it. It's not a decision, it's an institution.'

'I know, I know. He's very opinionated.'

'Most people who don't agree with university are. Still, never mind about that. You read often, don't you?'

'Oh, I read anything I can get my hands on.'

'Then I'm sure you'll get there, Victoria. I certainly hope you do. You should contact your old school and ask about A levels.'

Victoria nodded and mixed images flitted into her mind: Sally pushing notes into Victoria's fingers when they were at school, their battered wooden desks, her father's stormy face whenever Victoria mentioned university or books, her pages and pages of essays about Shakespeare and poetry, the rows of majestic red seats in the lecture theatre earlier that day and the hairsprayed students with their swinging bags and carefree conversations.

'If you want any help, do let me know,' Harry said, his voice breaking into her thoughts. 'I don't think you should stand in this shop for the rest of your life, Victoria. Not if there's so much more you want to do.'

There was a stillness between them then, a magical stillness, where all Victoria could hear was their slow, steady breathing and the ticking of clocks, and the distant rumblings of cars and people outside, and all she could see was Harry's face next to hers. When he leaned forward and kissed her, properly kissed her, she tried hard to think of how she would describe it to Sally when she told her all about it, but she couldn't think of anything, anything at all.

And as Harry spoke to her and listened to her and looked at her as if he'd never seen anyone like her before, Victoria still tried to find the words to describe the kiss. If she was to be a writer, she'd have to find words to describe things like that. But the kiss seemed too precious for words, too divine to pin down. She thought of it again and again, long after Harry had said goodbye and turned from her, towards the shop door; long after she had stared after him and realised that she hadn't offered him whisky or got him her copy of *The Blue Door* from upstairs or talked to him about a thousand things that she wanted to. But, she reasoned, as the golden day finally gave way to a pale-blue evening, there would be plenty of time for all that.

The night of Robert Bell's talk and the ice cream with Harry, Victoria dreamed of Harry all night: of his skin and his voice and his kiss that tasted of vanilla and a new world. She dreamed of walking next to him on the rocky sands, feeling cool ice cream slide down her throat. She dreamed of the day when she would marry him.

When Victoria woke up, it was to a car door slamming outside and a shout.

Her parents were home: the spell was broken.

Despite the shout that Victoria had heard from the car below, the auction that her parents had been to had actually gone very well: the clock that her father had travelled all that way for was now safely in the window of Lace Antiques, with a price tag of triple what he'd paid for it the day before. Mrs Lace appeared exhausted by the bustle of London, and the journeying to and fro. She gave Victoria an affectionate pat on the shoulder before sighing and disappearing up to bed for the day. Jack brooded in the shop, impatient for the clock to sell.

'You can go out somewhere, if you want,' he said to Victoria, waving his hand dismissively. He did that sometimes. Although Victoria was usually expected to run the shop alone for weeks on end, after Jack had bought something he thought might fetch a fortune, he sat tight behind the counter, like a fat cat waiting for a mouse to run out from under a cupboard. Victoria's very existence seemed to irritate him on these occasions, so that after she had done things like speak to him and breathe near him and perhaps cough she was told to leave him to it for the day.

Victoria went upstairs to her bedroom, squirted lacquer onto her hair, dabbed some of her mother's red lipstick on her lips and flew out of the back door of their house. When she arrived at Harry's office, she knocked gently. There was no answer. Everywhere seemed still and deserted. But Harry had said he still worked in his office marking exam scripts over the summer, even when there were no lectures, so he must be here. Perhaps she had knocked too gently on the door. She pushed it open, tentatively at first, then more firmly.

He was not there.

Victoria stood still for a moment in the middle of the room. Books lined the narrow walls: Aristotle, Shakespeare, Woolf, Dickens, Shelley and Stoker. She should read the classics; she would ask Harry which ones to start with. She'd always quite liked the sound of Dickens. She took *Great Expectations* down from the shelf and sat in Harry's chair, which was hard and green.

Victoria flicked open the first page to see an inscription.

*To remind you of what I almost was.*

*S*

Victoria frowned. What did that mean? Perhaps this was a student's copy of the book. As she placed the book back on the shelf, Harry was suddenly beside her, the door shut again, his arms around her.

'I didn't expect you,' he said. 'What a brilliant surprise for me.'

He kissed Victoria and she closed her eyes, unable to quite believe that this was happening to her. Harry's hands were firm around her waist, his lips pressed tightly against hers. He pulled away and they gazed at one another, giddy, energy crackling in the air between them.

'I've brought my writing with me,' Victoria said when her senses had returned to her, sitting down on Harry's chair and taking her crumpled papers from her satchel.

'Really? I'm impressed. You're serious about all this writing and studying business, aren't you? And I thought you just liked me for my good looks.'

Victoria laughed. 'I'd really like your opinion, too. Nobody has ever read my work before.'

Harry sat down opposite Victoria and touched the pages she had given him gently, as though they were fragile. 'Then I'm honoured, Victoria Lace. I'll read them tonight.'

'I want to know if you think I could manage A levels. Perhaps if you do, you could speak to my father and encourage him to let me leave the shop and study instead.'

Harry laughed, 'I doubt I could manage that. You told me that he doesn't believe in university, remember?'

'Maybe I should have kept that to myself,' Victoria said, grinning.

Harry looked down at the papers she had passed to him. 'I can't wait to read these. Are they short stories?'

'Yes. I did start a novel, too. But I want to finish it before you read it.'

'Good idea. You'll learn a lot from writing these. I'll give you my thoughts next week, perhaps.'

'Now I do feel like your student.'

Harry leaned forward across the desk and kissed Victoria. He tasted different today from the way he had last night: of morning and coffee, and secrets.

'And now?' he said as he leaned back and put his feet on the desk.

'I feel less like your student,' she said with a smile. She stood up and went over to Harry, and then he was kissing her again, more desperately than last time. His hands were everywhere, somehow under her clothes and on her bare skin and everything seemed to blur into nothing but feelings: she could feel so much and yet her mind was blank.

And then, a knock at the door.

Victoria sprung back from Harry so quickly that she stumbled, almost falling to the floor. Harry held his hand out to steady her and she took it, dizzy and breathless, feeling like she used to after she had ridden on the waltzer on the pier that had been torn down last year.

'Your blouse!' Harry whispered.

Victoria looked down, and saw that her blouse buttons were open, revealing her pale flesh underneath. She fumbled to do them up, trembling, as Harry brushed himself down and moved towards the door.

By the time he had opened it, Victoria had placed herself on the chair opposite the desk again. A bearded man with a ruddy complexion was visible through the crack in the door.

'Harry, do you have a copy of *Titus* I could borrow? Mine's gone bloody walkabout. I tell you, you can't leave a damn thing around in this... hello, who's this?' the man interrupted himself as he pushed into the office and saw Victoria.

'This is Victoria Lace. Victoria, this is Professor Michael Stone,' Harry said, his cheeks flushed.

Michael Stone frowned at Victoria. 'Don't you work in that little antique shop on Castle Street?'

'Yes, I do,' Victoria said, panicking a little. 'Do you know it?'

'Yes. I've done a bit of business with your father.'

'I was just going,' Victoria said, before Michael could say any more. 'I only came to borrow a book.' She sprung up and plastered a polite smile on her face; one that she hoped showed her as a stranger to Harry and his office and his chairs. 'So you were saying, you think *Great Expectations* is a good one to start with?'

Harry nodded emphatically. 'Oh yes. Yes. It's up there, on the shelf.'

Victoria reached up to grab the book, strangely aware of every part of her body, and of Harry and Michael Stone watching her. She pressed her hands around the rough spine of *Great Expectations* and pulled it down from the shelf.

'Thank you. I'll return this when I've finished it. I'd better get home. My parents are going out of town this afternoon,' she said, trying to be meaningful to Harry, though not to Michael Stone.

She turned around towards the door, squeezed past the rather unpleasant bulk of Michael Stone, and burst out into the hot air of the morning. Full of energy, she ran across the courtyard. Michael Stone's recognition of Victoria and her connection to Lace Antiques hovered in her mind as she rushed from the castle, the sharpness of apprehension about what he might say to her father blunted slightly by images of Harry in her mind and the taste of coffee and secrets on her lips. As angry as her father would be if he found out that Victoria had been spending time at Silenshore University, it was worth the risk for the thrill of the warm, adult touch of Harry's fingers still on her skin. She hugged *Great Expectations* to her chest tightly as she walked, and thought of nothing but Harry, Harry, Harry.

She was in her parents' bedroom when he arrived, sifting through her mother's cracked pots of orange powder and thick kohl pencils. All the pencils needed sharpening and there was no knife up here. She swept them up to take downstairs to the kitchen, but was distracted by an old compact of peach PanCake, which she dusted over her hand. Perhaps she would try this. Her skin was quite clear, but the powder might make her look older, somehow.

She had opened the window and the curtains were floating into the room softly, bringing with them hot, sour air that promised to turn stormy before evening fell. Although the screaming of gulls and buzz of conversations from outside were amplified, when Victoria heard the knock rise above all the other sounds, she knew it was his.

'I wasn't sure if your parents would have left yet. I waited outside until I saw them leave,' Harry said when she let him in.

The exquisite image of Harry lingering outside the shop, waiting for a chance to see her again, appeared in Victoria's mind as he followed her through the back of Lace Antiques, and then upstairs. She couldn't let Harry see her bedroom, with its piled-up issues of *Bunty* from years ago and childish stuffed rabbits and bears watching their every move. They'd have to stay in here. She leaned forward, into Harry. He kissed her as the first rumble of thunder rolled across the yellowed sky. Vibrations shuddered underneath them and rain began to hammer on the window. Harry's mouth moved down to Victoria's neck and his grip on her tightened slightly, their breaths mingling and sending Victoria to that hazy, blissful place where she had been before in Harry's office. The heat between them was thick and dizzying, and as the thunder roared closer and the brilliant light of electricity flashed into the room, their bodies melted into one another, and Victoria's life changed forever.

Afterwards, Victoria lay on the floor next to Harry, her pale arm lying across his chest. She kissed his bare skin, which was the colour of milky tea, and then laughed in delight.

'What are you laughing at?' he asked, turning to look at her, his green eyes bright and cat-like in the dark room. The storm was in the distance now, but the rain persisted, slamming down on the windows and staining the air yellow-grey.

'I'm happy. I'm incredibly, stupidly happy.'

'I am, too.' He took her hand and placed it next to his lips. She felt him take a breath, felt the air around her fingers tighten. His lips were slightly chapped and rough against her skin.

Victoria stood up shakily and smiled down at Harry. She was suddenly ravenous, and tried to remember when she had last eaten a proper meal. She wandered into the kitchen, where she clanged about, taking out pans and rifling through the scant food items in the cupboards. She inspected a piece of bread in a white bag from Blythe's Bakery and saw a fine layer of green mould flowering across the golden surface.

'Shall I make an omelette?' Victoria had never cooked anything before, but an omelette surely couldn't be that difficult. She cracked a couple of eggs into the frying pan that always sat on the cooker. Fragments of shell floated in the gluey yolk, and Victoria prodded at the pieces with her finger, trying to extract them. They wouldn't come out. She'd have to hope that Harry wouldn't notice. Did you stir an omelette or just leave it alone? Victoria watched as the eggs bubbled up in the centre and spread their white wings around the edges of the pan. Perhaps Harry would ask her to marry him quite soon, and then somebody would teach her to cook. Who, though? Her mother didn't ever cook, really. They lived off bread and tinned peaches and chips from Wheel's across the road. Victoria couldn't feed Harry those things. Perhaps Sally's mother would teach her. Sally's mother was a normal type of woman, who had her hair set every week and hosted civilised dinner parties, where Sally was allowed a small glass of wine and a prawn cocktail starter. Sally's mother was the kind of woman who would surely be happy to teach a newly married girl how to cook.

Victoria closed her eyes briefly and tried to picture her wedding day, but the sickly smell of the eggs and oil wafting beneath her nose distracted her and pulled her back to the present. She was only wearing her blouse because Harry had pulled her skirt off earlier, and she shivered in the newly fresh air that the storm had brought with it.

Harry stood up and wandered over to where Victoria stood. He peered into the pan, his arm around her waist, but said nothing. She sliced the wobbling mixture into two halves and slid each onto a plate.

'I'm not very good at cooking,' said Victoria as they sat in the lounge with the plates on their knees, hoping that Harry would admire her modest honesty. 'But I can learn. Once I'm a wife, I will learn very quickly.'

Harry paused with a fork lifted to his mouth. The brightness from his eyes disappeared for a moment, a fleeting shadow flickering across them. 'I don't want to think about that,' he said, putting his fork down.

'Why not? Is it my father? He won't like the idea at first, but surely, once he's got to know you, he will—'

'Victoria…' Harry's face was white. 'I'm already married.'

## CHAPTER 9

# *Isobel: 2010*

*My Queen,*

*I've had a letter from somebody anonymous warning me to get away from Silenshore.*

*I want to know where you've gone, and who it is that I might need to protect myself from. Has somebody hurt you, too? If they have, then I need to know. You must tell me.*

*Victoria, I am barely living without you. I dream of you, and the day that we can be together, always.*

*H*

On Friday evening, the rain comes down in slicing sheets. Isobel pauses for a moment to reposition the bright blue hood of her coat, which has blown down from her head in a hostile gust of wind. Her face is frozen with water. She slams the boot of her Corsa shut and then hurries around to the driver's side.

As she arrives at Broadsands and swings her car onto the wide gravel driveway, Daphne's words from when Isobel first met her ring in the air, mingling with the engine and the rain on the windscreen. She stops the car on the drive and sits for a moment.

*This is a gift for you both.*

But as she listens to the words in her mind over and over

again, she remembers Daphne's face, cool and still. Even the next day, when Isobel and Tom visited Daphne again to tell her that they would like to accept her offer of moving in, she remained unreadable. Isobel thought then, without warning, of her own mother, her feelings painted on her face as brightly as her lipstick. Daphne is another breed altogether.

Isobel sighs and shakes her head, then opens the car door to the pummeling rain and wind. Tom is the only one she really needs to be behind her. And Daphne is just quiet and a bit guarded: one of those people it takes time to get to know. Plus, Isobel reasons as she lugs out some heavy bags from the boot and staggers to the front door, she'll have all the time in the world to get to know Daphne now that they'll be living together.

Isobel hammers on the black front door and then tries to push it open. It's locked. She stands in the pouring rain and surveys the street where she is going to be living, the roads that she will push a pram along. Isobel noticed in the daylight last time they came that Daphne's house is painted a pastel pink. The one to the left of Daphne's is powder blue; the one to the right a pale yellow. In the fading sun, the houses looked like a trail of sugared almonds.

The houses opposite look as though they belong in another street, another time altogether: crammed-together terraces that are browned, tired and poor. The road between the two rows of houses is wide, and now Isobel squints across it through the rain. At one of the terraced houses directly opposite Daphne's, an old woman hunches at her bowing front door. Although the rain is stinging and unrelenting, the woman does not move. With growing unease, Isobel realises that the old woman is staring at her, watching her. Her bright eyes penetrate across the wide, flooded road.

'Isobel, come in. I didn't realise the door was locked.' Daphne's voice takes a few moments to interrupt Isobel's gaze across the road. She hurries into the house and is met by the same heavy scent of lavender and polish that she noticed the first time she came.

'You shouldn't be carrying those bags. Where's Tom?'

'He's loading up his car at his place. He'll be here in a minute.'

There's a silence as the two women stand facing one another. 'Thanks so much for offering to let us stay,' Isobel says eventually. 'We're really determined to save as much as we can and get somewhere of our own as quickly as possible.'

Daphne shakes her head. 'You don't have to worry. I'm rattling around in this house. It's too big for one person, and I spend a lot of my time in the garden and walking in the summer, so it's empty a lot of the time.'

Isobel nods. 'Still, I'm so grateful.'

She follows Daphne into the kitchen and takes a seat at the pine table. Daphne stands at the Aga and waits for the kettle to boil, glancing through to the hall every few seconds. Her pale jeans bear slight splatters of mud, the sign of an earlier walk with Hugh, the chocolate Lab, who wanders around the kitchen in search of something invisible.

'Have you got much in your car to bring in?' Daphne asks, running her hand through her short grey hair.

'Yes, quite a bit. But I might wait until this rain dies down a bit before I unload any more.'

'Good idea.'

Daphne busies herself with three sturdy blue mugs and some coffee. As she puts one of the mugs down in front of Isobel, the back door creaks open and Tom comes in, rainwater dripping down from his dark hair onto his face. He smiles when he sees Isobel sitting at the table, his eyebrows raised in subtle question.

*Are you okay?* his face asks, his eyes darting quickly from Daphne back to Isobel.

Isobel smiles back at him and nods subtly. They'll have to get used to secret code now that they live with his mother.

'Isobel's car still needs unloading, Tom. She didn't want to go out in the rain. Not in her condition,' she says. Isobel looks down into the remnants of her coffee.

'It's okay. I'll get the stuff out. Just let me unload mine first. Are we in the front bedroom?'

'Yes. That's the one I've made up. It's a bit bigger than the other spare, and it's got those wardrobes. They're quite old, but they'll do the trick.'

Tom nods and opens the door again, grimacing as the sharp, wet wind bites at him through the gap. As he leaves, Daphne grins at Isobel. Her smile is wolfish and sharp, disappearing as soon as it's arrived.

'Saves you getting wet. Shall I get us some dinner?'

Isobel steals one last glance at the back door, which remains closed. Tom is probably unloading methodically, slowly, in spite of the horrendous rain. And last time Isobel skipped a meal, she felt horribly nauseous and threw up on her carpet. She can't throw up here, in front of Daphne.

'Yes, that'd be nice.'

Daphne bends to open the fridge and takes out some chicken, a quiche and some salad. She puts the food out on the table with some hunks of brown, crusty loaf and a tub of hard butter.

'Might as well tuck in. Tom can get something once he's finished bringing the things in,' Daphne says, snatching a piece of chicken and popping it into her mouth. 'Help yourself. Can't have you going hungry.'

Tom appears at the door, drenched and dragging two suitcases behind him, as Isobel is loading some chicken onto some bread. He crams a triangle of quiche into his mouth before heading back outside.

'I don't mind helping,' Isobel calls as he ducks back into the wet night.

Tom sticks his head inside again, a faint line of pastry on his upper lip. 'No need. It won't take long. You have some more food and relax. It's been a hectic day.'

When Tom has come back in with her boxes of toiletries and books, and carried all their things upstairs to the bedroom they will be sleeping in, Isobel stands up, her muscles aching from sitting in the hard-backed dining chair.

'I think I might go to bed, if that's okay? I can help clear up first, if you like.'

'No, don't be silly. There isn't much to clear,' Daphne says. 'I hope you sleep well. I'll get you a glass of water to take up. Tom, show Isobel the front bedroom, will you?'

Tom shows Isobel the bedroom that they'll be having, his gentle hand on the small of her back as he guides her upstairs. The room is big and comfortable. Daphne has put a vase of carnations on the deep windowsill. The dusky, honeyed fragrance of the flowers mixes with the hint of freshly washed sheets. There's a neat, compact en suite to the right of the bed, and to the left there is enough room for the mahogany crib that is back in its box and ready to be reassembled.

Tom takes Isobel's hand and motions for her to sit on the bed. 'Well?' he asks. 'What do you think?'

Isobel smiles. 'I think things will work out. It all seems okay.'

'It does. And anyway, we're just staying here short-term. As soon as we have some money saved up, we'll buy somewhere of our own. It's a means to an end.'

Isobel turns to face Tom. Is it really going to be this simple? She looks at his clear green eyes; his calm, stolid expression. It seems as if it could be. She kisses him and he presses her into him. The warm scent of his musky aftershave, dampened by the rain, envelops her.

Once Tom's left the room and Isobel has undressed, she wanders into the bathroom. Daphne has left out a new bar of soap, and after running the peach sink full of warm water, Isobel lathers the smooth bar into her hands and runs them over her face, then pats herself dry with one of the towels that Daphne has left on the bed. When she hangs the towel back on the radiator, she sees that her mascara has left steel-grey scores on it. Her skin is taut and tingling with the scent of the unfamiliar.

She crawls beneath the tightly tucked duvet, her eyes open and alert in the strange darkness. The window is slightly ajar and the sounds of the sea linger in the room. She turns over and touches her belly. The bed is warm, and she can hear the lull of Tom's voice below. He'll be saying positive things to Daphne, nice things about Isobel, about the baby. The rise and fall of his undistinguishable words are comforting, and she feels herself being swept into the tide of sleep. Broken images flit through her mind, pulling her from the day.

And then suddenly, she is awake again, sitting bolt upright. She swallows and forces herself to take a lungful of air. What has woken her so suddenly? It's a few seconds before she realises what it was; a moment until she remembers the last image to dart into her subconscious.

The old lady from across the road, silver-haired, ethereal, staring.

Isobel pulls the covers up to her chin like a frightened child. The bed creaks. The room is chilly all of a sudden, the open window letting in icy air. Isobel releases the soft covers and swings her legs out of bed. As she reaches the window, she parts the heavy pink curtains and glances out into the inky street below, the ghost of her reflection watching her. The street is empty, the houses opposite in darkness. She shuts the window with a bang and, shivering, returns to bed.

'First baby?' the sonographer asks as she rubs cool gel onto Isobel's pale skin. The first few weeks at Daphne's have passed quickly and quietly, and today is the day of Isobel's first dating scan.

'Yeah,' Isobel and Tom answer in nervous unison.

The sonographer gives a fleeting nod and then turns towards the monitor next to Isobel. 'Let's have a look.'

The screen shows a grey, flitting mass. Isobel strains to see it, to watch the wispy shapes blur in and out of view.

'I can see it,' Tom whispers, his eyes strangely still as he stares at the jumping image.

The sonographer frowns as she flicks through some notes, one hand still rolling the scanner over Isobel's skin. 'How far along did you think you were?'

Every muscle in Isobel tightens. 'I wasn't sure, but I thought I was about twelve weeks?'

'I think you're a bit further than that. I'll take some measurements, but I think you're about four months.'

'But everything's fine? The baby's okay?'

The sonographer doesn't answer for a few seconds, squinting at the screen and looking down at her notes and scribbling down letters and numbers that Isobel can't see. Isobel sees Tom glance subtly at the notes, his face pale with apprehension, and squeezes her eyes shut.

Everything will be okay, she tells herself, chanting the words over and over again in her mind until the sonographer touches her shoulder and she opens her eyes again.

'So everything's fine?' Daphne says that night as she dishes out sausage casserole. Her voice is shaken. It seems she's been worried too.

'Yes. We were a bit anxious because the woman who did the scan seemed a bit confused at first. But it turns out that was because I'm further along than we thought. I'm due at the end of May.'

Daphne motions for them to sit at the table. The sweet, fatty smell of the sausages permeates the kitchen and Isobel's stomach twists with something that is difficult to label as either nausea or hunger. She sits down next to Tom, and as she looks over at Daphne she sees that her eyes have suddenly become blurred with tears.

'Don't mind me,' Daphne says, turning and moving swiftly over to the Aga. 'I get emotional too easily these days. It must be old age.'

Isobel stands up and follows her. The Aga's dry heat buzzes around them.

'I'm the same. I barely cried before I was pregnant, but now it's all the time. And it's over silly things like adverts or songs.' She holds out her arms and gives Daphne a small, awkward hug. The smell of the house, the polish and fresh flowers, is stronger this close to Daphne. It clings to her, mingling with the faint smell of Hugh and the outdoors. Isobel realises as soon as she puts her arms around Daphne that she probably isn't the kind of woman who wants a hug from Isobel, that she should have stayed sitting at the table next to Tom.

'We'll have enough crying when the baby's here,' Daphne replies, pulling away and clearing her throat. She runs a hand through her hair. 'I'll pull myself together. You two eat and I'll have something later. You need some time just the two of you anyway.'

'Mum, come and sit with us,' Tom says, rising from his place at the table.

'No. Eat, Tom,' Daphne says, her voice clipped with the threat of more tears.

Tom sits down again, shrugs, and motions for Isobel to start eating.

'I think the baby has got her a little worked up,' he whispers, once Daphne has left the kitchen.

'Is that really all it is?' Isobel asks. 'It seems as if so something's bothering her. I hope it's not my being here, or the baby.'

'She's always like this. But she's harmless. She means well, and she told me she really likes you.'

'Really? What did she say?'

Tom shrugs. 'I can't remember. Something about you being good for me. So she's fine with us. It's just a big thing, having a baby on the way. It's her first grandchild, so she's probably feeling a bit anxious or something.'

'Well she's not the only one,' Isobel points out, pushing the sausage and tomatoes around her plate, then putting down her fork. She pulls her chair closer to Tom's, nestling herself into his broad chest. 'I was so nervous at the scan when I thought there might be a problem. It made it even clearer to me how much I want it all. I know it's all happened quickly but it feels right, somehow. I do wonder if I'm being a bit naïve, though. Is it going to be much harder than we think?'

'Well, we'll find out soon, I suppose. It can't be that difficult, surely, otherwise nobody would ever have more than one.'

'Yes, but don't forget that we're biologically tricked.'

'Tricked?'

'Yes! Didn't you know? We're tricked into having babies, and then more and more.'

'Ah. So I've been tricked? I must admit, I have heard of this type of scenario before. Girl meets boy, falls in love, wants to keep him, has baby in order to do so.'

Isobel jabs Tom gently in the ribs, through his grey shirt that is still crisp and still smells of his musky aftershave, even though he's been wearing it all day. 'Not tricked by me! Tricked by *biology*.'

'Biology? Well, this is getting interesting.'

As they draw together and kiss, the rattle of Hugh's lead and the slam of the front door as Daphne goes out interrupt them.

'Shall we go after her?' Isobel asks, pulling away.

'No,' Tom says. 'She probably does just want to give us some space. Don't worry about her.' He picks up Isobel's fork and hands it to her, smiling. 'Let's eat.'

The next day, Isobel sits in the small staffroom of Silenshore Castle High School, her head bowed over a mock exam script and the tip of a biro between her teeth.

'Everything okay?'

Isobel hears the voice, but doesn't register it for a while. She's engrossed in the words of the year-ten pupil who describes Seamus Heaney's poems exactly as Isobel hoped. She peers at the marking scheme on the table in front of her and then returns to the neatly printed script. *A** she marks in green. Always green pen, never red.

'Isobel? Are you okay?'

Isobel turns to Simone, who stares at Isobel with curiosity unsuccessfully masked by a vague attempt at concern. Simone teaches geography and has worked at Silenshore Castle High School since it opened in the late 1980s. She's not somebody Isobel would normally chat to at work. The only person Isobel has told about the baby is Lucy, another English teacher, who Isobel felt, at the time of conspiratorial whispering, that she could trust. Now, she's beginning to doubt that she can trust anyone here. As she thinks about all the secrets she's heard in her time here: people's affairs and redundancies and broken hearts, it dawns on Isobel that nobody at this school is particularly fastidious about keeping secrets.

'I'm good, thanks,' Isobel replies now, flipping the script over to reveal another. It's Cassie's. This pupil is on an eternal brink of D/C grades. She scans the angular, scratchy writing to look for concepts she's tried to drum into the class in the past few months: *metaphor, symbolism, simile.* Some are there. Isobel ticks quickly, then looks back up at Simone.

'I hope you don't mind me saying, but I hear congratulations are in order?' Simone's voice rises in question, her face desperate to know more.

Isobel smiles and shuffles her papers. 'Yeah. News travels fast here.'

'I didn't even know you were seeing anybody,' Simone steamrollers on. 'Is he a nice man?'

'He's amazing,' Isobel said. 'It was a bit of a shock, I'll admit.

But we're really happy about it. I had my scan yesterday and I'm due in May.'

Simone picks up her mug again and then sits back slightly, disappointment at the lack of drama spreading over her pallid features. Obviously, the version she has already heard of Isobel's pregnancy from someone else at the school was more thrilling. 'That's good. Is he local?'

'Yes. We're staying with his mother at the moment, actually. She lives on West Street.'

'Oooh!' comes another voice from behind them. Lily, the music teacher, looms behind Isobel's shoulder. 'Are we talking about Isobel's new man?'

'He's not that new,' Isobel points out, picking up her marking again and looking down at Cassie's answer. 'I've known him for quite a few months now.'

'He's older, isn't he?' Lily asks, going over to the kitchen area and opening the drawer where she keeps her fruit tea bags. She drops one into a mug and the air fills with the floral, sugary scent of raspberries and orange. 'I'd love an older man. They just have a bit more about them, don't they?'

Simone is intrigued by this offering. She puts her mug down again. 'So he's older, is he? Has he got any other children?'

Isobel bristles. 'No. He was married, but he's divorced now and he has no children.'

'Married?' Simone repeats, the glow of satisfaction brightening her features. 'So there's an ex?'

Lily drops her teaspoon into the sink with a clatter. 'Oh, everyone's got an ex these days, Simone. It's no big deal.'

Simone shrugs huffily. 'I was just saying. It normally gets tricky with an ex.'

'Tom's ex doesn't live round here,' Isobel says curtly, but she can feel herself colouring. 'It's definitely over with.'

'It's never been really over with mine. Ex-wives are never fully in the past, Isobel. I'm just saying, maybe you should slow down a bit. Do your homework on him, so to speak,' she finishes as she snatches her bag and pulls the staffroom door open.

'Ignore her,' Lily instructs in a whisper as Simone disappears. 'She always wants everyone to be as miserable as her.'

Isobel rolls her eyes. 'I know. She's always the same.' But that afternoon, as she hands out flipchart paper and stickers to her boisterous classes, logs quiz scores, marks role-plays and confiscates mobile phones, Simone's words niggle her.

Tom told Isobel, when they first got together, that his ex-wife, Georgia, was living in Australia, and that he never really speaks to her now. They got married when they were quite young and both ended up wanting different things, so they split up. That's all. Isobel has never felt as though Georgia is an issue. She seems as though she's in the past: Tom never mentions her.

Now, Simone's words echo in her mind.

*Ex-wives are never fully in the past, Isobel.*

*Slow down.*

Isobel doesn't ever slow down. And there's no way the baby is going to slow down, either, not for anything. She might ask Tom for a more detailed version of what happened with Georgia at some point. But his answers won't change how she feels about him, anyway. She trusts him. And not because she's stupid or doesn't know him, or needs to slow down, or is desperate. She's just completely crazy about him. She can't help it. She's crazy about Tom, the baby, the whole thing. And she's in too deep for anything to change her mind now.

## CHAPTER 10

# *Evelyn: 1948*

All morning, the castle had been buzzing with an electric atmosphere. Evelyn was meant to stay in her bedroom, but she just couldn't. Excitement fizzed up inside of her, making it impossible to sit serenely, like a bride was meant to do.

A bride.

Evelyn du Rêve was to be a bride. And after being a bride, she was to be swept away to London, to a life of parties and champagne and, Jack assured her, fame. He would give her everything she had ever wanted.

After that day when she had met Jack; when the 12.05 train to London had chugged along merrily without her whilst she perched on a stool that Jack pulled out for her, Evelyn had seen him rather a lot. She'd spent hours in the shop with him as he worked, and she'd taken Jack to the castle, where he charmed her parents and looked around in awe at where Evelyn had come from. Jack had proposed after a month, as they sat on the cool rocky beach with a bottle of golden champagne. Evelyn had jumped to her feet and squealed her answer, pleasure bolting through her blood. She drank more, and more, and asked Jack to dance with her. When they had danced, and when there was no more champagne left, he set down an old fur rug on the uneven rocks, and lay Evelyn down beneath him. She closed her eyes and put her hands on his firm, warm skin that was gritty with flecks of sand. He had made Evelyn into a woman, and now she was about to be his wife. She simply couldn't wait.

The suitcase that she had packed to go to London on her own was still standing in her bedroom, packed again, but this time with her things, to move into Lace Antiques with Jack, as his wife. And once the wedding was done with, Jack was going to sell the shop and they were going to buy their very own flat in London above a bigger and better antique store.

Evelyn stepped out of the castle's front entrance into the crisp January air. Her mother was outside too, arranging flowers around the imposing archway. Evelyn frowned. When her parents had offered to hold the wedding reception at the castle, Evelyn had expected that they would have staff to arrange flowers and set out wine glasses and do all the other things that her mother had seemed to spend all morning doing,

'Mother! What are you doing that for?'

Mrs du Rêve glanced away from her work. Her face was drawn, pale. She smiled at Evelyn, but the smile was a flicker of light on an otherwise dark expression.

'I'm just helping out. People never do a proper job of anything these days. Anyway,' she said, touching Evelyn's shoulder lightly. 'Why aren't you getting dressed yet? Shall I come up and help you? You can't be late for your own wedding!'

A flutter of nerves swept through Evelyn as she thought about the day to come. 'Yes, please.'

They climbed the wide stone stairs back into the castle together, Evelyn leading the way.

An hour later, Evelyn gazed at herself in the full-length mirror in her bedroom. She hadn't wanted to wear this dress. It was her mother's wedding dress, and it was too short, dotted with strange feathers and not at all what Evelyn had imagined. She'd thought that perhaps she'd have gone shopping with her mother for a grand and elegant gown. But at this idea, her mother had frowned and murmured something about the best shops closing down during the war. Surely there had been some left, Evelyn had wanted to know. But then Mrs du Rêve had appeared with this dress, and all but begged Evelyn to try it.

It didn't look so bad, Evelyn supposed. And it might bring her good luck in her marriage: her parents had been so very fortunate since their own wedding.

'All ready,' she said brightly to her mother, her fingers entwined tightly around a sharp feather on her waist.

Mrs du Rêve nodded and walked over to Evelyn, putting her arms around her without warning and hugging her so tightly that Evelyn thought her bones might break.

'Mother! What's the matter?'

Mrs du Rêve shook her head. 'Nothing. Nothing at all. Please, Evelyn. Enjoy your day and don't worry about me.'

Evelyn pulled away from her mother, taking in her tight mouth, her eyes clouded with tears. 'I can't,' Evelyn said. 'Not until I know what's wrong. You've been acting strangely all day. Do you not want me to marry Jack? Do you not like him? Is that it?'

Mrs du Rêve stared at Evelyn for a moment, saying nothing, her features still tight, fearful. Then a sob erupted from her, tears suddenly rushing down her cheeks. 'Oh, Evelyn! Evelyn!'

'What?' Evelyn said, her voice shaking. 'What is it?' She pulled her mother upright, taking her over to the bed and sitting her on it like a child.

'It's not Jack at all. It's nothing to do with him. I'm so pleased that you have him, because we have nothing left for you. It's all gone Evelyn! It's all gone!'

Evelyn put her hands up to her face. 'What's all gone?' she asked, although she knew.

'The money. The castle.' Her mother slumped back on the bed. 'It's all gone. We've run out. The castle is too big to keep up with. Your father and I have tried, but it's just impossible.'

'But how has it happened? I don't understand!' Evelyn thought of their grand parties not so long ago; her proud father; of their dresses and china and crystal that had all gone missing over the last year or so to be repaired or valued, and never returned.

'Oh, Evelyn! The war changed everything. We're in debt to so many people who've done things for us. We thought we'd be able to pay them all off somehow, but we can't. There are just too many bills, and our taxes are higher than ever. Before long the castle will be falling down around us. We just can't afford to keep going like this.'

'It can't be true. I'm sure if you sold some things, you could make enough money to pay what you owe.'

Her mother shook her head, taking Evelyn's hands in hers and gripping them tightly. 'I didn't want to tell you this today, Evelyn. But we agreed a sale on the castle yesterday. A consortium has kept offering to buy it, to make it into a university, and we've always said no. But now we've no choice. Some of your father's relatives in France have offered to take us in for a while. It'll do us good to have some time to think about what to do. We'll go next week.' Evelyn's mother began to cry again. 'I'm so sorry, Evelyn.'

'France? But when will I see you again? Evelyn asked, questions tumbling from her mouth before she had even thought about them. 'How am I meant to live in a different country from you? Without the castle? How can it be changed into something so different?' Images of the castle, of her home, as a university, flew into her mind, making her feel sick. 'I can't take all of it in.'

'Your father and I have thought about what you should do, Evelyn. Come with us! Bring Jack. He can start up a new shop. I'm sure your father's family would help him along.'

Evelyn faltered. She thought of the plans she'd made with Jack, of the glittering life ahead of her in the city, of her bright future with her handsome husband. 'I can't,' she said, the words surprising her. 'Why don't you come to London?'

Mrs du Rêve sighed. 'We don't have enough money to move to London. Your father's family are our only chance.'

Evelyn thought frantically, desperately. If only there were a way they could all be together. Then she saw it from across the room, twinkling in the light.

'The mirror!' she said, racing over to her bedside table. 'I have your mirror! We can sell it!'

Evelyn's mother snatched the mirror away. 'Evelyn! I didn't know you had this! I warned you off it!'

Evelyn stared at her mother. Surely none of that mattered. Not now.

'We can't sell it.'

'Why not?'

'It's been in the family for generations. It's been passed down to whoever has lived here. We can't take it away from the castle.'

'Nonsense,' said Evelyn, reaching for the mirror, but her mother cradled it tightly, as though it was a precious baby.

'Evelyn. Listen to me. This mirror is a legacy of the castle. If it leaves these walls, whoever has taken it will be cursed.'

Evelyn frowned. 'That's so silly!'

'Anyway, it wouldn't be worth enough to make a difference. We owe all sorts of debts. We've tried lately to sell things and make some money. But it doesn't stretch far enough, and there's very little left to use up now. The only thing to do is sell the castle. We've already agreed to it. So the mirror isn't even worth arguing about. Promise me you'll leave it here, Evelyn.'

Evelyn thought about when she had packed the mirror in her suitcase to take to London, the day she had met Jack. It had left the castle then, and nothing bad had happened to her. But she stayed quiet. She knew she wasn't going to begin her new life with Jack without it.

'I'm so sorry, Evelyn. I can't quite believe I've had to tell you all this on your wedding day. It's not what I wanted for you. I wanted you to have a perfect day.'

Evelyn stood up and brushed her strange wedding dress down, her fingers catching on rough feathers and smooth pearls. She wiped a tear from her mother's cheek and smiled. 'I still will have a perfect day. And tonight, I will tell Jack and we'll face it all as a family. He'll help you decide what to do.'

Mrs du Rêve nodded, finally releasing her grasp on the mirror and leaving it on Evelyn's bed. 'And please, Evelyn. Tell nobody other than Jack about this. Nobody in Silenshore can know what has become of us. I couldn't bear the shame.'

'I won't tell anybody else. Perhaps Jack and I will be able to visit you in France. Or perhaps we could even send you some money, once we're settled in London. Jack's sure that he can get me a job in the theatre, and I know his new shop will do well. Perhaps eventually you'll be able to come back home.'

'I hope so.'

'Just wait. You'll see,' Evelyn said, her voice suddenly full of hope and light. 'It will all turn out in the end.'

The wedding, at least, turned out well. It was only small, because since they had thrown fewer parties, the du Rêves appeared to have fewer friends. But that, as Mr du Rêve pointed out, was just the way the world went round. Jack's parents had died years ago, so they weren't there. A few men who knew Jack from his nights in the Smuggler's Ship brought their wives, who wore things that were obviously modelled on the outfits of Princess Elizabeth's wedding guests a few months before. Evelyn felt like rather a letdown when she saw their carefully chosen cheap furs and jewels, for in her mother's old wedding dress she certainly didn't look anything like a princess. A few people from Silenshore came to the church to flutter rose petals over them as they came out, and Evelyn wondered if she should ask them to the castle afterwards, but then she thought of her mother's secret and stayed quiet. The reception in the castle, then, was a quiet affair. Evelyn didn't have any friends to speak of, so the day was perhaps a little too quiet, and the dull January weather made it a little bit gloomy and cold. But if Evelyn felt cold; if she thought about the fact that it might be the last time she would ever sit in the castle dining room; if she felt a strange, twisting sensation low in her stomach every time she thought of her parents, then she would simply look across at her new husband, and smile and he would smile back, and Evelyn would think of all that she had before her.

On the night of her wedding to Jack, Evelyn lay stiffly in his bed above his shop. This, she had to remind herself, was her home now. Yet although she loved Jack, and had imagined living here so very often over the past few weeks, now that this was it, Evelyn felt frozen somehow. She thought of her bedroom in the castle, empty, all her things packed away; all her parents' things being hurriedly stuffed into boxes. The castle had been so stripped of its valuables since the war that there wasn't much at all for them to pack. Evelyn shivered and pulled Jack's blanket – *their* blanket – over her cool skin.

When Jack appeared in the room and climbed into the bed next to her, Evelyn breathed in his foreign, meaty scent and tried not to think too much about all that was changing. He tugged at her nightdress gently, and she let him. But as he touched her, her skin seemed to recoil, and to her horror, tears gathered in her eyes.

Stop it, she told herself. Don't be afraid, and don't think about the castle.

But it was too late. Jack had noticed. He sat up, frowning.

'What's the matter?' he asked, a sigh escaping from his lips.

Evelyn shook her head tightly. 'We'll talk afterwards.'

'No,' Jack said, frowning. 'Tell me.'

Evelyn sat up too, hugging her knees to her chest. She had been stern with herself about this: she would tell Jack in the morning, and let him have her to himself, without her family's problems, tonight. But now, in this strange room full of scents and feelings she hadn't even known existed before now, she felt her resolve crumbling into sand.

'My parents,' she wailed, unable to contain it any longer. 'They've lost the castle! It's gone, Jack. Their fortune, their home. It's all gone, swallowed up by the war.' She took a clumsy breath and managed to calm herself, quieten her words. 'They've sold it, and they've nowhere to live. We need to help them.'

She looked at her new husband. In the darkness of the bedroom, he looked like a different man to the one she'd known up to now. He said nothing.

'Jack,' Evelyn said, tears catching in her throat. 'Can we help them?'

Jack sighed again, more sharply this time. In the dim light of the bedside lamp, Evelyn saw something change in his eyes: a subtle shift from light to dark.

'You're telling me now?' he asked quietly.

Evelyn nodded. 'Yes. I meant to wait until tomorrow.'

Jack's shout was unexpected: Evelyn had never heard him shout before. When it came, she covered her ears, found herself trembling underneath his blankets.

'You've trapped me!' The words seemed to swoop around the room, echoing and reverberating in Evelyn's mind again and again.

She shook her head wildly. 'No! No, Jack. I just didn't want to ruin the day. My mother told me just before the ceremony. I couldn't tell you at the church, could I?'

'You married me on purpose,' Jack stormed. 'You knew you'd soon have nothing, so you married me.'

Evelyn shook her head again and again. 'No!' she shouted, her voice flying high in the room and matching Jack's. 'You're wrong. That's not what happened!'

'You do know, Evelyn, that we have nothing? That I can't help your parents? That I can barely get us by?'

Evelyn put her head in her hands, her body shuddering with

sobs. Jack had promised her wealth and beautiful dresses, and a new flat in London. He'd told her that they didn't need a honeymoon, because their new life in the best flat in the best part of the city would be like a honeymoon that would last forever. He told her all sorts of things, and she'd believed him, only now she saw that she was a stupid, stupid girl, because none of it was ever going to be true.

'Oh, you're wondering about the lies I told you?' Jack laughed. 'You're wondering about all the things I said you could have? Well, they're not real, Evelyn. So that leaves both of us disappointed.' He leaned close to her, suddenly grotesque: his naked, hairy body repulsive. 'And now you're as trapped as I am.'

'This came for you,' Jack said, tossing a parcel onto the Formica table in the kitchen.

Evelyn glanced up from her untouched, grey porridge. It was only a few weeks since she'd become Jack's wife, and already the sight of him wore her out. She pulled the parcel towards her, noting that the brown paper had already been torn into. Her heart seemed to stop as she saw the things inside: things that belonged to her old life. She took out a bottle of her mother's Chanel perfume, half empty; a blood-red lipstick; a tiny photograph of her parents.

'Was there an address? A note?' Evelyn asked as Jack shovelled his own porridge into his mouth.

He shook his head.

'But you opened it. Mother wouldn't forget to tell me where she was. She knows I need her.'

Jack frowned. 'They disappeared, Evelyn. Without telling you.'

Evelyn thought back to the day after her wedding, when she'd sneaked out of her new house as the sun sank in the grey sky. She'd only spent one lonely day in the shop as Jack came and went on errands, one night in his bed, and already she knew that she'd made a terrible, terrible mistake, and she needed to see her mother. Perhaps, she'd thought, she would go to France after all.

She'd run softly up the hill, from Jack's shop, up to the elegant gates of the castle, but when she reached them, they were locked. Evelyn squinted, peering between the wrought-iron petals, and in an instant, she knew.

Her parents were gone.

'My parents wouldn't have disappeared suddenly like that if they could have helped it. They told me they were going the week after the wedding. Not the very next day,' she said now to Jack, as he clattered his spoon clumsily around his bowl.

Jack shrugged. 'They were probably chased away. I heard something at the Smuggler's last week about them owing money all over the place.'

Evelyn's cheeks burned at the thought of her parents being discussed by leery men who smelt of beer. 'Why didn't you tell me?'

'I'm telling you now,' Jack said simply, standing up and brushing past her roughly before disappearing downstairs into the shop.

Evelyn stared after him, then sat back down at the table, pulling the box from her parents towards her again. There must have been more in the package: a letter or a card that Jack had hidden. They had left Evelyn their address: of course they had. She knew it. It was somewhere in this house. And as soon as she found it, she could find her parents again, and this nightmare would be over.

She searched the kitchen first, finding odd plates and chipped bowls and even a few pound notes, but no letter. She moved quickly, deftly, from one room to another: the lounge, the bedroom, the ugly cabinet on the landing, even the little pink bathroom. But she found nothing.

She sat on the strange, hard bed that was now hers, thinking and thinking. Perhaps somebody at the castle would know where her parents had gone. Jumping up again, she listened at the bedroom door for the sounds of Jack she had grown used to in the weeks since their marriage: his short, impatient cough; his stomping, his clanking and clattering of things for his shop downstairs.

She could hear nothing. Breathing a sigh of relief, she crept downstairs, and, silent as a cat, sneaked out of the back door into the golden afternoon.

Evelyn's heart plummeted as soon as she slipped through the side entrance to the castle. Already the soul of her old home was being cut away, making way for something quite different. The university had already erected a large, unpleasant sign outside the gates, and the windows were bare, stripped of their drapes and character. It was as though there had never been elegant parties, grand games and music and fun inside.

A tall, lanky man was painting one of the tired-looking doorways. She watched him for a moment, swallowing down her mortification at suddenly being an outsider at the castle. Ignoring her flaming cheeks, she cleared her throat so that the man glanced at her, his dripping paintbrush dotting the floor with tiny mossy green splatters as he paused.

'I'm sorry to bother you,' Evelyn said, trying not to look at the mess the paintbrush was making. 'I was wondering if you had any information on the previous owners? Where they went?'

The man turned back to his painting. 'They were off as soon as the deal had been done. Glad for the castle to be taken off their hands. That's it, really.'

*That's it.* Evelyn shuddered. So simple, to someone who wasn't experiencing it all, someone who hadn't made an awful choice and lost everything.

'But do you know why? I've heard they went sooner than they were meant to,' she pressed, her voice beginning to break.

'I suppose they were in a hurry. Maybe someone was after them,' the man said, shrugging. 'These rich people aren't always what they seem.'

Evelyn felt something thud down inside her. 'Oh, I see,' she tried to make her voice sound less rich, as if it hadn't been part of the castle for all of her life, and took a step away from the newly painted glossy doorway.

'Their daughter's still around, you know. My pal said she's still here in Silenshore. She got married to someone local, apparently. You could try and find her, if you really wanted to know the full story.'

Evelyn took another step away. Part of her wanted so badly to stay there for as long as she could, so that she was somehow absorbed back into the castle, into who she used to be. But the man kept glancing back at her as though he wondered what on earth she was still there for, so in the end she thanked him and turned away from her old life, and walked slowly back to her new one.

'Do you think it's true?' she asked Jack that night. She'd managed to make them some sandwiches and bake a small, simple cake for tea and they had spoken about an original painting that Jack had managed to get his hands on that morning for the shop. Evelyn felt calmer than she had earlier, and now, as she looked at Jack, she wondered if things might not be as bad as she'd thought. He might be someone she could bear, if she tried. After all, he had made her so many promises. He couldn't possibly go back on every single one of them.

'Do I think what's true?'

'About my parents being chased away by someone. I wonder if that's really why they went.'

'Probably. I don't know why else they'd go. Maybe they'd got on the wrong side of someone and needed to get away to be safe.'

Evelyn's sense of calm crumbled as she suddenly realised what that might mean. 'I might not be safe either, then,' she said quietly. 'People might recognise me. They might expect me to pay what my parents owed.'

Jack glanced at her, scorn quickly passing over his features. 'With what?'

'I don't know. They won't know I have nothing, will they?'

Jack sighed and Evelyn felt the cake she had made lying heavy in her stomach. Perhaps she hadn't done a very good job of baking it after all.

'Maybe,' Jack said, 'you should stay indoors for the next week or so. Just in case.'

Evelyn nodded. But although she wasn't altogether bothered about going out: visiting the castle now that it wasn't hers had been so peculiar that she didn't much like the thought of going out in Silenshore again anyway, uneasiness still prickled inside her.

'Jack,' she said, her hands reaching out for his across their table. 'Do you think I should ask the police about my parents? They might help me find out what happened to them.'

'The police? Don't be stupid. You'd be wasting their time.'

Evelyn frowned. 'Would I really? I can't imagine they'd mind. In fact, they'd probably be glad to help. My parents did a lot for this town in their time. They looked after people during the war and they always threw such wonderful parties. They were very generous. Maybe people here should go some way to trying to help them out. The police could ask around, perhaps. I could walk down to the station tomorrow.'

The pain was sharp and sudden, the blow unexpected. Jack seemed to be sitting opposite her one minute, and beside her within an instant, his hand stinging her cheek.

'No,' he breathed. 'You never, ever bring the police sniffing round here. I have things I don't want them poking their noses into. You ask them about your parents, you invite trouble to our door.'

Evelyn nodded, stunned, her shaking hand touching her cheek.

## CHAPTER 11

# *Isobel: 2010*

*My Queen,*

*I walked along the coast today, and stood for a while in the very spot where we ate our ice creams together in the summer. It was so very odd being in the same place without you, and not knowing why you weren't there with me.*

*Once I'd had enough of standing and being melancholy, I turned down West Street. Then I realised I needed to get back to the university for a meeting, so I turned around again.*

*It was as I looped around the houses like a lost man, going back on myself, that I realised.*

*There's somebody following me.*

*Please, if you are reading this, take care. Watch behind you, and where you are going. You are so very precious to me.*

*H.*

On Christmas Eve, Isobel and Iris sit in Mayor's coffee shop on Silenshore High Street, a tray crammed with lattes and mince pies between them. Iris tells Isobel about the man she's recently met through her work at the local gallery. She talks quickly and excitedly, smiling her narrow, secretive smile each time she pauses to have a sip of coffee.

'Seth's taking me out for dinner tonight, although I'm not sure where,' Iris says as she picks a tiny piece of pastry from her pie.

'Is he surprising you?'

'Yeah. He seems to be a fan of grand gestures. I mean, I know the first date I told you about was just in the gallery café, but he brought with him this huge bunch of lilacs for me. I was a bit embarrassed, because I had to put them on their own seat whilst we had our drinks. It was like a whole other person was sitting there with us. Anyway,' Iris says with a wave of her hand. 'Enough about me. What are you doing with Tom tonight? Anything special for Christmas Eve?'

'I'm not sure. He's at the restaurant till about eight, and then Daphne said something about cooking a meal. She's invited my dad, but he doesn't want to come. He's coming tomorrow for Christmas dinner because I didn't really give him much choice, but he'll probably stay late in the office tonight. I have a feeling that's for the best anyway.'

Iris looks at Isobel sympathetically. 'What do you mean?'

'I don't know. I just get the impression Daphne doesn't really want him to come. She was fine about it a few weeks ago when she first invited him, but now she seems to be backpedalling, as though she's gone off the idea.'

Daphne's usual awkward countenance had been more pronounced when she asked Isobel about her dad's plans this morning. She had fired question after question at Isobel: wanted to know about his office and his flat, how long he'd lived there, what he knew of Silenshore and the people in it. Isobel had told Daphne the bare bones of the facts of his life, wondering if her answers were the ones Daphne wanted. Tom rolled his eyes behind his mother, out of Daphne's view, trying to make light of her interrogation.

'If it's too short notice, I understand. Same with tomorrow. I know it's strange spending Christmas with somebody else's family,' Daphne had said, her words cool in the warmth of the kitchen.

‘No, he wants to come tomorrow. Let me double-check about tonight, too. He struggles a bit at this time of year, though, and doesn’t always want to do social things. He spends most of his time working.’

Daphne nodded almost exuberantly, her grey hair swishing around her face uncharacteristically. ‘I understand. That’s fine. If he doesn’t want to come, then he mustn’t.’

‘I’m sure it’ll go well,’ Iris says now. ‘The main thing is that he’s not on his own on Christmas day. And if it’s that awkward having him with you at Daphne’s, text me. You can come and watch the Queen’s speech with my family. Then you’ll be begging us to take you back to Daphne’s.’

Isobel laughs. ‘Oh Iris, I miss you. Oh! I nearly forgot! I’ve got your Christmas present here.’ She digs around in her oversized green leather handbag and takes out the compact mirror she bought on Portobello Road. She’s wrapped it in brown paper and tied it with magenta taffeta.

Iris places a gift on the table too and gestures for Isobel to open it. Isobel leans forward to see what’s inside. A silver box nestles in a mass of shredded gold paper. She lifts out the box gently and places it on the table, then waits as Iris tugs at the taffeta of her present.

‘Oh, Isobel! It’s beautiful!’ Iris says as she tears the paper open carefully to reveal the rose-shaped compact. She opens it and smiles at her reflection. ‘I love it! Sixties?’

‘I think so. It’s from Portobello Road.’

‘Thank you. I’m going to take it out with me tonight. Open yours,’ Iris says as she gestures towards the box. Isobel pulls the lid open. Inside, there is a brooch, peacock blue and glittering in the fairy lights that are twisted around the walls of the café.

‘I love it!’ Isobel says as she lifts it from the box and pins it onto her dress. It’s light and delicate, and sits perfectly on the twisted black wool. ‘Forties?’

Iris nods excitedly. 'Yeah. Etsy. I don't have someone sweeping me off to vintage markets, so I had to make do with online.'

'Well, by the sounds of things, Seth will be sweeping you off to all sorts of amazing places before too long!'

They sit for a few minutes in peaceful silence, Isobel looking down at her brooch and fingering the jagged blue edges of the stones; Iris clicking her mirror open and shut before putting it into a side pocket of her bag. The café murmurs around them, the electricity of Christmas anticipation almost tangible in the air. Children writhe in their seats, too excited to sit still, baristas smile widely as tips clank into the glass jar on the counter, and outside the afternoon light turns luminous blue then black, golden car headlights sweeping through the window every few minutes.

'So, how is it living with Daphne in general?' Iris asks.

'It's okay. She can be hard to read sometimes, which makes things a bit awkward. But she's nice enough, I suppose.' She takes her coat from the back of the chair. 'You'd better get going and glam up for your night with Seth!'

'I should,' Iris says. She stacks their saucers and shuffles into her coat.

Outside, in the freezing still air, Isobel hugs Iris and smells her familiar lemon scent. 'I'm so glad I've seen you. I'll call round to the flat this week and get the gossip on your date.'

'That'll be great. Any time,' Iris says, pulling her purple coat around her body and hopping from one foot to the other to keep warm.

Isobel watches Iris as she disappears up the hill and begins to merge with shops and trees and other people. She looks up to the very top of the hill, at the elegant, pointed turrets of Silenshore Castle High School, and the blue-black sky above them. Then she hurries across the road, her hands buried deep in her pockets, her chin nuzzled down into her scarf.

As she turns onto West Street, Isobel sees the old lady from across the road. She's standing outside her house, her arms folded against the cold. Her hair, silver grey, blows across her face. Isobel lowers her gaze when the woman's eyes meet hers, but it's too late: the woman takes small, quick steps towards Isobel until they are face to face. The woman moves closer and closer, until Isobel can see all of her faded features: the greying skin, the browning teeth that reveal themselves as she opens her mouth to speak.

'You're nicer than the other one,' she says, her voice rasping.

The words make no sense. Isobel waits for more, and when nothing comes she raises her eyebrows in question, trying to look friendly. She's probably talking about Georgia. *The other one.* Isobel imagines telling Tom, teasing him about his never-ending line of women.

'I shouldn't have said,' the woman says eventually, her face crumpling with worry. 'I was just trying to be nice to you. Tom doesn't know I saw him. I didn't mean to watch, it's just that I saw him.' The woman's words bleed into one another, and she wrings her hands as she talks. Isobel glances at the woman's face again, and sees that her eyes are pale and watery. 'The thing is,' she continues, 'I'd want to be his number one. I wouldn't want to share him.'

Isobel shakes her head. Share him?

But the old woman is turning around, muttering apologies and Christmas wishes as she heads back to her house. Isobel dashes across the road, wanting to be away from her, wanting to ring Tom and tell him what's just happened. She takes her phone out of her pocket. They've already spoken about the old woman after she made Isobel feel uneasy on her first night at Broadsands. Isobel asked Tom what he knew about her. She was strange, he said, and Daphne had always told him to avoid her. She'd always lived across the road, and was harmless enough, if a bit nosy. Isobel brings Tom's number to the screen and smiles at the little picture of him that comes up. She's about to press call when she remembers that it's Christmas Eve, which means that Tom's shift is a really busy one.

She'll tell him later, when he gets home.

Christmas Day is silver with frost. Isobel drives to her dad's, her car skidding perilously over the glittering roads, and lets herself into the office. Her dad is sitting at his desk, the only person in the whole of Silenshore to be working.

'Merry Christmas,' Isobel says when he looks up from his papers. She sees his hand tremble slightly as he pulls his coat from the back of his chair. He's nervous.

'Thanks for coming today, Dad. I'm so glad you're not going to be on your own. And I can't wait for you to meet Tom.'

Graham doesn't answer, but pats his coat pockets to check for his keys, and mutters to himself about the office and what still needs to be done.

'Come on,' Isobel says quickly as she moves towards the door.

This time three years ago, Graham was a different person. The office would have been shut for days by now, locked and forgotten about, in favour of festivities. This time three years ago, he was suitably pleased with the mug that said 'I Love Spreadsheets' and stack of CDs that Isobel bought for him, and he laughed at the jokes from the crackers that weren't funny. Her mother had always worn the same perfume, but her father had bought her a different one that year.

'Time for change!' her mother had said with a smile as she squirted it on. The cloud of fragrance was sharper than her mother's usual sweet scent, almost bitter, and Isobel had felt a twinge of anxious disappointment for her father. Why hadn't he just bought her mother's usual perfume? Surely she didn't like this one as much?

But her mother had smiled and spritzed, and kissed Isobel's father's cheek when he came in the bedroom, and Isobel had thought how much her mother must love him.

Now, three years on from a time for change that nobody could have predicted, Isobel opens the car door for Graham, her body pulled tight with cold and apprehension.

'Daphne's a really good cook. You'll like her food,' Isobel says as the car climbs the main road of Silenshore.

'Turkey?' he asks, staring out of the window, up at the castle. His arms are crossed tightly across his chest, ready to defend himself from whatever madness the world is bound to fling at him.

'No. She's cooking duck, I think.'

'Duck? At Christmas?'

'Yep. I know Mum never did duck at Christmas. But I bet she'd have liked it. Maybe you should try it on her behalf.' Isobel steals a glance at her dad, wondering if she's gone too far, as usual. But his expression is unchanged.

'Maybe I will,' he says, his arms still crossed firmly and tightly across his chest.

Broadsands twinkles with the bright white lights that Tom helped Daphne to put up a few weeks before. They throw a luminous dapple onto the driveway as Isobel and her father walk up to the front door. Isobel pushes open the door, but it catches on something. She bends down and picks up a small red envelope that is jammed between the door and the mat. It's obviously a Christmas card. She glances down at the name on it.

*Tom*

'You're here!' Daphne says as she wanders down the hall to greet them. She holds out her willowy arms to take their coats. 'It's lovely to finally meet you, Graham. Merry Christmas.'

Graham hands over his coat and smiles. 'You too, Daphne. You needn't have invited me. I would have been fine at the office, you know. I don't really like Christmas.'

Daphne nods and takes Graham's duffel coat and the red envelope that Isobel holds out before ushering them into the kitchen. 'It's no problem. Dinner's almost ready.'

The air in the kitchen is thick and white with heat and steam and Isobel feels sweat prickle her underneath the black lace blouse she squeezed into this morning. The smell of duck crisping in the Aga is bitter and syrupy. Tom is moving over from the cooking to the doorway of the kitchen to greet them, and Isobel searches his face for signs of anxiety at meeting her father for the first time. But there's nothing, just a faint line of perspiration on his forehead from standing at the Aga.

'Dad, this is Tom. Tom, Dad.' Isobel says.

'So you're going to take care of her and the baby?' Graham asks, his eyes scrunching up as he takes in Tom: the snowflake-patterned jumper that Isobel bought him as an ironic nod to Christmas, his short dark hair, his wide, uncomplicated smile. Isobel cringes, but Tom replies smoothly, unruffled.

'Definitely. Your daughter's amazing, Mr Blythe.'

Graham nods. 'Call me Graham.' He sits down at the table and is silent, leaving Isobel to watch her strange new family: Daphne crouching at the Aga to check on the duck and whispering to herself about the timings of the potatoes, Tom stirring gravy slowly and cautiously, her father sitting silently in Daphne's spindly pine chair at the head of the table. When dinner is brought to the table in huge, steaming dishes, everybody is quiet. The sounds of the clanking of spoons against plates, the calm tones of the carol-singing CD that is playing, the hopeful padding of Hugh the Labrador under the table, the wind from outside tapping meekly at the back door, all rise in the air and fill in the empty spaces where there should be conversation. After a few quiet minutes, Isobel can't stand it any more.

'Just think, next Christmas, we'll have a baby with us!'

Tom makes an amusing mock-frightened face, and then meets Isobel's eye and grins. 'A bit scary. But I can't wait. Another member of the family.'

Isobel and Tom continue chatting about the baby, about the

year to come. Graham chips in now and again, recalling stories about when Isobel was a baby.

'She was a crier,' Graham says. 'Just as feisty as she is now. As soon as she was born and I saw that red hair, I knew I had trouble.'

Isobel shakes her head and smiles. 'I can't believe that for a minute.'

'Well, we could have another redhead on its way. So we'd better prepare ourselves,' Tom says, and Graham laughs.

Daphne stares across the table, a little stonily, Isobel notices. But perhaps she's not even listening. She watches Daphne until their eyes meet, and Daphne smiles thinly, then stands suddenly to clear the plates.

Later that night, after Isobel has taken her father home and returned to Broadsands to eat too many mint crèmes and play two quiet games of Scrabble with Daphne and Tom, she lies in bed, curled into Tom.

'I'm sorry if today's been a bit dull.' Tom says.

'It's been fine,' Isobel replies, her words stretched out by a yawn.

'It's always quiet here at Christmas these days.'

Isobel laughs, a whispery laugh that hisses in the darkness. 'I must admit, I was waiting for your mum to turn the *Eastenders Christmas Special* on tonight.'

'When did you realise she wasn't going to?'

'About eight-thirty. When we were setting up for the second game of Scrabble.'

They laugh and Isobel pulls herself closer to Tom. 'I don't mind, really. I'm grateful to your mum for having my dad here, and for letting me stay. At least we're getting to live together, and spend Christmas together. I can't believe that this time last year I didn't know you. It's unimaginable now, isn't it?'

Tom kisses Isobel and pulls her even closer towards him. 'Yes. Unthinkable.'

'Did you get the card that came through the door for you?'

'I don't think so.'

There's silence and Isobel's mind wanders. Before she can help herself, she's whispering to Tom again.

'Tom? I know this isn't very festive, but can I ask you something?'

'Hmm,' Tom murmurs, his breath warm on her cheek. 'Depends what it is.'

Isobel squeezes her eyes shut and speaks. 'It's just about Georgia. I know you told me that you just grew apart. But I feel like I don't properly know what happened. Was there anything else?'

Tom shuffles and then sits up, propping himself against the old-fashioned headboard. 'It's as I told you,' he says. His voice is neutral. 'I don't say anything about those days because there really isn't much to say. We'd only been together for about two years when we got married, and most of that time we were travelling around France, so I suppose it wasn't really like real life.' He looks at Isobel and she can see his face move in the dark, into a smile. 'Once we'd been back in Silenshore for a few months, I could tell Georgia was annoyed that we weren't in New Zealand or Australia like she wanted to be. She was itching to get away again, whereas I was happy to stay in Silenshore. I enjoyed travelling, but I felt a pull to come back at the end of it. It was probably because my dad was becoming quite ill and so I knew I needed to stick around. Georgia didn't really understand that because she wasn't very close to her family. I just don't think we were very compatible, in the end. And now she's back in Australia, it's a bit like she never happened.'

He lies back down, and Isobel puts her head on his chest. 'I can't believe she let you go,' she says.

Tom laughs loudly, the sound at odds with the darkness and the silence around them. 'I'm glad she did. What made you think of Georgia tonight, anyway?'

'Just something the old lady across the road said.'

'Oh, she talks nonsense. Ignore her.'

They lie together, Tom's breathing becoming steadier and slower, his chest rising and falling with approaching sleep. Isobel closes her eyes, but they spring back open, alert and unwilling to rest. She turns in bed, her newly rounded belly making it a little more awkward than it used to be. The air is stuffy and she feels too full. She sticks out a foot from the soft warmth of the duvet, savouring the cool air that touches her skin, and waits for sleep to come.

## CHAPTER 12

# *Victoria: 1964*

*I'm already married.*

As his words rang around the room, Harry's expression was frozen with horror. It was as though, Victoria noticed bitterly, he had only just found out himself, as though he was the one who had just had his heart pulled from his chest and hurled out of the window so that it splattered onto the concrete beneath.

Victoria put down her plate on the floor and suddenly remembered that she'd left her parents' bedroom window open, and that there was probably going to be a huge rain stain on their green carpet.

'I don't understand,' she said, picking up her plate again, because to leave it on the floor would mean the end of things, it would mean that this conversation was too big to carry on eating through. She held it steady on her bare knee, the white china cold on her skin. She stared down at the gooey, raw egg, the sickly white and yellow that had merged into one another.

'I thought you knew, Victoria. I don't know why, but I thought you knew. I have a wife.' Harry put his head in his hands, in his wonderful hands that a few moments ago Victoria had thought were hers.

'You don't wear a wedding ring,' Victoria said, then hurled her plate across the room at him. Egg flew and rained down onto the floor, onto the furniture. A drop of yolk landed in Harry's almost-black hair and melted into it like snow.

Harry moved towards her and put his arms on Victoria's shoulders, which were shaking now with huge, uncontrolled sobs.

'I'm sorry. I'm so sorry, my darling. I should have made it clear, and I started to tell you a number of times, but in all honesty I probably didn't want to because I didn't want to lose you. I've never known anybody like you before, Victoria.'

'I want you to myself,' Victoria said quietly, her sobs subsiding, her shoulders stilling.

Harry stared at her, and Victoria saw that there was a tear working its way out of his left eye. He blinked it away, 'I know.'

'You don't know, because you have me to yourself. I'm the one who has to share.'

'I'm sorry. I've thought and I've thought, but I don't know how to solve it,' Harry said. His chin began to tremble and Victoria watched as the tear that had threatened a few seconds ago began to spill from his eye. He did not cry like Victoria did, or like anyone she knew. His face did not turn red, and he did not bat the tear away. He let it fall and carried on speaking, even though his voice was shaking and his cheek was stained with the single wet track. 'I'm stuck, Victoria. I've already asked her about a divorce. She simply won't agree to it, and so the courts would deny it.'

Victoria shook her head slowly, and the new, sharp idea of Harry belonging to somebody else rattled around, making her brain ache. 'What's her name?' she asked, not really wanting to know, but unable to focus on anything until she did.

'It's Sarah,' Harry sighed.

'So the note in *Great Expectations* was meant for you, then.' It was like a crushing weight on her chest, like when Frederick the cat sometimes sat on her in the middle of the night, so that she woke up suddenly with a heavy weight bearing down upon her.

But much, much worse. 'What does the message from your wife mean? What was she 'almost'?'

'I don't know what you're talking about. What have you seen?'

Victoria ran to her bedroom, not caring if he followed, not caring if he saw her *Bunty* comics and stuffed rabbits and bears, because what difference would it make now? She snatched *Great Expectations* from under her bed, brushing away the balls of matted dust that had attached themselves to it.

'Here. The inscription on this page says, '*to remind you of what I almost was. S*'. What did she mean when she wrote it?' Victoria's words were high and loud, ripped from her with no control.

Harry followed her back from her bedroom to the lounge and pulled his shirt over his chest. That milky-tea skin that she'd thought was hers, locked away again. Unbearable.

'We met when we were very young. We were just friends, really, and we never should have been anything else but we drank too much one night at a party and she…Well, suddenly we were going to have a baby. So I asked her to marry me. I didn't love her, but she obviously couldn't have the baby all by herself, without a husband. We planned a wedding straight away. But the day before we were going to get married, I found out that there was no baby. There never had been. It was just an elaborate plan to get me to marry her. I threatened to walk away from her, the wedding, everything. But she begged me not to. All of her friends were married and she didn't want to be left behind. She said that if I cancelled the wedding she'd turn into Miss Havisham, waiting for love for all eternity. That's what the inscription in my copy of *Great Expectations* means. But I grew to see over time that she didn't really love me at all. She just wanted a husband and the life that all her friends had.'

'Have you forgiven her?'

'For lying to me? No, I haven't. I don't love her, Victoria. And I never could after what she did. But she'll never agree to a divorce. I don't quite know what to do.' Harry's jaw was set tightly, but

Victoria could see a slight tremor fighting to make itself known. 'I never dreamed there'd be someone like you in my future when I married Sarah. I just wanted to do the right thing.'

Victoria sighed, her breath trembling as it left her body. 'How can you teach all the classics and such great literature day after day, and think that marrying somebody you don't love is the right thing to do? Maybe what my father says is true after all. Maybe university doesn't teach you anything.'

Harry took her hand and held it tightly, so tightly that it hurt. Victoria could feel the bones of her fingers crushed against one another, but when she looked at Harry's face she could tell that he didn't mean to hurt her, that he was lost in his own world, so she grimaced and stayed quiet.

So this was it. She could stay quiet, have contact with Harry's skin, his beautiful big hands and his milky-tea skin, and ignore her body shouting out in pain. Or she could leave him to his wife, and have nothing.

No pain, no pleasure.

'Are you really glad it rained on the day we met?' she asked. 'Or do you wish it'd stayed fine, so that you'd walked straight past Lace Antiques, and straight past me, and kept things simple?'

Harry pulled Victoria to him, kissing her over and over again: the skin of her neck, her cheeks, her forehead. 'I thank all the stars in the world that it rained that day. And I think it rained so that I would come into Lace Antiques and meet you. I needed you.' His words trembled, his voice breaking. He held her tightly, his chest broad and strong against her. 'I know I'm asking a lot of you, Victoria. Too much. But I need you to wait for me until we can somehow work this out. I can't live without you now.'

'I don't think I can live without you. And I'm not sure I want to try,' Victoria said slowly, picking at the sticky patch of yolk in his dark hair.

Harry smiled at her and Victoria felt a strange prickle of relief. He couldn't possibly smile at Sarah like that, with his whole being.

Perhaps Victoria *could* be the only one, then, in her own way. The shock was still smarting, but maybe Victoria could let time soften it, and maybe they could somehow work out a way to be together.

And that's when they heard it. The car skidding up to the shop, her father's shout. Victoria was on her hands and knees before she knew it, picking up pieces of broken plate and wiping unpleasant, cold egg from the blazing orange carpet with her bare hands. Harry was buttoning his shirt back up to the top, his face pale.

'My skirt!' Victoria hissed at him. 'Where's my skirt?' Hysteria rose up inside her, the urge to do more than cry or laugh, but the need to unleash a torrent of emotion from her body.

Downstairs, the shop door clicked open. There were rumbles of conversation, her father shouting about a clock. His heavy footsteps on the stairs. Her mother's sighs floating through the air. Victoria saw her skirt, at last, a flash of burgundy under the couch. She pulled it on, swatting Harry away as he tried to fasten the buttons at the back because his hands were too big and he was being too slow and there just wasn't enough *time*.

When her parents entered the room, Harry and Victoria were sitting at opposite ends of the couch, *Great Expectations* between them, the heavy smell of fat and eggs lingering in the air.

'Why aren't you in the shop?' Jack said, his mouth downturned in disappointment. Obviously, he hadn't managed to win the clock at today's auction. As he noticed Harry, his face tensed in irritation. 'Who's this?'

'This is Harry. He's here to talk to me about A levels,' said Victoria loudly. Better A levels than what had really happened.

'A levels?' Mrs Lace said, taking off her string of pearls and dangling them from her delicate hand. 'What on earth for?'

'Oh, I just wanted some information on them. I was thinking about perhaps going back to school in September, and then one day to university,' said Victoria, emboldened by the sight of her pale, fragile mother, the woman who never told anybody what she wanted or did anything of her own.

Her father gave a laugh: an empty, echoing bellow that stopped as suddenly as it had started. 'Nonsense. Absolute nonsense. Forgive us,' he said, beckoning for Harry to stand and then placing his hand on Harry's back to direct him to the door. 'My daughter is full of fads and fancies. She's silly, like her mother. She's wasted your time. If you'd like to have a look around our shop on your way out, I'd be happy to show you some of our best pieces.'

Harry shook his head. 'I'm afraid I don't collect antiques. I didn't mind talking to Victoria about her education. She's welcome to visit me at Silenshore University if she wants any more information.'

'She won't be wanting any more information, and she certainly won't be wanting to go to your university. I'll see you out.'

Victoria sat still and watched her father followed Harry out of the room and shut the door behind them. Her mother dropped her pearls on the floor.

'Victoria, I hope you—'

'Don't, Mum. Please don't.'

Mrs Lace stared at Victoria, her blue eyes draped with makeup that was starting to flake with the wear of the day. Victoria stared back indignantly, her cheeks beginning to flame. Her mother knew. Her mother knew that Victoria's skirt wasn't fastened properly at the back, that her blouse wasn't quite straight, that her skin was still warm from being so close to Harry's. But *so what*? Victoria wanted to scream. So what? What she had done with Harry was better than anything that her mother had ever done, because Harry was nothing like Victoria's father and Victoria was nothing like her mother.

'Be careful, darling,' her mother said, stepping over her pearls and leaving the room.

It was a whole week before Victoria saw Harry again, after he'd met her parents and she'd made him an omelette, then thrown it at him and there'd been sultry thunder clouds ripping through the sky.

'I've missed you so much. I was desperate to come and see you but after the way your father reacted to me, I thought I should avoid the shop,' Harry said as he and Victoria sat opposite one another in The Golden Egg in Soho. Harry had taken Victoria to London and she had told her parents that she was going out for the day with Sally.

'I hope my father doesn't go into Clover's and see Sally working,' Victoria said, her stomach turning at the thought of being found out. How many lies had she told since she had met Harry? The thought was an unpleasant one and she squashed it so that it lay like a dead spider in the corner of her mind.

'He won't. He's in the shop. And your mother won't go to Clover's, will she? It doesn't seem like she goes out much alone.'

'She never goes out alone. It's his fault. He's a bully,' Victoria said vehemently. 'He makes her so very unhappy.'

'What do you think would make her happier?' Harry asked, frowning.

Victoria sighed. She looked up around at the bright colours that lined the walls. 'I don't know. I don't know what she wants. I just know what she doesn't want, and that's my father and me, and I don't blame her.'

'I hope that's not true. How could she not want somebody so beautiful?'

Victoria grinned. 'I hadn't realised you were so taken with my father.'

Harry laughed loudly, and dropped his fork so that it clattered onto his plate. 'It's his eyes I love the most,' he said with a wicked grin. 'They're like the stars.'

Victoria laughed and drank the last of the wine that Harry had ordered for them. It was red: dark, sweet and warm. 'Thanks for bringing me to London, Harry. I've not been since I was very young, and I think that was only to auctions. I love it here.

I love how lively it is. Silenshore is so small and nothing ever happens there.' Victoria grabbed Harry's hands suddenly, dragging them clumsily across the table. 'Please let's live in London one day!'

'I would love that. I will do everything I can to make it happen. It might take some time, but I promise that I'll try.'

'I don't want a promise. I want a dream. I want to dream of living here, with you, in a messy flat full of friends and books and colour.'

Harry squeezed Victoria's hands, then brought her fingers up to his lips and dotted them with soft kisses. 'Then let's dream.'

They walked along the river after their early dinner, hand in hand. Nobody looked at Victoria as though she might not belong to Harry, as though she had lied to her parents and should really be behind the counter of Lace Antiques. They simply accepted that Harry might be hers, that she might be his.

'So tell me, Victoria Lace. What else do you dream of?' Harry asked.

Victoria looked out at the glittering Thames. 'Oh, I dream about lots of things. I dream of drinking champagne with you, and reading lots more books. I dream of learning to cook, and meeting more writers, and writing my own books, and dancing, and wearing beautiful dresses.'

'Well!' Harry linked his arm into Victoria's and pulled her towards him. 'I do have a lot to organise for you!'

'And France!' Victoria went on. 'I want to go to France! My mother used to talk about France all the time. I think her family came from France, a long time ago. I would like to go to Paris, and visit my long-lost relatives, and find out that I am a French Queen.' She stopped speaking, breathless with the excitement of the future that suddenly lay before her, twinkling and beckoning like the gentle waves of the river beside them.

'I'll spend the rest of my life trying to make those things

happen for you, Victoria,' Harry said. He did not mention his wife and his ties to Silenshore, and Victoria was glad.

'I meant to bring my old copy of *The Blue Door* back for you,' Victoria said as they walked alongside the salty river, gazing up at Big Ben and the cloudless, pale sky. 'I've finally finished it.'

'And what did you think?'

'I was wrong, wasn't I? I couldn't believe that she wasn't even kidnapped. She hid herself away and sent the ransom notes herself, just to make some money! And the music man from the street had only tried to help find her. I had him down as strange. I got it all completely wrong.'

'I had a feeling from the start that she was a fake,' Harry said with a wink.

'Oh, and I suppose you also knew that the mysterious blue door was actually a trap door?'

'Of course I did.'

'I liked the old house that the girl was found in. If that was a real place, I'd like to go there. I wonder if Robert Bell had been somewhere like that in real life. He didn't say in his talk.'

'You liked it? I think it's meant to be haunted and frightening.'

Victoria let go of Harry's hand and sidestepped as they were divided by an oncoming crowd of men in crisp brown suits. As they walked past, a cloud of bitter aftershave lingered in the breeze. 'I wasn't frightened at all,' Victoria continued. 'My mother used to talk about spirits and spells when I was little, and I quite liked the idea of there being people around us who we can't see. I like to think I'll be one of them, one day.'

'I'm never sure what to believe,' said Harry as they walked on and on. He took Victoria's hand again and squeezed it. 'All of Robert Bell's books have some kind of ghostly place in them. Perhaps if he comes to visit us again at the University, we can ask him about it. He might tell us about the house that inspired him, and if it was actually haunted.'

'I'd like that,' Victoria said, her heart aching with something like longing with the memory of Robert Bell and his talk that she'd attended with Harry. It had only been a few weeks ago but already, that clear, perfect point in time when she'd thought that Harry could be her husband within a few months seemed like another lifetime. How had time made her feelings swell so much? She glanced at Harry, who walked along as he had done that day at the university, his back straight, his head high, his tie flapping in the breeze from the Thames.

'The thing with the mystery of the supernatural,' he said, still talking about ghosts and ghouls and the haunted house in *The Blue Door*, 'is that if you haven't ever seen something, it's tempting to believe that it doesn't exist.'

Victoria thought of Harry's wife, *S*, with her jagged handwriting in his copy of *Great Expectations* and her tricks to make Harry marry her all those years ago. She thought of her own mother, blinded by a swollen eye and insisting that she'd walked into a door, and of the thoughts of what might have happened to her that Victoria constantly banished from her mind because she hadn't seen it with her own eyes and therefore didn't always have to believe that it had happened.

'You're right,' she said, as she stared up at the looming face of Big Ben.

It was after they had been walking for a while, after their steps had fallen into perfect synch with one another, that Harry stopped and looked into the distance.

'Can you wait here for a minute?' he asked Victoria, squinting over her head at something.

Victoria nodded, and placed her hand on the railings by the river as Harry disappeared into the crowd of people before them. Late-afternoon sun blazed down onto the crown of her head and she lifted her hand to her burning hair. Minutes passed and Harry didn't return. He wasn't visible in the crowd of people, and

Victoria's heart began to flutter in the early stages of panic. He would come back to her, wouldn't he?

Fifteen minutes later, Victoria still stood alone, the Thames glinting beside her. If he didn't come back, perhaps she would throw herself in. She would have to do it quickly, otherwise some tiresome interferer might try to save her, and bring her up, dripping wet and still alone. She squinted into the water, wondering how deep it might be. It would pull her deeper and deeper, cocooning her into a place where she didn't hurt so much…

'I'm back, Victoria. Queues are bloody eternal here.'

Victoria spun around to see Harry. 'I was starting to wonder about throwing myself into the water. I thought you would never come back.'

Harry stroked Victoria's hair. 'How very romantic that you were going to drown rather than live without me.' He leaned forward and kissed her forehead. 'But thankfully, that's not necessary. I only went to the shop over there to buy you something. Here you go.'

Victoria opened the little paper bag that Harry had given her. Inside was a sepia photograph printed on a postcard.

'It's Queen Victoria! Oh Harry, I love it.'

'It's to remind you, whenever I'm not there to do it myself,' Harry said, as they began to walk again, 'that you, and only you, are my Queen.'

A few weeks later, Victoria sniffed as she spritzed Chanel onto her pale wrists. She wanted to smell luxury and femininity, but she could only smell her mother. Still, it was better than nothing.

She'd agreed to meet Harry outside the university. His car was a red Monza, and when Victoria got in, the smell of Chanel dissipated and she could smell a sort of concentrated version of Harry's scent instead: ink and coffee and cleverness. They were going to Concetta's, a new coffee bar in Ashwood that Sally had been talking about lately.

'I hope you like it there,' Victoria said, as Harry sped out of Silenshore. Ashwood was a much newer, greyer town than Silenshore, about fifteen minutes away in the car. It had more shops and more people and sounds than Victoria was used to, and she preferred it to Silenshore.

'I'm sure I will. We'll get a good seat and sit all night drinking coffee and talking about books. In fact, that reminds me. I looked at that writing you left with me.'

'And?'

'I thought your short stories were quite brilliant. I can tell you've been influenced by Robert Bell.'

'Yes, I definitely have. Even more so since his talk.'

'I like the way you describe places and people. You obviously have excellent skills of observation.'

Victoria stared at Harry. What did she observe about him? A man in his late twenties, his jaw ever so slightly darkened with hair that if she reached out and touched would be softer than it looked.

'Is there anything you think I could do better?'

Harry shrugged. 'Nothing comes to mind.'

'Oh, Harry. You're a teacher! You have to tell me to do something differently. I won't be offended, I promise. I want to learn.'

Harry laughed. 'You're a rather ideal student. Most want me to think their work is perfection. They want me to tell them to leave their essays exactly as they are, and go out and have fun instead of working.'

'Well, I want to get better. Go on. Tell me.'

'I'll have a think. I didn't read your stories as a teacher. I read them as a reader. It's a different thing.'

Victoria rested her head back on the seat of the car as they flew towards Ashwood. She wondered if the coffee bar would be crowded. She couldn't imagine Harry in the ones she'd been to before with Sally, because they had all been full of young people, and Harry was so much more mature and refined than the skinny little boys Victoria used to talk to and dance with. A flicker of excitement fizzed inside her as she thought of being on Harry's arm, and she hummed as he parked the car.

'Sally said it's on Wood Street,' Victoria said as they walked along the wide pavement, past a neat row of new council houses. 'So it must be just along here.'

They found Concetta's straight away, and sat in a dark corner.

'I've had an idea,' Harry said after their frothy coffees had been set down on their table. 'I don't want you to change the stories you've already written. I want you to write something new.'

'Go on,' Victoria said.

'Well, I really think you could write something wonderful about the castle. Just a short piece. I could tell you what I know about it, and then you could come up with a sort of biographical story about it. I could see about having it put up in the University foyer, if you'd like.'

'Oh, I'd love to write about the castle!' Victoria put her elbow on the table and rested her chin on her palm. 'I remember a few things that you told me about it. I remember you saying about the evacuees who were sent there. I thought how wonderful it would be to be sent to such a place to live. If I were sent there, I wouldn't ever want to go home. It seems magical there, somehow.'

'Some people say it's magical and some say it's a place of doom. But that's what'll make it so fascinating as a subject.' Harry took a paper napkin and a pen from his pocket and scribbled down some notes. 'So, yes, perhaps a bit of history, and a bit of mystery, all in that lovely romantic voice you use in your stories. I don't know everything about it, but I know that it was built just after the Norman Conquest. The same family owned it, until they disappeared just after the war. That's when the University took it over.'

'What did you say it was called before the University bought it?' Victoria asked.

'It was called Castle du Rêve.'

'That's French, isn't it?'

'Yes. It is. Roughly translates to Castle of the Dream.'

'That's what I'll call my piece of writing,' Victoria said, pulling the napkin towards her as Harry put his pen back in his pocket. She gazed around her, at the cappuccinos and Pepsi floats, the sticky tables and the bored waitresses that reminded her of Sally, and the boys and the grey streets beyond the window, and all the other things that one day she would leave behind for a life with Harry. 'The Castle of Dreams.'

The hot summer gave way to a drizzling end. Silenshore lay emptier than it ever had before: the sea thrashing alone with nobody to watch it. When Victoria awoke on the second Saturday of the month, she sat up in bed, an unpleasant anxiety flooding through her. She heard her mother in the bathroom, clanking the taps on and off. Victoria swallowed, nausea swimming through her body. She lay back down, but that made it worse. She stared up at the ceiling. Everything she looked at made her feel more sick. She sat up again, clutching her stomach in misery.

Harry had taken her out last night. They had gone to a bar she hadn't even known was there, in a town beyond Ashwood that was wide and clean and full of people that Victoria knew she would never see again. He had given her a glass of glittering yellow champagne, and then another, and another, until Victoria's words blurred into each other and she laughed at everything Harry said, and then laughter blurred into tears and the tears blurred into staggering into her bedroom and falling into bed.

Now, her clothes were crumpled and stale with the champagne that had slopped over Victoria's glass. Her mouth tasted of rot. She wondered if she'd said anything she shouldn't, if she had shown Harry up. The thought of showing him up was what did it: she lurched out of bed, tripping on her discarded shoes on the floor, and vomited into her red leather handbag.

She threw the handbag away, which was a shame. Her mother had bought it her for Christmas years before, when Victoria had started to take an interest in her mother's things. She had put a little comb in it, and a bracelet. The bracelet had disappeared over time, as things sometimes do, and the comb had lost most of its teeth when it was used on a doll with particularly stiff hair. But the bag had remained: a reminder that Victoria did have a mother, one who had, at some point, cared about Victoria being happy and had wrapped up a present that she would love in brown paper decorated with hand-drawn stars. As she wrapped the acid-drenched bag in a towel, and dumped it into the bin, covering it carefully with some newspaper, Victoria said a silent farewell.

*No more champagne*, she told herself as she trudged into the shop, feeling as though she needed to sit down. The urge to vomit again lingered, and when a man came into the shop who smelt ever so slightly of onions, Victoria had to excuse herself and take some careful, measured breaths behind the back door. She bent over, her hands on her knees, her stomach pulsing to expel anything that was left in it. She stayed in the hallway that led from the shop to the flat until she heard the huff of an impatient sigh from the onion man, and the bang of the front door as he left.

But although Victoria didn't have any more champagne that week, although Harry didn't take her to a restaurant and fill her with rich food, shiny with oil again, every day when Victoria woke, the heavy weight of sickness returned.

*Be careful, darling*

*I just don't want you getting into trouble*

The words stung Victoria's mind, hot and sharp as needles. She sat in her bed on Wednesday morning, knowing that champagne did not make you sick for five days, knowing that something else did, something that she couldn't even consider. She held her breath, wanting to keep everything in. Her father dawdled in the pink-tiled bathroom. Her mother lay in bed, her head lolling against the wall that adjoined her bedroom to the bathroom.

Victoria held her breath for as long as possible, but it was no good. The sickness burst from her. She climbed out of bed weakly and took off her bedsheets, twisting them into a knot and stuffing them into a paper bag. It was lucky that her mother wasn't very good at housework. Victoria would never have got away with this if she had a normal mother who knew what sheets she'd made the bed up with and might want to know what had happened to them.

'Victoria!' Jack's voice vibrated through her bedroom door. 'Shop, please!'

Victoria brushed her hair in front of her sapphire hand mirror, which was propped up on her bedside. She thought of Harry, of Sarah, of Sally, of her parents. She thought of the woman across the road who ran Blythe's Bakery, who had a squirming baby boy, all wrinkles and skin and jerky little movements. She touched her belly, and then was sick again, managing to narrowly avoiding the carpet and aim for her bin.

'Victoria! Shop! Now!' her father yelled, his heavy footsteps passing her bedroom door.

She scraped her hair into a high ponytail, pinched her cheeks to give them some colour and then, plastering on the face of a person who hadn't been sick, who wasn't fearing for her life, walked slowly down the stairs, and into Lace Antiques.

'You know,' Sally said as they sat at table six of Clover's, tapping her cigarette into the ashtray on the table, 'there's a rumour that this place is being taken over by somebody new.'

Victoria stared down at her egg custard. The sickness had faded in the last few weeks, leaving behind a bitter scent on Victoria's bedroom carpet, and the pleasant feeling that she might have imagined it all. She took up her spoon and dug into the pastry, cutting into it with mean, hard blows. It crumbled, and the custard spurted out messily from the centre. She dipped her finger into the cold yellow jelly and licked it. Perhaps it had been a nasty illness and nothing more. She had heard that the sure sign of a baby was a missed monthly, but to tell the truth, Victoria didn't have regular ones anyway. They came every now and again like the way distant friends might turn up to stay: unexpected, infrequent but very inconvenient. She couldn't remember the last one she'd had, so there was no way she knew when her next was due. She spooned up a huge chunk of custard and crammed it into her mouth. Delicious.

'Really? Will you be able to keep your job?'

'I don't know. It's a man called Eric Mayor. He keeps coming in all the time, asking if we do cappuccinos and when we say no, he asks why on earth not? He looks around with a real glint in his eye as though he has big plans, and everyone says he's going to buy it.'

Victoria frowned and glanced down at the mess of custard in front of her. The overpowering aroma of sugar and nutmeg drifted up from the plate, suddenly making her feel sick again.

'I'm sure if he does buy Clover's, he'll keep you on. He'd be a fool not to,' she said, pushing away her plate. This couldn't be happening.

There was a pause as Sally put her cigarette in her mouth and took a long drag, staring out stonily over the crowded café. 'I don't even like cappuccino,' she muttered, grey clouds puffing from her lips as she spoke.

'Sally,' Victoria blurted out, suddenly sure that if she told her friend her worries, they could somehow be sorted out. Sally knew about these things, didn't she? She would know just what to do.

'Yes?'

Victoria stalled, knowing that if she said anything now, then it would be real and she would sob, and everyone would look at them and wonder what had happened. So she said nothing. But in the end, Sally brought it up.

'I need cheering up. I need to hear something exciting. Tell me about Harry! Has he kissed you again? Is he still as handsome as you first thought?'

Victoria shuffled in her seat and nodded. 'Yes. He's kissed me again. And he's so handsome, I don't quite know what to do about it.'

Sally laughed. 'There's not much you can do. Victoria,' she said, her voice turning serious all of a sudden. 'You do know… you know about getting caught, don't you? You know how it happens?'

Victoria flinched. A memory flickered into her mind. Her mother, sighing when they heard about some girl who'd had a baby without getting married. *She got caught too early. Make sure you know, Victoria.* There had been no elaboration when her mother had said this years ago, just the sting of the words and the dull ache of confusion about what they might mean. Now, their meaning grew inside Victoria each day.

'Of course I know,' Victoria said, taking the cigarette from Sally and sucking on it so quickly that she felt quite dizzy. She couldn't say anything else. The words slipped out all on their own.

Sally nodded curtly, then looked around her before whispering. 'You know, I heard that Barbara Reynolds managed to go to a doctor outside of Silenshore, and told this new doctor that she was married. She wore a Woolworth's wedding ring. The doctor believed her, because why wouldn't he, and gave Barbara all kinds of information on artificial checks.'

'Sally, don't compare me to Barbara Reynolds. I'm nothing like her. I love Harry. I think he loves me too.'

Sally looked at Victoria shrewdly and snatched her cigarette back. 'I'm not comparing you to anybody. I just don't want you getting into trouble.'

'I won't,' Victoria said, sitting back in her chair and wondering when Sally's break might be over.

And so that was it. She couldn't tell Harry, of course. She couldn't even go through with telling Sally. The idea of a baby was like poisonous lead, weighing her body down everywhere she went. The sickness came and went, and after each day looking after the shop, Victoria began to go straight to bed, where she would lie quite still until the next morning, when the nightmare would start all over again. Day after day, night after night, she wondered and worried: what was going to become of her?

## CHAPTER 13

# *Isobel: 2011*

*My Queen,*

*I don't know why I still write. I've never had a reply, but perhaps my soul is somehow carrying my thoughts to you. Do you believe in souls? This very question reminds me that there is so much more I want to ask you. Have you read the new Robert Bell book? Have you been to London? Have you worn the green dress that I bought you? Do you think you might risk shame and live with a man who is married only in name? Do you think you can only truly love one person? Do you believe in spells and dreams coming true? Who might have told me to leave Silenshore? And why?*

*Write to me, answer me.*

*I'm still being followed.*

*H*

The day after her due date, Isobel stands in front of the mirror in the front bedroom at Broadsands. Her ruby ring lies on the carpet where she's just dropped it, staring up at her helplessly.

Why is it that now she can't bend down, she drops things so often?

As she's bracing herself for the almost impossible task of

retrieving the ring, she hears Daphne on the landing outside her room.

'Isobel? Everything okay?' she asks. Her voice is the same as always: too small and quiet for such a tall woman.

Since Isobel finished work to begin her maternity leave a few weeks ago, she and Daphne have lived relatively peacefully together. Isobel has joined Daphne on some walks along the promenade, Hugh bounding ahead of them, the women walking quietly. Daphne is mostly silent and cool. But the companionship is fairly peaceful and sometimes even pleasant. Maternity leave from the school has crept up suddenly on Isobel, and because the baby isn't here yet, she feels like she's straddling old life and new.

'I'm fine, thanks,' Isobel says to Daphne. 'I've dropped my ring, though.'

Daphne swoops down and picks up the ring, handing it to Isobel, the red stone twinkling as she does. Then she bends again, retrieving a hairbrush from under the bed.

'Oh thanks, I was wondering where that'd gone. I never would have found it.'

Daphne smiles and stands at the door, but doesn't reply.

'I feel like this last part of my pregnancy seems never-ending,' Isobel continues as she pulls the brush through her thick hair. Her good hairbrush is packed in her hospital bag, which waits in her wardrobe. This brush is plastic and static-inducing, and snags her coarse hair, pulling at her scalp.

Daphne nods, moving over to the window, staring outside.

'I'm going for a walk with Iris. It's her day off,' Isobel says. 'The midwife says I should keep active.'

Daphne nods again, still watching something outside.

'Where's Tom? Is he at work?' she asks sharply, not turning to Isobel as she speaks.

Without thinking, Isobel moves over to Daphne and places a hand on the woman's bony shoulder. She looks down through the window. The street is deserted. A hearse is pulled up across the road and Isobel wonders if Daphne is thinking of Tom's dad, of the day when a somber black car pulled up outside Broadsands.

'Yes. Tom's doing the early shift today. He'll be back at about three o'clock. Are you alright?' she asks.

Daphne swings around suddenly, her eyes wide, the yellowing whites giving her a ghoulish look for a moment that passes as quickly as it arrives.

'I'm fine,' she snaps. 'Have a nice walk,' she says as she leaves the room, her face pale.

'No twinges?' Iris asks an hour or so later as she and Isobel pick their way over pebbles on Silenshore beach. The air has changed from sharp to smooth as spring has gently taken a hold of the town. The tide crashes in the distance, dark and frothing, as though the sea is trapped in another season to the beach altogether, an eternal winter.

Isobel breathes in the salty, golden air. 'Nothing yet. I had a few pains in the night, but they didn't amount to anything. I'm desperate for the baby to just come now. I'm too impatient to be overdue,' she grins, pulling her hair back from her face. 'I'm so glad you're off work today. It's lovely to be with you. Daphne's nice enough, but she makes me feel a bit awkward sometimes.'

'In what way?'

'She just acts a bit oddly sometimes. Tom thinks she's overwhelmed by the idea of a baby, which does makes sense.'

Isobel looks away from the sea, up to the top of Silenshore, where the castle looms above the town. She imagines the lessons going on inside the turrets, the secrets being whispered about in the staffroom, the echoes of shouts from pupils in the courtyard. It's not even a year since she stood in the courtyard behind her bookstall at the school fair, since she met Tom and her life suddenly bloomed into full colour.

'How's it going with Seth?' she asks Iris. 'Is he still lovely?'

Iris grabs Isobel's hand in hers excitedly. They walk hand in hand along the beach for a second. Isobel is transported back to their childhood, when she used to run along the uneven sands with Iris, their red hair streaming behind them both like two bright kites.

'Oh Isobel, he's brilliant. I've got something to tell you!' There's excitement in Iris's voice: a freedom and lightness that tells Isobel her news isn't pregnancy or even marriage. She knows what it is before Iris says it. She thinks of the dream box that she left behind at the flat.

'Seth's taking me to Paris!' Iris says eventually. She squeezes Isobel's hand as she says it. 'I didn't know how to tell you. But he's surprised me. We're going in June. He's spoken to the gallery and booked time off for me and everything. He's visiting a gallery whilst we're there, because they are considering exhibiting his work.' She drops Isobel's hand and stops, pulling Isobel to face her. 'I know we were going to go to Paris together. And we still can at some point. Vienna too. But with your baby and everything, it just seems…' she stops talking, searching Isobel's face, concerned.

Isobel reaches out to hug Iris. 'Of course you should go. I'm so happy for you.'

'I'm so glad you're not upset,' Iris says. 'I was looking in our dream box last night. I found all my Paris things. My map is probably out of date now, but I'm going to take it anyway.'

'You should definitely take your map. I'm sure most places will be the same. Just keep my Vienna things safe and I will come and get them when I can.'

'I will. Vienna will always be there, Isobel. You still need to go. But you have a more pressing concern first.' Iris grins, and reaches out to touch Isobel's large, firm belly.

They turn back and walk towards the promenade. There's very little there, and hasn't been since the 1980s, when the prosperity and popularity of Silenshore began slipping away like the tide itself.

'So tell me all your Paris plans,' Isobel says, her breath tight with the effort of walking and talking. Iris begins chattering quickly and excitedly. But the flow of words about the Eiffel Tower and the Louvre and Arc de Triomphe are suddenly drowned by a flood of pain that rips through Isobel's body as they climb up the steps to the promenade path. She bends over, the concrete glittering beneath her, dangerously near as she sways towards the ground. The tearing pain soars through her again, and she moans, unable to formulate anything other than sounds. She feels Iris's arm around her, hears vague sounds that merge together: her own groaning, Iris's calm voice, seagulls crying overhead, and the faint sound of sirens becoming louder and louder, and then nothing at all.

# PART TWO

## CHAPTER 14

# *Victoria: 1964*

'Are you alright?' Harry asked Victoria in early October, when glowing orange leaves lined Silenshore's pavements, blowing into Lace Antiques every time the door opened. 'You're very quiet.'

'Of course I'm alright. It's the cold. It makes me feel a little gloomy, that's all,' Victoria said. That morning had been a dreadful one. Harry had bought her a new green shift dress about three weeks before as a surprise. She'd gone to try it on today, only to find that the zip at the back wouldn't do up. She had tugged at it, red-faced and hot, until there was a frightening snap and the zip pull broke off in her hands.

'I wanted you to have this,' Harry had said when he gave the dress to her. She'd admired it the day he had taken her to London in a window on Carnaby Street.

'I don't know if green would suit me,' she'd said when she had first seen it, staring up at the stiff mannequin, who was modeling it indifferently.

'Green for a Queen,' Harry smiled. 'Shall I buy it for you?'

Victoria moved towards the window, then shrank back. 'It's ten pounds! Come on, let's go. I don't want it.'

But of course she did want it, and when Harry arrived at Lace Antiques with a shiny cream gift box a few days after they'd been to London, a bubble of excitement had popped inside her. She'd known exactly what was in the box. When she lifted the lid and saw the bright-green material she jumped up and down and hugged Harry.

'We'll go to London again and you can wear it,' he'd said.

But they hadn't gone to London yet because the new term had started and Harry became busy with new students and marking and muttering things about grammatical errors and attendance. Then, when he began to emerge from the chaos of the new term and mentioned London, Victoria was busy trying to cover up the scent of vomit and hide from Harry the fact that she couldn't go a day without throwing up or having to sit down every ten minutes.

And now the dress was too small.

Victoria folded it up and placed it in the dustbin, dry-eyed and numb with panic.

Now, Harry glanced behind him at the door to check that nobody was there, then hugged Victoria. She could barely breathe, he squeezed her that tightly, but that didn't matter.

'Warm enough now?' he asked, his voice in her ear.

She nodded into the rough tweed of his suit. The truth was, she was boiling hot, even though the air was crisp with the lurking winter. He took her hand and looked at her, making her want to cry.

'Victoria, I am so sorry that we're living like this. I can't imagine how difficult it is for you. I want it to change so much. I do wish I wasn't stuck.'

*Stuck. Like the zip. Force it, and it will break.*

'I know,' Victoria said.

Harry took Victoria's hands, his features tight with frustration. 'I have practically begged Sarah. She still won't agree to a divorce. But I won't give up.'

'You're cold too,' Victoria said, feeling the cool skin of Harry's hand. 'You could have come upstairs, but my mother's up there in bed.'

Harry looked at his watch and sighed. 'I should get back to work. Will you walk with me a little way or do you have to stay here?'

Tiredness weighed Victoria down. She thought of her bed, the house silent around her, heavy, sleeping dreams of when everything was simple. 'I have to stay,' she said.

As she watched Harry's tall figure disappear from view, Victoria gripped the counter and fought the tears that threatened to spill out. If she started, she would never stop.

'Victoria, where's this dress from and why is it in the dustbin?'

Victoria swung around. Her mother stood behind her in a white cotton nightdress that hung down to the floor. In her hands was the folded green dress. How long had her mother been standing there? Victoria quickly recalled everything she'd said to Harry before he had left. He had kissed her: how long ago had that been? Her mind whirred, slow and tangled with secrets.

'It was Sally's dress. It doesn't fit her any more. She's put on some weight since she bought it. But it doesn't fit me either.'

'It's brand new. It still has the tags.'

Then there was a silence, big enough to fall into and never return from.

'Victoria? I want to know what's happening to you. Please, darling, speak to me.'

A black eye and a week in bed. Victoria's mother knew what it was like to be snapped in half by life. Victoria, overcome by an urge she hadn't had for so many years, leaned forward and hugged her mother. Her skin was cool, her nightdress soft from being slept in. Stale Chanel mixed with skin, and a faint smell of apples and wine, sour and sweet. She held onto Victoria weakly but determinedly, like a child.

'Darling, oh darling, what's the matter? What's the matter? Tell me, tell me.'

'I can't,' Victoria said, pulling away, her black hair tangling with her mother's and her tears, hot and stinging, leaking oily black mascara onto the white cotton nightdress.

Victoria's mother took hold of her hands, and the green shift dress dropped to the floor in a heap.

'The dress isn't Sally's. It's mine. But it doesn't fit me,' Victoria wailed suddenly. 'It's too small.'

Mrs Lace's blue eyes darting over her daughter's body, seeing everything.

'Was it the university man?' she asked, still holding Victoria's hands.

Victoria nodded, dizzy with the release of her secret.

'We will go to the doctor.'

Victoria wailed again, a howl of fear bursting from her soul.

'We must. He will give you advice. You mustn't tell your father. He can't ever know.'

'How on earth will we keep it from him? I'm already getting too big for my clothes!'

Mrs Lace brought her fingers to her mouth and began chewing ferociously on her nails. Victoria had never seen her mother bite her nails, and seeing it now made everything worse, made her mother seem like a frightened animal.

'I don't know,' she said eventually. 'We will go to Dr Bright, and then we will decide what to do.'

*What to do, what to do.* The words circled in Victoria's mind like rooks over a ruined castle. The cawing sound of the words followed Victoria around, but it was only when she was sitting beside her mother, in the hot, cramped doctor's office that smelt of germs, that their meaning screamed out at her.

'Sixteen years old, and unmarried. I see,' Dr Bright said after a few silent, staring moments. 'Do you have stairs in your house?' His pen was poised carefully over his notepad, making no contact with the paper. The room seemed to contract with his words. Mrs Lace inhaled sharply. And that's when the screaming began in Victoria's head. She didn't know if she was actually doing the screaming, or if it was only in her mind. She focused on the doctor's pen. It quivered slightly in his hand.

'We do,' Victoria's mother said quietly. 'But we won't be using them.'

Dr Bright dropped his pen abruptly. It bounced off his pad and landed on the floor. He didn't move: made no attempt to pick it up. He would, it seemed, be making no note of this meeting.

'There are homes for this sort of thing, as far as I'm aware,' he said next, standing and opening the door. 'Good day,' he said loudly as the door swung open.

The walk back downhill was cold and grey. Victoria closed her eyes as they walked, knowing the Silenshore streets so well that she didn't need them open. The cobbles didn't trip her, the slope didn't force her forward. She opened her eyes again when she heard her mother speak next to her. She had forgotten her mother was with her; she had forgotten everything apart from the feel of the ground under her feet and the slicing cold air on her face.

'You'll have to marry him,' Victoria's mother was saying, her breathy voice being swirled around in the autumn breeze.

Victoria walked a little longer, then stopped and faced her mother. Time stilled. People passed them, talking about things they thought mattered, but didn't, because nothing mattered at all, nothing but this.

'He's already married,' she whispered, looking into her mother's watering eyes. The whisper was lost in the blur of the breeze and the street and other people's sounds, but Victoria's mother heard. Her eyes flooded, tears drenching her pale face, turning it to melting wax. Her hand, trembling, reached out and took Victoria's.

'Oh, darling. My darling, darling girl.'

Victoria's mother told Jack about Victoria's situation on the evening of the first day of December. Victoria lay in bed, her bedroom door locked by her mother. She heard shouts and the ugly thud of something heavy being thrown across the room. Her door rattled then, her father shouting through it that she'd ruined them all and ruined the business, that Lace Antiques was down the drain, that she'd have to come up with some other way of housing them and putting food on the table.

And then the worst came. The quiet was always the worst. Victoria lay under her eiderdown, a hand on her swollen belly. She could feel the baby move. It flipped around haphazardly, stretching her skin like rubber. Victoria rolled over onto her side and listened again for the sounds of her parents. None came. Her mother might be asleep, and her father would be out at the Smuggler's. A tight wire of anxiety pulled through Victoria's body as she pulled the eiderdown up to her chin. Jack would be home just after 11pm, reeking of beer and anger. It was about eight o'clock now. Three hours of waiting, of lying stiffly as a corpse until he came back. Impossible.

She threw off the cover and heaved herself out of bed, trembling in the sharp, cold air. She tried her bedroom door, but it was still locked. She tapped on it lightly, pressing her head to the bright wood to listen for her mother. When no sound came, Victoria tapped again. If Jack was out, then her mother might rescue her. She might take her to Harry, or to Sally, or to anybody who understood that Victoria never meant for this to happen and would take her in and keep her warm and safe until the baby came. Once the baby had come, her father might prove himself different to how they had all thought. A baby might soften him. And something might be done about Harry's marriage to Sarah. Victoria stood shivering at the door, waiting and listening, urging her mother to come. But there was no sound except her own juddering breaths. When she was too cold to stand there any longer, she returned to bed and squeezed her eyes shut, praying for sleep to wrap itself around her, and when it did, dreaming strange, mixed-up dreams of prams and horror and love.

It was when the dreams had stopped, and Victoria was deep in a blank, heavy sleep that the crash of her father through the house woke her up. She shuffled up and propped herself up against her headboard, vaguely aware that she'd been waiting for him to return. His boots thudded up the stairs at the back of the shop, the thuds uneven as he stumbled closer. When he reached Victoria's bedroom door, she held her breath. He tried to open it, but it stuck fast, still locked.

She heard him shout to her mother, the rumble of a drawer opening and closing. And then her door was opened.

Jack wasn't a tall man. He was wide, his black hair and skin both coarse with years of alcohol. His tie was loose around his neck tonight, and for a horrible moment Victoria imagined leaping out of bed and tugging on it harder and harder until his neck cracked and his head hung forward like a broken flower.

'I've spoken to somebody,' he said, before Victoria could move. The image in her mind of his mouth drooping open, his eyes glazed with death, vanished and she tried to focus on his words. They weren't slurred. He was so used to drinking that he never slurred his words.

'There's a place for girls like you. You'll go and have the baby there. Nobody will know.' He turned around and then glanced back at Victoria. In the pale light of the landing, she could see a flicker of something other than tyrant in his bloodshot eyes. Not hate or anger, as Victoria had come to expect, but something else. As she lay in her bed after her father had staggered to his own room, she realised with a jolt what it was she had seen.

Fear.

'Victoria?'

The knock on Victoria's bedroom door was soft, the voice hoarse. When she swung the door open, her mother lingered on the landing, saying nothing, her eyes wide. She was holding a small blue suitcase with a gold zip that curved over the rounded edge. In another circumstance, it would have been a pretty little case.

'What's that for? I'm not going away yet, am I?'

Mrs Lace shook her head slowly. 'No. Not yet. Have a look inside. I've managed to find you a few dresses. I bought you the suitcase to put your things in, when you do go.'

Silence hung over them.

'Thank you,' Victoria sighed as she took the case from her mother's delicate, pale fingers.

Her mother stayed there for a few minutes, leaning her willowy body against the doorframe. Her fingers, now that they didn't have the case to occupy them, flitted about, making unpleasant flicking noises.

'Have you seen Harry?' Victoria said, before it was too late and her mother disappeared to bed for a week again.

Her mother blinked, her fingers suddenly still.

'No. Don't mention his name.'

Hot tears burnt Victoria's eyes. She thought of Harry's eyes and his skin, and his books and his little office, where he had kissed her. 'Can't I see him?'

Mrs Lace shook her head. 'No, darling. You must forget about him. Your father mustn't know his name. It would put Harry in great danger.'

Victoria sank onto her bed, her prison. She hadn't been out for weeks. Her parents barely spoke to her. She hadn't seen Harry since the day of the green dress. She hadn't said goodbye to him. She wondered about going to see Sally, but Sally might tell somebody about the baby. She was a good friend, but Victoria didn't know if she could trust her. That hadn't mattered so much before, when all there was to trust her with was the loan of a new headband or a secret about somebody's stuffed bra. But now, everything, oh everything, was different.

'Hasn't Harry been looking for me?' she asked her mother miserably.

Mrs Lace shook her head again. She gestured to the suitcase. 'Have a look what's in there and try some of it on.'

Victoria nodded, and tensed as her mother moved forward and stroked her cheek with ice-cold fingertips. When her mother had drifted down the landing, back to her own bedroom, Victoria unfastened the gold zip and lifted the top of the suitcase open. In it were three white dresses, billowy and humiliating, the kind of thing that Mrs Lace wore to bed, only five sizes bigger. Victoria folded them up and put them back into the case. She noticed her initials embroidered onto the cream lining.

*VL*

It was her mother's embroidery: shaky and uncertain. She had never been any good at stitching things for Victoria, like all the other mothers had. Victoria reached out and touched the raised letters, the satin lining cool on her skin. It was odd that her mother had given Victoria the suitcase today, when she was barely about to set foot out of her bedroom, let alone the county.

But as Victoria climbed back onto her bed, picking up Harry's copy of *The Blue Door,* she realised why her mother had chosen today, why she had lingered in Victoria's doorway for longer than usual and why she had given her the dresses and the suitcase and the wobbly embroidered initials.

The sky was heavy with evening mist and ice, the light fading into a velvet-blue darkness.

It was almost over now.

But today had been Christmas Day.

The shop lay empty and untouched between Christmas and New Year. Silenshore Hill was sleek with frost and silence.

On one of the last evenings of December, when her parents had gone out for dinner with somebody Jack was trying to sell an ugly old rocking horse to, Victoria heard a banging on the shop's door. The rattling of the glass in the door vibrated up into the flat above, and Victoria knew without looking who was there.

She reached for her duffle coat and pulled it over her shoulders, fastened it, then stood for a moment in her bedroom. She looked down at her belly. The duffle coat covered it nicely. Nobody would know, unless she took the coat off. She unbuttoned the coat quickly, her fingers cold and stiff. She stepped out of her blue smock dress, the constant banging on the door downstairs making her tremble. She *had* to get this right.

Victoria pulled on her old girdle that she had worn to parties last year, before everything was different, and winced as she fastened it, the stiff material straining over her skin.

'Victoria!' she heard Harry shout through the shop's letterbox. She imagined him crouching down to call her and ached to see him. She zipped up her dress and put her coat back on, stuffed a piece of paper from the floor into her pocket, then ran from her bedroom down the stairs.

The girdle pinched her skin and her secret blasted through her body. When she opened the door to the shop, Harry stepped in, his nose and cheeks pink from the nip of cold air he'd been standing in as he waited for her. The sight of him made Victoria's heart ache. His kind eyes, his strong hands, his soft hair.

*Tell him*, a voice inside her insisted.

She took out the piece of paper from her pocket and gave it to him. 'Here's my piece on the castle. I used the article you found for me, as well as your notes. And I tried to do as you said and make it mysterious. I hope you like it.' Victoria's voice cracked as she spoke and she bit her lip and looked down.

Harry gazed down at the paper for a moment, taking in her words. 'Victoria,' he said as he looked up again and took her hands in his. 'I'm so glad you've given this to me. It feels like so long since we spoke about it, so long since I've heard you talk about things like your writing. I've been so worried about you. I've missed you. I've tried to come and see you here, but today is the first time I was sure that your father wasn't here. I don't want to make him angry with you. I don't want to make things harder than they already are for you.'

'I've not been well,' Victoria said, looking down at the polished wooden toggles on her coat.

Harry touched her cheek. 'What's been the matter?'

Victoria hadn't cried since that day at the doctor's office. Every day she had sat in her bedroom, reading magazines and trying to knit and writing the piece on Silenshore Castle, she had tried not to think of much. Her feelings had been still, paused by pure horror. But now, seeing Harry, they somehow came to life again, and pain screamed around her and sliced through her.

'How was your Christmas?' she asked, brushing away a cool tear that was ambling down her cheek.

Harry frowned. 'Victoria, what's the matter?'

'Nothing's the matter. I just want to know how your Christmas was.'

'It was horrible. I wanted to spend it with you. I love you, Victoria.'

*Then tell him.*

'Harry, I…' she began. But as she looked into his deep eyes, his expression of perfect concern, she stopped. She had one chance to get this right. She couldn't lose him. She dropped Harry's hands.

'I'm going away with Sally. Next month. We are going to work for Sally's old aunt. She's dying and needs some help around the house. I'll be back in the summer, and we can see each other then. We can pick up where we left off.'

It was all lies. The aunt, the illness, the dying. None of it existed, yet still, it all came flooding through Victoria's lips more easily than the truth would have done.

Harry took Victoria's hand again. 'The summer?'

'Yes.'

She'd worked it out. She'd heard her parents talking about it the other night. Jack couldn't ever lower his voice; it was beyond him to make himself more subtle, it wouldn't occur to him. So a few weeks ago, when he'd been talking about the mother- and-baby home he'd found out about, every one of his words had seeped through Victoria's bedroom wall. *She'll go to the home six weeks before she has the damned thing. Then she'll get rid six weeks after and come back to us.*

May, Victoria had worked out. The baby was due to come in April, and so she'd be leaving for the home in February and she'd be back in May. The sun would be shining and somehow, everything would be alright.

'I thought Sally had a waitressing job?' Harry said, a frown creasing his face.

'Oh, she's leaving Clover's. She'd rather look after her aunt. It'll be better money,' Victoria said with a dismissive wave of her arm. 'This Mayor man is buying Clover's and so everything will change there soon anyway.'

'I see.' Harry stepped back and looked away, out of the window to the deserted streets outside. Tired Christmas decorations hung forlornly in the few shops that hadn't yet been prepared for the business of the New Year. 'Well, that's that, then. If you've already decided on going, then there's nothing I can do to change it. I'll miss you terribly though, Victoria.'

Victoria nodded. He'd probably find out it was all lies. She didn't know what her parents were going to tell people about her absence; he'd probably hear another story before long that would pull apart the thin, fragile tale about Sally's aunt. But Victoria's whole body ached with tiredness and sickness and misery. All of this just needed to be over and done with. And the sooner Harry left the shop and left her life, the sooner he would be able to come back.

'Let me kiss you goodbye,' Harry said after a cold pause filled the shop.

Victoria leaned into him and tried not to weep as the scent of him flooded through her. His broad arms were tight around her.

*May. Just get through until May. And then he will hold you like this again.*

On the fourteenth of February, St Valentine's Day, Victoria woke early. She ambled over to her bedroom window after managing to lie still for only a few seconds. The sloped cobbles of Silenshore glittered with blue frost. The narrow windows that Victoria's bedroom faced were still dark. Everyone in Silenshore, it seemed, was still asleep and warm in bed. Everyone except her. The dark-grey buildings stared at Victoria mournfully through the darkness of the morning. It was as though they knew that she was leaving them behind.

'I'll be back,' she whispered, her breath clouding on the window so that she couldn't see anything but a plume of white on glass.

There were two hours until they were due to leave. Victoria hadn't even tried to leave her bedroom in the last few days. She had been to Blythe's bakery across the road a few weeks before, but since then she hadn't dared to meet her father on the landing, or on the stairs. She hadn't wanted to see the shop, or customers or the slanting streets of Silenshore, or the dramatic castle that reminded her of so much. But today, she must.

Her parents were still asleep. They'd stopped locking her bedroom door a few days after they had started, their initial bright panic faded and soured. She stood alone for a moment on the landing, taking in the worn carpets and pale-grey and green flowers that exploded across the walls. Would she miss this house while she was away? She shook her head. It didn't matter.

The crumpled address that Victoria clutched in the pocket of her coat was, she had estimated, about a forty-minute walk away, out of the main streets of Silenshore and beyond the castle. Victoria's cheeks burned in the cold violet morning as she ambled slowly uphill. She could feel her baby twisting inside her as she walked. The land that she had seen being dug up with Harry was flat and neat now, dotted with the skeletons of wide, low houses.

She looked away from them, not wanting to think of that golden day with ice cream and Harry and the sweet, insatiable feeling that had bloomed inside her. She had known nothing then. Nothing at all.

Victoria glanced up as she passed the castle. It stood majestically, and she thought of the piece she had written about it for Harry. As she gazed up at the golden stone, sorrow that she wouldn't be near the castle for the next three months, or near Harry or anything else that she knew, flooded through her.

*Don't*, she told herself, looking ahead and trying to straighten her thoughts. She had studied the map voraciously every day and night since she had found the address in her father's telephone directory. Now, she knew the order of streets by heart.

Back Castle Street

Tide Street

Hill Street

Finally, Victoria saw it.

Stone Street

Her breath caught in her throat. Questions pecked at her like birds. *What will he say? Will he still want you? Will everything turn out after today? What about Sarah?* She blocked them from her mind, pushing her legs forward, her eyes flitting over the numbers on the glossy front doors. Four, six, eight. She marched on until she reached the forties, and then slowed. The morning had become lighter now, the violet sky turning to a pale lilac as weak sun emerged over the horizon in the distance. She squinted at the row of doors to her left. Forty-four. Forty-six. Forty-eight.

She placed a hand on her covered belly and stared at the house. It was unremarkable, its door the dark green of holly leaves. Victoria swallowed as she reached up for the brass knocker. As she waited, Victoria let herself imagine, for a moment, that Harry might be hers soon, that he might have an answer to all of the questions that she had barricaded from getting into her mind.

But when it came, the figure through the mottled silver glass of the door was not Harry's.

Out of all the questions she'd had to suffer, she had stupidly missed out one: perhaps the most important of them all.

What if Harry was not there?

When the door swung open, Victoria stepped back slowly, wanting to run. She had never let herself imagine Sarah. She had never asked Harry what she looked like, and he had never told her. She didn't want to know. But now, Sarah stood before her. She was taller and thinner than Victoria, her face pulled down at being disturbed, her light-brown fringe curling slightly at the edges, her skin pale and freckled.

'Yes?'

Victoria stared. This was the woman who got to say Harry was her husband, who saw him every day, who could touch him whenever she liked.

'Can I help?' the woman asked.

'I've come to see Harry.'

Sarah's face snapped, her features becoming sharp and unpleasant. 'Oh. I see. I suppose you're the girl he's been nagging me about?'

Victoria suddenly felt as though she was being pulled down into deep mud, sinking, her limbs heavy. 'I – yes.' She took another step backwards. 'I'm sorry to come here. Harry didn't ask me to. I just really need to see him. It's very urgent.'

She noticed Sarah staring downwards then, at Victoria's belly. She'd thought the coat covered it well, and perhaps it had when she last saw Harry. But now, she saw, it covered nothing.

'He's not here,' Sarah said, her eyes crawling back up to Victoria's.

'Will he be back in the next few hours?'

'No.'

They stared at one another. Sarah's eyes were narrowed in scorn, or perhaps hatred.

'I really am very sorry,' Victoria said again, mud pulling her down and down. 'I wouldn't have come here if it wasn't very important.'

'I'll tell you what's important,' Sarah said. 'My home. My name. My pride. And I won't have you coming here, threatening to snatch them all away.'

'Do you love him?' Victoria heard herself ask. Her voice was brisk, assured, not her own. But the bravado deserted her as soon as it had arrived. She felt her legs weaken and shake, and she held her hand out to grab at the low brick wall that ran along the path.

Sarah frowned, her whole face contorted in irritation. 'I beg your pardon?'

'Do you love Harry? I want to know. If you do, then I will leave you alone.'

Sarah stared past Victoria somewhere.

'Do you love him?' Victoria's voice was rising now; she could hear herself wailing like a hungry gull. Time was everything. She needed to know. If this woman didn't love Harry, then surely they could come to some sort of arrangement.

Sarah suddenly jerked her head and looked straight at Victoria. 'It's bad enough that he was stupid enough to get you into such a mess. But making you want him for yourself!' Sarah laughed, revealing pointed teeth. 'I don't know how he managed it. Did he not talk you to death about his students? About that bloody castle? Did he not bore you to tears?'

Victoria shook her head. 'No,' she said quietly. Here was Sarah's answer, then, as clear as the sun that was beginning to emerge in the distance. But the answer alone meant nothing.

Sarah stopped laughing and sighed, waving away Victoria with her hand. 'Go away. I don't want you here. I don't want people talking.'

'Please,' Victoria said. 'Please, just tell him that I want to see him.'

Sarah shook her head. 'No.'

She closed the door softly and retreated back into the darkness of the house without hesitation, as though Victoria had been a passing salesman or a Christmas caroler, nothing more.

Victoria stared up at the holly-green door. There was nothing left to do now. Nothing left but to turn around, face the long walk home and begin this strange new life alone.

The drive to the home was silent. Victoria's mother came along, which was a surprise, but she didn't say a lot. Her father's leather gloves squeaked on the steering wheel, making Victoria simmer with irritation. She stared out at the passing streets and twisted her neck so that she could see the hill disappearing out of sight. As soon as the spires of the university and the crooked row of ascending shops vanished around the corner, Victoria turned again and shut her eyes, not wanting to see anything that lay before her.

If only she had tried to tell Harry before this morning, it might have all been different. If only, if only.

Gaspings House was a red-brick Victorian building with jutting leaded windows. As Victoria sat in her father's car, an irrepressible urge to yank the door open and run away tore through her body. But then her father was suddenly there, beside her door, taking her hand and helping her out of the car. He looked down at her, a strange, pinched expression on his face.

He didn't want to leave her, Victoria realised with a start. She gazed up into Jack's eyes, but the moment of softness passed, leaving Victoria wondering if it had ever been there to begin with.

The air, once out of the car, was still and silent. The front garden of the house was bare and pale with a week's worth of frost, the ground soft under Victoria's feet. As she stood with her father at the wide front door, Victoria felt her mother drifting behind her like a shadow. She turned to look at her. Something seemed not quite right, but before Victoria could work out what it was, the scene shifted as it might in a dream and they were all of a sudden standing in the hallway of Gaspings House.

It was clear that it had been a beautiful home once. A twisting staircase spilled out from the centre of the hallway, its imposing dark bannister polished but worn. There was plenty of furniture: plastic, mismatched chairs in the large hall; a tired rug; a vase of artificial flowers on the windowsill. But something seemed missing somehow. The house had that aloof, detached feel of a school or a hospital. It wasn't somewhere you might want to sleep or wash your hair or brush your teeth.

The woman who had let them in was silent for a few moments as Victoria and her parents shuffled in and looked around.

'I'm Matron,' she barked eventually, in a voice that seemed too loud for her frail body.

There was a smell of eggs floating in the air, and without warning Victoria was transported back to that day last summer with Harry and the omelettes and the thunderstorm. Harry, with his kind eyes and his confidence in Victoria's writing and his disappointment on the day she told him she was going away to stay with Sally and her aunt. A surge of heavy guilt swept through her. Why had she lied to him that day? Why hadn't she just *told* him then, before it was too late? Sorrow lurched forwards in her, bringing back the urge to run home, to Harry, to anywhere but here and now.

'I need Harry to know,' she said, turning to her mother and finding herself tugging at her dress like a child.

Her mother paled. 'That's enough, darling. Don't cause a scene, now.'

Matron coughed like a teacher, not to clear her throat but to make the point that she was in control and that things were on the verge of getting out of hand and she'd like them back in hand, please.

Jack turned, swivelling his broad body around to face his wife. 'What's she saying?'

'Nothing. Nothing at all.'

Victoria breathed through her mouth to avoid the smell of eggs. In, out, in, out. Keep breathing, and all of this will somehow evaporate into another time, she told herself.

'Come upstairs,' Matron said briskly, gesturing for Victoria to pick up her case from where she had left it on the floor. 'You need to see where you'll be sleeping.'

The house was split over three floors. Victoria lugged the blue suitcase up as she followed Matron up the stairs. Her parents lagged behind. Her father didn't touch anything, didn't hold onto the bannister, didn't offer to help Victoria carry her things. The brittle thread that had floated between them previously, before Victoria had met Harry and got into this state, was broken.

'This is where you'll stay,' Matron said loudly as she opened the door to a room in which four beds were lined against the back wall. 'There's a bed spare. That one, by the window.'

Victoria gazed over to where Matron was pointing. The window ran along the whole length of the bed. The net curtains moved softly in the draught, even though the air outside had been still. It was going to be freezing in here tonight. It was impossible to imagine lying in that bed. What on earth would it be like sharing a room with three other girls? Victoria thought of Sally. She imagined her friend sitting on the assigned bed, jiggling about and commenting on the state of the mattress and the ugly green blankets. A sickening longing for Sally floated down onto Victoria's shoulders. If only she were here now.

'Some of the girls have finished their jobs for today, and so they're in the common room,' Matron said, snapping Victoria out of her thoughts and making the vision of Sally sitting on the bed vanish into a stark nothing. 'If your parents are happy to leave now, I'll take you down and you can introduce yourself.'

Victoria stared at Matron. There it was. In those perfectly pleasant words was a trace of what she had expected: disapproval. She looked past the small, greying woman to her mother, who stared out of the window to the frozen hills beyond. Her father looked down at the floor: an orange carpet that Victoria knew would make her feet itch if she went barefoot.

Victoria touched her belly fleetingly and behind her duffle coat felt her bump. The baby had been still for most of the day, but now it flipped around like an eel. Even the baby knew that things were changing: that an end, or a beginning, was hurtling towards them like an angry bull.

Matron's eyes flickered down to where Victoria's hand rested and she gave a small sigh of irritation. 'Come on. I'll see you out now, Mr and Mrs Lace.'

This would surely be it. This would be the moment where Victoria's parents took her by the hand and told her that she had been punished enough. Any second now they would seize her sleeve and pull her down the musty corridor, bundle her back into the car and whizz off into a future with Harry and the baby and a new Silver Cross pram. They would.

Any minute now.

Victoria waited, but the moment never came. Instead, her parents walked softly in Matron's aggressive footsteps to the front door of Gaspings House. When they reached the door, Jack stood well back and nodded at Matron, his eyes never reaching Victoria's. The smell of Chanel wafted over Victoria as her mother gave her a brief hug. Victoria clung to her mother, her nails digging into her bony back, but her mother retracted them carefully. As she did, Victoria felt her fingers being quickly prized open, and something cool and sharp being placed into them.

'For the baby. For hope,' her mother whispered, the milky scent of her breath covering the words and making them sweet.

The door opened, an unpleasant swirl of icy air swept into the hallway and her parents moved out into the mist. As she stood in a painless, strange horror, Victoria remembered her mother's gift. She opened her fingers and stared down. There lay a fragment of bright-green emerald that she remembered always dangling from a chain around her mother's neck, a chain that she now realised hadn't been there today. That's what had been different. She clasped her fingers around the stone again, the edges pricking at her skin like needles. Her parents' car coughed to a start so slowly that Victoria wondered if she might have time to run out and climb in, but before she could make her shaking limbs move, the car was gone and she was alone with Matron in the fading light of the corridor.

# CHAPTER 15

## *Isobel: 2011*

*My Queen,*
*I've been re-reading the short stories that you left with me all those months ago, before you wrote the Castle piece. I like holding your paper, seeing the strokes of your pen and creating your own images in my mind. I remember that you asked me to tell you what I honestly thought of them. I honestly think they are excellent. But you also made me promise that I'd tell you what you could work on, and make better.*

*There's only one thing to make better now, Victoria. Come back and read them with me.*

*H*

It feels as though Isobel has been asleep for a hundred years. When her eyes flicker open, she sees white curtains and a grey ceiling. Her eyes close again and her mind begins to whir with memories that are only half-formed: the tangy smell of blood, wetness between her thighs, people gripping her hand then leaving her and then coming back again. She remembers the feeling of pain pulsing through her, as though it was going to rip her apart. There was beeping, wheeling of trollies, the steady murmur of voices. A sharp sting in her back, and then an uncomfortable, heavy numbness that spread through her legs and is still there now. As her eyes begin to open again, a sense of something surreal flutters down on her.

The baby.

She tries to sit up, but can't. The bed she is in is hard and so infuriatingly smooth that when she manages to ease herself up on the pillows, she slides back down again.

'Hey, Isobel, Isobel. It's me.' Tom is standing over her, his face grey.

'What happened?' Isobel manages to say, her voice rasping and not her own. She swallows and presses her lips together. They are dry and hard.

'You're okay, Isobel. You've had a bad time.'

'But the baby?'

Tom's face transforms, lifts. 'It's a girl,' he says.

'She's okay?'

'She's absolutely fine. You both did so well. But it was a bad labour and you lost a lot of blood.'

Isobel touches her stomach. It's baggy and stretched, like an old water balloon that's almost empty.

'Where is she?'

Tom grins and gestures next to Isobel. There, in a transparent cot, is a tiny bundle. Isobel forces herself up on her elbows and gazes down. The baby's lips are full and pink, its eyes squeezed shut as if to block out the life it has been thrust into.

'I can't believe it's happened.'

'You were out of it on drugs for most of it. Iris called me and told me you'd gone into labour on the beach while you were out walking together. She's gone home to get some rest. She stayed here the whole time, to make sure that you were okay.'

'I remember her talking to you on the phone. That was just after the pain started. We were walking on the beach and then I was suddenly in agony. Everything after that is a bit of a haze. I can just about remember the labour, but it feels like a dream.'

Tom strokes Isobel's arm and she stares up at him. His expression is not like his usual one. He looks jagged and tense. Her eyes move to the cot and Tom wanders over to it and gazes at the bundle inside. 'So her name…' he begins.

Isobel looks at him cautiously. 'You're sure you're fine with it?'

'I love it. Honestly.'

Isobel smiles at him, her lips cracking and burning with the movement. She turns awkwardly to dangle her hand in the cot and stroke her daughter's cheek. 'Hello, Beatrice. Happy birthday,' she says.

Beatrice writhes a little and then lets out a soft snort. She reminds Isobel of a piglet: pink and new, snuffling into the mustard hospital blanket.

'Your dad is on his way,' Tom says after a moment.

Isobel lies back on the hard, high bed. 'Really?'

'Of course. He's coming with my mum for visiting hours.'

'I didn't think he'd come here. He's funny about hospitals.'

'I think people who are funny about hospitals make allowances for babies. It's an exception to the rule.' He hands Isobel a drink of water from the jug on her bedside locker. It's warm and metallic. Tap water. It reminds her of childhood, of home, of her mother. She turns to the cot and looks again at Beatrice.

*I won't mess things up for you*, she says silently. *I won't fade out of your life before you're ready for me to and I won't let anybody let you down.*

Isobel is lying with her eyes closed when Daphne and her father arrive. They think she's asleep and whisper, their words hissing in the air.

'How's she doing?'

'They're both doing well.'

'She's beautiful.'

'Get a photo.'

'Have they checked her over?'

'Yes, everything's fine.'

Isobel hears the soft bounce of a helium balloon and the rustle of a carrier bag. She hears Tom walk over to the cot and lift out Beatrice. Beatrice begins to yowl like a hungry cat.

Isobel opens her eyes and sees her father holding Beatrice awkwardly. The sight makes a lump appear in her throat, stings her eyes, makes her whole face ache.

'I didn't think you'd come, Dad.'

He doesn't move his eyes from Beatrice. 'Of course I came.'

'So don't you want to know what we've called her?' Tom says to the small group eventually as quiet falls like snow over the room.

'Yes!' Graham's cheeks are red. He looks like he's been out in the sun. He is more excited about hearing the baby's name than he has been about anything in the last three years.

'It's Beatrice,' Isobel says, watching her father cautiously.

'I love it,' he says.

'It's quite unusual,' adds Daphne, peering at Beatrice.

'It's popular these days. And it was Isobel's mum's name,' Tom tells her, his hand resting on Isobel's shoulder.

Graham holds Beatrice out to Daphne. 'Do you want to hold her?' he asks.

Daphne takes Beatrice awkwardly, slowly, her face collapsing. Isobel can see tears gathering in her eyes, her fingers turning white beneath the nail as she clutches at the blanket tightly. Daphne turns from everybody, rocking Beatrice in her arms and singing a strange, strangled lullaby. When she turns back around, her face is puffed and pink. She hands Beatrice back to Tom.

'I hope you're going to take very good care of her,' Daphne says as Tom readjusts Beatrice's hat.

He looks up. 'Of course I am.'

But it seems Daphne hasn't finished. 'You can't be changing your mind about what you want, you know. Not now. You need to focus on Isobel and Beatrice.' Her voice is quiet as always, but it's sharpened by an unpleasant, insistent tone.

Tom frowns at his mother and takes Beatrice from her. Isobel tries to work out if his face betrays any knowledge of why Daphne is being so accusing, so harsh. She tries to think why her words pull at a cord of anxiety. But her head aches and her mind is strangely slow and heavy. She can see nothing. She closes her eyes, hoping that there is nothing to see.

She didn't think they would let her go home so soon.

But they do. They don't seem to be concerned that neither she nor Tom know what they are doing: how to change a nappy, how to be responsible for all eternity, how to work out why the baby keeps wailing like a faulty siren.

So home they go, to Broadsands. Tom leans gently over the just-unpacked car seat, working out the buckles and straps while Beatrice screams blue murder in his face. He drives home slowly, meticulously, glancing every couple of seconds into the back of the car. Isobel closes her eyes as they wind through the uneven roads of Silenshore, trying to sleep, if only for an instant.

'Looking forward to getting back?' Tom asks, when there is a lull in Beatrice's crying.

Isobel nods, although she knows he probably doesn't see her. But her words seem to have all gone. Perhaps her words are all still on the beach, where the pain ripped the life she knew away. Perhaps they are wandering around with the old versions of Isobel, floating along the coastline like ghosts.

When they get back, Daphne loiters in the corner of the kitchen.

'Do you want to hold her?' Tom asks as they bring Beatrice in and set down their bags on the table.

Daphne shakes her head. She looks tired: her eyes are weighted with lines and grey shadows.

Tom shrugs and takes Beatrice from her car seat himself.

'You go and have a lie down, if you like,' he says to Isobel, motioning to the lounge.

Even though it's a warm day, Daphne has lit the woodburning stove and it glows luminous in the centre of the wall. Isobel sinks down onto the sofa carefully. She watches as Tom rocks Beatrice gently and sees her pale-pink translucent eyelids droop. Once Beatrice is in the crib in the corner of the room, Tom disappears and then returns with a pile of pink congratulations cards. Isobel stretches out on the sofa as Tom puts all the cards up on the oak mantlepiece. The sight of him carefully displaying them all next to one another in a neat row makes her ache with something, although she's too tired to identify exactly what it is. He puts up the last card, a huge creation involving a pop-up stork, and then wanders over to the couch. He bends over and kisses Isobel, and she smells the not altogether unpleasant stale smell of him, of his unwashed hair and skin. He hasn't showered today because he rushed to the hospital first thing this morning and stayed with Isobel all day, chatting to her as she held Beatrice to her breast, wincing along with her at the ferocity of the relentless little mouth on her nipple.

'You know, you should get some sleep before Beatrice wakes up again,' Tom says.

Isobel nods and Tom stands up. He pulls a fleece blanket over her and draws the curtains. It's still light and the room is bright with early summer sunshine that glows through Daphne's yellow curtains. Isobel closes her eyes, but once she hears Tom leave the room, her insides begin to slowly whirl around in a panic that she can't seem to grasp or stop.

Sleep seems a million miles away.

She sits up and looks across at the outline of the little bundle in the crib next to the couch. She's been staring at Beatrice for most of the day, trying to relate what she sees to the shifting, growing belly that she's had for the past six months; the hopeful, excited glances that she and Tom shared the weeks before the birth. But she can't relate to it at all. She can't relate this, this intensity of feeling, this little shrimp in a blanket, this blur of exhaustion and shock, to anything that has ever gone before.

She lies back on the sofa and stares into space until the bundle next to her begins wriggling and mewling. Tom appears.

'Is she hungry?' he asks.

'I don't know.'

'Here you go.' Tom hands Beatrice over to Isobel. The baby's head wobbles next to Isobel's shoulder and Isobel lifts her hand higher up to give it some support.

*Don't forget to support her head, love,* the midwife or one of the nurses, or somebody, said to Isobel this morning in the hospital. Isobel had burned with humiliation as she scooped up Beatrice's lolling head in her arms. How had she forgotten to support the baby's head? Everybody knows you have to do that.

'Did you get some sleep before?' Tom asks as Isobel unclips her bra and begins to feed Beatrice.

'Not really. But it doesn't matter. I had a rest.'

'Iris called. She's going to come round later. Is that okay?'

'Of course. I want to see her.' At the thought of Iris, Isobel wants to cry. She shakes her head. What's wrong with her? If this is how she's going to be as a mother, then she isn't going to do a very good job.

Tom puts a hand on Isobel's shoulder. 'Isobel, is something bothering you? Or are you just a bit overwhelmed by everything?'

Isobel smiles, her lips cracking again, her face hurting, everything seeming to be such hard work. 'I'm not sure.'

'Do you want me to run you a bath before Iris comes?'

Beatrice has stopped feeding, so Isobel stands up and pats her on the back like the nurses showed her, and then puts her back in the crib. She's asleep again now, her little face frowning with the effort. 'Thank you. I'd love that.'

Tom puts lavender in the bath, and the woody, soapy smell rises up in the steam of the bathroom as Isobel enters. Daphne's main bathroom is painted a deep blue. Seahorses and shells adorn the walls and a blue wicker chair sits in the corner. Tom perches on it for a moment.

'You will feel like yourself again soon,' he says, although it isn't clear if he's trying to convince Isobel or himself.

'I hope so.' Isobel peels her clothes from her strange, baggy body, stepping carefully into the oily bathwater. She brings up her knees to her chest. 'I keep panicking that I'm going to be no good as a mum,' she blurts out. Tom springs up and moves over to Isobel. His shirt is wet as he leans against the cool ceramic side.

'You mustn't think that. It's rubbish.'

'I can't help it.' Isobel's voice cracks like glass, and tears mingle with the water on her face. 'I just don't feel ready. And I won't be a good mum, because I keep thinking horrible things,' Isobel says, unable to stop the torrent of quiet words spilling from her lips. 'I keep thinking that there's so much I was going to do. I keep thinking of the dream box at Iris's, and how I need to throw all my things in there away.'

'What dream box?'

'We have a box. We *had* a box,' Isobel says, correcting herself carefully. 'And in it was all the things we were going to do. Like places we wanted to go. I told you about it. Or I told you that Iris and me were planning to go to Paris and Vienna together. I had maps and pictures of Vienna. And Iris had things about Paris. And I've just had a beautiful baby girl, and I can't seem to focus on her at all. Yet I can focus on that box and what was in it! What's wrong with me?' Her words are high and loud, and she wonders if Daphne might hear her.

'Isobel, that's not horrible. It's probably normal. It'll just take some time to adjust, that's all. But we'll manage it.'

There's a knock on the bathroom door: quiet, reluctant.

'Isobel? Are you both in there? Beatrice is awake. She needs you.'

Tom hands Isobel a towel and she stands slowly, the cooled water dripping down from her distorted body, suds sliding over her stretched skin. She catches sight of herself in the mirror.

*Somebody's mother.*

*Beatrice's mother.*

The reflection is ghostly with fatigue, blotchy with upset, somebody Isobel cannot recognise.

Iris brings with her a bunch of magenta peonies and the smell of fresh air and freedom. She sets them down on Daphne's coffee table and then moves to the crib, where Beatrice is still sleeping.

'Oh!' She covers her mouth with her slim, freckled hand. 'Isobel, she's so beautiful! How are you feeling? How's it all going?' She looks around furtively and then lowers her voice to a whisper. 'I hope Daphne isn't interfering too much?'

Isobel shakes her head. 'No. Actually, she's having very little to do with us. She's barely even held Beatrice. She's out at the moment. She's walking the dog a lot since we got home. It's like she doesn't want to be here with us.'

Iris frowns but she says nothing, just puts her hand to her mouth again as Beatrice wriggles and stretches in her loosely swaddled blankets.

'She's a little dream.'

'Iris,' Isobel begins. Iris looks up, her green eyes expectant, her face open, ready to accept anything.

What is it that Isobel wants Iris to accept? That she doesn't feel like herself any more? That her mind is moving more slowly than it used to, that her words have all gone? It doesn't even make any sense.

'Thanks for my peonies.'

Iris grins, her face relaxing. 'You're welcome. I've not bought Beatrice anything yet. I wanted to get to know her first.'

'I feel like I need to get to know her, too,' Isobel says carefully.

Iris sits down next to Isobel on the sofa. The scent of outdoors has faded, and now she smells just like Iris again: lemony and familiar.

'You need to give yourself time,' she says firmly, taking hold of Isobel's hand. Isobel looks down at their hands. Iris's have always been delicate, china-like. Isobel's are stockier, with sturdier fingers that Iris's rings won't fit on. Iris's fingernails are glossy, painted dark red, almost black. Isobel's are bright red and chipped. She wonders where her ruby-coloured ring is that she was wearing when she went into hospital to have Beatrice. There's so much she doesn't know. So much she can't remember.

'That's what Tom said. I'm just a bit worried about it all,' Isobel says, and then stops. She's read about the baby blues, fleetingly glanced over websites and NHS leaflets that talked about day three: crying, fearing, fretting. But this doesn't bear any relation to those websites. It's darker and bigger, and feels like more than just a few hormonal tears.

'Isobel, this is all huge. You have just had a baby. You will adjust soon, in your own time. Tom will help you, and so will I. Okay?'

Isobel looks at Iris, at the face she has known for so long: watched as it has changed from gap-toothed and freckled to slender and expertly made up with delicate kohl and highlighter. Iris knows Isobel more than anyone. If Iris thinks everything will be fine, then Isobel has to believe her.

'Okay,' she says, smiling and standing up. She peers into the basket and tries to summon her strongest feelings of love. She thinks about her mother, and how much she loved her, and tries to reverse the feeling inside of her, so that it's flipped on its head: mother to daughter.

Iris makes them tea and brings it in on one of Daphne's floral trays. They sip and dunk in some elaborate chocolate and ginger biscuits that Tom finds in the cupboard behind the teabags and jars of expensive coffee.

'I'd better get going,' Iris says after about an hour, standing up and brushing some gold biscuit crumbs from her floral tea dress. 'I've got another exhibition to organise.' Iris leans down and kisses the air next to Beatrice's cheek, then gives Isobel a tight hug.

'I'll see you out, Iris,' Tom says, gesturing for Isobel to sit back down on the sofa. She obeys and waves as Iris leaves the room. It's only after, when she hears the hissing of Iris and Tom whispering from the hall, and Tom disappears straight upstairs after the front door bangs shut, that Isobel wonders why she didn't see Iris out herself.

Beatrice's first days blur past like the view from a train. Isobel can't sleep when Beatrice does. Tom closes his eyes whenever it's quiet, and appears to fall asleep promptly and efficiently. A midwife sits in the lounge with Isobel and asks her questions about how she feels and ticks and scribbles in a file and offers a concerned expression of well-practiced sympathy to Isobel. A health visitor comes and does the same, her head inclined, her brows low with textbook concern, which Isobel finds unbearable, and so she finds herself telling them both that she is doing very well, all things considered, and managing to feed Beatrice well, and sleep well, and is looking forward to getting out and about a bit.

By the time Beatrice is a week old, Isobel is fractured with exhaustion. Everything she touches seems to fall to the floor. Her skin aches and her head pounds with each sound she hears: the wail of Beatrice, the clearing of Tom's throat, the clatter of pans from the kitchen in the rare moments when Daphne is home.

'I have to pop out,' Tom says. He's been off work for a week and isn't due back there for another few days.

'Not to the restaurant?'

'No. I just need to pick something up.'

'From where?' She's interrogating him. She can see he doesn't want her to. His eyes flicker, a rare instant of uneasiness.

'From Lucas, the guy who lives below my old flat. He kept a

few of my things stored at his for me. You just try and get some rest while Beatrice is asleep. I won't be long. Mum might be back soon too.'

Daphne doesn't return while Tom is out. Isobel lies on the sofa, pulls the blanket over her, closes her eyes. But the strange, animal snorts and grunts that rise from Beatrice's crib and hang in the air make it impossible for Isobel to drift away into her own sleep. She sits up and stares across the room. She could do all sorts of things while Beatrice sleeps. All the things she hasn't done since her life cracked like an egg. She could read something, or watch television, or cook something so that Daphne doesn't have to bother later. But she can't make herself do anything, except stay in the room and listen tensely to Beatrice's foreign sounds.

Eventually, Tom comes home.

'Everything alright?' he asks.

Isobel nods. She has no idea how long he has been out for. But her muscles ache, rigid with remaining in one position on the sofa.

'I'll make us some tea,' she says, slowly getting to her feet. She's still doing everything slowly. She forces herself to make the tea at a pace more like her own. She darts about the kitchen, filling the kettle, squashing teabags down into the mugs, pouring the steaming water and the milk. But in her haste, somehow, she drops one of the cups of tea, gasping as the hot water hits her leg.

'You must have a sleep,' Tom says, appearing suddenly behind her. Hot brown liquid scalds Isobel's knees, clinging to her jeans. She takes them off while she's still in the kitchen to reveal angry red skin on her thighs. It's the second time she's burned herself in two days.

'You're not functioning properly,' he continues, taking hold of her hand and pulling her up. 'You're not sleeping at all, are you? You didn't sleep while I was out?'

Isobel shakes her head. Whenever Beatrice wakes up, Isobel is waiting for her with an intensity she's never felt before. When Beatrice goes back to sleep, Isobel lies stiffly next to the crib, tensing with every snuffle and creak of the darkened wood.

Tom eases Isobel up gently from the sofa. 'Come on. You have to sleep.'

Isobel says nothing, but lets herself be taken upstairs by Tom. Once she's in their bedroom, she pulls on some pyjama trousers and climbs into bed. Tom kisses her forehead and strokes a strand of auburn hair from her eyes.

'Sleep,' he commands. 'You'll feel so much better for it.' His phone rings from his pocket as he leaves the room and Isobel sits up in bed. Tom's words creep into her bedroom, but they are blurred together and she can't hear what they are.

Who is he talking to? She wants to get up and ask him, but Daphne is downstairs, and Isobel doesn't want Daphne to know about any of the worry that is coursing through her. Yesterday Tom left his phone on the sofa next to Isobel and when it began to ring, he launched himself across her to grab it, fumbled with the keys to cancel the call. She raised her eyebrows at him, but he slipped the phone into his pocket and left the room, and when he returned Daphne was there and Isobel stayed silent.

Now, Isobel closes her eyes and waits for sleep to wash over her. She feels as though a part of her has been asleep for days and days. That part of her lies dormant, oblivious, but doesn't make her any less tired.

*Sleep. Sleep. Sleep.* The word loses meaning and she turns over in bed. Her thoughts drift by like clouds: thoughts of Beatrice and her mother, images of Tom and Iris and Daphne and midwives and doctors. The beeping and wailing and dizzy blur of the labour floats in her mind. New scenes that she hasn't seen before somehow emerge. Beatrice is handed to her, slippery and purple. Tom leans down and kisses her, his lips pressing down on her slick, sweating forehead. Iris asks Tom about the name for the baby. And Daphne weeps, muttering a string of broken words about Tom not being who Isobel thinks he is.

Isobel sits up in bed. The room spins around her. Downstairs Beatrice starts to cry.

'Was your mum there when I was in labour?' Isobel asks Tom as she stands at the door of the sitting room.

He looks up from Beatrice. She is on his knee, her pink scaly fingers gripping his thumb.

'Yes, I thought you knew? Iris was there too. It was all quite frantic.'

'I don't mind,' Isobel says, seeing worry dart over Tom's face. 'It's just that I'm having these sort of flashbacks about it all. I'm remembering things I didn't really take in at the time. I've remembered that your mum was crying.'

Tom shrugs. 'Of course she was. It's her first grandchild.'

'I know, but it was more than that. She was saying strange things.'

'About what?'

'About you. How you're not who I think you are, or something.' Isobel tries to wrench the accusatory note from the words, but they are inseparable. The tone and the words hang in the air like a sour smell and she wishes she hadn't said anything.

Tom shakes his head. He's tired too: his skin is pale with dry patches around the chin. Normally he moisturises and Isobel mocks him affectionately for it. He must have forgotten, or not wanted to bother, or perhaps the cream just isn't good enough to balance out all the broken sleep.

'I really don't know what you're talking about. Have you just remembered this?'

Isobel nods.

'Well, then, isn't there a chance you drifted off to sleep and just dreamt it?'

'I don't think so. It seems so real.'

Tom stands up and passes Beatrice to Isobel. She smells of sour milk, of sickly sweet baby-friendly washing powder, of another world completely.

'Where are you going?' Isobel asks him.

'I'm going to pack Beatrice some things. I think we need to go out. We need a change of scenery.'

Isobel nods. She carries Beatrice upstairs with her and lays her on the middle of the bed before opening her wardrobe. She's worn only jeans and pyjamas for the last few days. Today, she's going to dress like Isobel. She takes one of her favourite outfits from before she had the baby, an olive-green dress from Topshop. It skims her protruding belly kindly.

She rifles through her makeup bag. She hasn't looked in there since bringing Beatrice home from hospital. She rubs some foundation into her cheeks, across her nose and forehead. Already she looks better. She picks through the rest of the bag and finds her mascara. Her lashes aren't quite black, but cocoa brown. Black makes her eyes look rounder and bigger, and she strokes the wand over her lashes again and again. As she's zipping her makeup bag up again, she sees a gold tube of lipstick. She picks it out. She collects red lipsticks. Her mum had a thing for red lips.

*People say red is a no-go for us redheads. But that makes me want to wear it more.*

Isobel was about five when her mother told her this. *Us redheads* had stuck in her mind. She was the same as her glamorous, grown-up mother? She'd hugged the words close to her, never forgetting them. As an adult, she'd admired the punch of the words, the determination to go against sober advice. Brick, Pillarbox, Rose, Crimson, Blood. Isobel has all the reds. This one is called Scarlett Kiss. She slicks it onto her lips and then stares at herself in the mirror until Tom appears in the en suite.

'You look lovely,' he says.

They walk through the narrow streets to the main stretch of Silenshore. Beatrice is impeccable in her pram, sleeping gracefully as they wheel her over uneven cobbles. It feels good being outside. The air is warm and golden, the salt from the sea tangy on Isobel's lips. She walks slowly beside Tom, still sore and stiff from the labour. They head uphill, towards the castle. Its turrets glow with the sunlight behind them, the stone glinting gold.

'Let's sit down for a minute,' Isobel says when they reach the bench outside Harpers. She rocks the pram gently with one hand as she sits down, and Tom nods towards Beatrice and smiles.

'Look, you're a natural, rocking her like that.'

Isobel sighs. 'I'm not sure.' She stares into the pram, where Beatrice is lost in white blankets. A pale-pink rabbit toy rests next to her cheek, bigger than her head.

*My daughter.*

She looks over to Tom, to try and gauge whether his expression betrays a better understanding of having a daughter than Isobel's. But he's turned away, rooting in Beatrice's changing bag.

'I love her,' Isobel says. She listens to the words before they drift away down Silenshore Hill, tries them on like a dress she's not sure suits her. Beatrice doesn't show any sign of hearing, or caring. Her full strawberry-coloured pout and her miniature nose, her tuft of dark hair like Tom's, her tiny fingers, peep from the depths of the pram.

'I love her,' she repeats. 'My daughter.'

The words won't penetrate Isobel's mind. They float on the surface, like leaves on a lake.

## CHAPTER 16

# *Evelyn: 1948*

The day that her daughter was born, Evelyn gazed down at her, a fireball of love forming rapidly in her chest. The baby had shining black hair and a tiny pink scrunched-up face. Evelyn could see Jack in her new baby, but she could also see her mother and father. She was a true du Rêve. She was special, beautiful. And to prove it, Evelyn gave her the name of a queen.

This could be it, Evelyn thought. Now that she had Victoria, everything might be better. Her world might become brighter again. Because the world for the past year, since her wedding day, had simply been Lace Antiques, and what lay behind its white door: the dark, narrow staircase, the carpet that swirled with roses and smelled of old cigarette ash and trodden-in Chanel and secret footsteps. The pink-tiled bathroom, square and cold. Evelyn's bedroom, reeking of sleep, and now, the darling pink skin of her baby.

But now, perhaps Evelyn could start to go out more. Now that she had a huge navy-blue pram and wasn't heavy and tired she could perhaps walk around Silenshore and feel more like herself again. When her parents had first disappeared, and the rumours were flying around the town about who they might have owed money to, who might have chased them away, she'd stayed inside all the time because she'd been frightened that somebody might recognise her. One stale, slow day, when Jack was out buying strange things covered in dust, Evelyn had even told a lone customer that she came from far away, just to see if he would believe her. It seemed that he did. So she told another person, and another, until everybody thought the same. There was no reason to doubt Evelyn's lack of connection with the castle. She knew she didn't look like a princess or a film star any more. How could she, surrounded by old things, standing at a square counter day after day, week after week?

But even when enough time had passed that the rumours about the du Rêve girl being left behind had faded, and people were less likely to remember her as the old Evelyn du Rêve with the bright-gold hair and the brilliant blue eyes, Evelyn still stayed behind the dusty curtains of Lace Antiques. It was as though she'd forgotten how to go out.

She'd waited for London, of course. But the month they were meant to go, Jack had heard that there was a man in Silenshore who wanted to buy a caseload of antiques, and had said that going to London just then would be stupid. So they'd waited for a better time to move away: Evelyn upstairs hunting for hidden notes from her parents that she never found; Jack downstairs in the shop. Marriage was strange and lonely. It wasn't at all how Evelyn had imagined it to be. If they could just get to London, she'd thought at first, then her life would be the glittering party she'd intended. But as the months went by, Evelyn realised that they weren't going to London now, or any time soon. Jack probably had never even planned to go. He'd just said it so that Evelyn would marry him, although she wasn't sure why he'd wanted that so much because he didn't seem to particularly like her, except for at night, when he grunted and tugged at her and thrust against her as though they were animals.

But now, Evelyn thought, as she stared down her darling Victoria with her raven-black hair, perhaps none of that mattered. Perhaps now life would finally begin.

Evelyn managed to take care of the baby, who was rather subdued from the moment she was born. She slept easily in her wooden crib next to Evelyn, and when she cried, Evelyn took her in her arms, or latched her onto her breast until Victoria's miniature eyelids fluttered closed once more and Evelyn could sleep again.

Jack did not involve himself with Evelyn or Victoria. He took to sleeping in the spare bedroom, because Victoria snuffled and shuffled in her sleep, and it was not easy attending auctions and keeping on top of the shop and its stock when he was tired.

When Victoria was a few months old, Evelyn decided to try on some of her old dresses that she'd brought with her from the castle when she married Jack, before she'd blown up like a balloon to carry Victoria. Her stomach had returned nicely to its original shape without much coaxing at all because Evelyn never really ate much these days. Her face, she knew, had lost the plumpness that Victoria had brought to it. It was time, she decided, to be herself again.

She took out some skirts and blouses that she hadn't worn at all that year, and placed them, together with her yellow crepe dress, on her bed. This was the dress she'd worn the day she'd met Jack. She needed to find her matching shoes to wear too, now that her ankles were back to their normal size. Evelyn dragged a chair across the room and clambered onto it, pulling down a small suitcase from on top of the wardrobe. Perhaps they would be in there: she still hadn't properly unpacked all of her things since living with Jack.

As Evelyn pulled the case open, she saw not shoes, but a doll: a round head fringed with shimmering hair. As she pulled the doll from the case, an image of Mary, the evacuee, filled her mind. Evelyn pushed its black hair from its glassy eyes, then held it tight as though it was a real child. Although she'd brought the doll with her when she'd moved to the flat above Lace Antiques, she hadn't really looked at it since she'd been here. Now, holding the doll transported her back to the times when she'd stormed through the castle playing games with the evacuees, the times when she'd believed that the castle and its riches was something to be left behind for a more exciting life.

Mary and the other children had only stayed with them in the castle for a few months in the end. London was as safe as anywhere, it appeared. Nothing was happening. It was a phony war. And so battered suitcases were packed, parents were telegrammed and suddenly Evelyn was alone in the castle again. She wrote to Mary often. Wonderful Mary, who gave away her only doll because she knew Evelyn loved the way its dress and hair sparkled in the light.

Once it was clear that the war was perhaps not so phony, another batch of sniffing, amazed children were dispatched to Castle du Rêve. None of them were like Mary. These were all young boys with grey shorts and scabbed knees, who spoke to Evelyn so infrequently that in the end she often forgot that they were there. She had stuffed the doll away, and, along with the millions of other people whose letters had suddenly stopped, tried to forget. She'd thought about Mary again when she'd told her mother that she was going to stay with her in London, then ended up meeting Jack and staying and marrying him instead. Now, the thought of how that white lie had turned dark and black made Evelyn feel quite sick.

Pressing the doll to her flat chest, Evelyn remembered pieces of conversation with Mary; precious words that she had turned over and over in her mind for months after Mary had left the castle.

*You're glamorous, Evelyn. That's why I think you'll end up in Hollywood, covered head to toe in diamonds.*

*The war's going to change everything, Evelyn. And when it does, you should be ready.*

Mary would be disappointed to see Evelyn now, her only company a doll that should never have been hers. She placed the doll back into the suitcase gently, and pulled the crepe dress from the bed, fingering the thick yellow fabric before pulling it over her pale shoulders. She would make something of her life, for Mary if nobody else.

As she stared in the mirror in the corner of the bedroom, she saw Jack appear behind her. His eyes locked onto hers.

'You look beautiful,' he said. His words weren't soft, but sharp. 'Come to London with me. You can come to the auction. You might have your uses there.'

It was as though wearing the yellow dress again and thinking about Mary and her own old dreams of being a star had unlocked something; it was as though even Jack knew that now was the time for their lives to really begin. Evelyn packed a little case for her and Victoria, her heart singing.

Jack was attentive to them both as they sat on the juddering train, his arm hooked around Evelyn's shoulders the whole way. When they arrived, he took her to Oxford Street, bought her more lipsticks and another bottle of Chanel No 5 perfume, and a new red dress from Horrockses Fashions. Maybe, now that he had brought Evelyn to London for the day and treated her nicely, he was finally considering moving here? Maybe he had almost saved enough money for the move, and would tell her that she needed to pack up any day now. They could be in London for Christmas, and perhaps, in London, Jack would be a happier man.

When they went into a shop that was brimming with paintings of fields and dogs and horses, and golden frames stacked one on top of another, Jack nodded at the man behind the counter.

'Lace,' the man muttered to Jack in greeting, his eyes on Evelyn. 'What can I do for you?'

Evelyn took Victoria from her pram, bouncing her in her arms while the men talked. Victoria wrapped her plump little fingers around Evelyn's as they muttered about prices and artists and the costs of framing. Eventually, the men shook hands on a deal and Jack and Evelyn stepped back out of the shop into the bustling street. It was beginning to rain, the sky black with unspent showers.

'I got that painting for half the price he had it marked for. I'll make a nice amount on that. Bastards like him never took me seriously before,' he said to Evelyn as she pushed the pram along, weaving it through the crowds and the umbrellas and puddles. 'They thought I was worthless. I've shown them today.'

Evelyn nodded, knowing that this wasn't altogether true. She'd seen the way that the man in the shop had looked at her. She'd seen them both glance at her, heard Jack promise him something in a whisper, although she couldn't hear exactly what. They still thought Jack was worthless. But they would give him half-price paintings if they thought he might give something in return. She looked down at her yellow dress, her fitted coat, suddenly hating them.

As time went on, Jack took Evelyn to more shops, more auctions, and introduced her to more men, who stared at her as though she were a painting herself. Nothing ever happened to her that she could really say much about: just the odd calloused old hand of a seller around her waist, or resting lightly on her bottom. She'd look across at Jack when this happened, but he'd always be in the middle of a deal. Sometimes, Jack paid the baker across the road from Lace Antiques to look after Victoria while they both went to London. Evelyn came to dread those days, for those were the ones where she had to have strange hands around her shoulders as she stood in auctions and sat in dirty little cafés. Those were the days when she always felt as though a promise that Jack had given might materialise, for when she was without Victoria she was without a reason to disappear outside or sit in a quiet corner alone. She grew more and more fond of being in Silenshore, away from London. She knew now that London wasn't the sparkling, bright place for a life of adventure to begin. London was a place of fear and dark alleyways that Jack made her take shortcuts through, and strange men with their leering eyes and wandering hands and their glazed expressions when Evelyn asked how she might go about finding a missing couple in France. When Jack wasn't watching, and sometimes even when he was, men would sidle up to Evelyn and whisper in her ear their promises about better lives with them, about happiness and diamonds and anything her pretty heart desired. Once, Evelyn knew, she would have fallen for it. She would have believed them.

'What was a woman like you doing marrying Jack Lace?' asked one man with a white smile and shiny blond hair. 'Did he give you a gift or a potion of some kind? Bewitch you, did he?'

Evelyn shook her head, watching Jack across the auction hall that they were in. 'No. Nothing like that. I just loved him.' But then she thought of the glinting, jewel-encrusted mirror that she had taken from her mother. The stones that Evelyn had thought were blue diamonds as a child were actually sapphires. The gems of new love. Never mind that she fell in love with a man who turned out to be all wrong for her: she'd still fallen in love. 'I wasn't bewitched. I fell in love,' she said firmly.

'Ah, but maybe those two are the same thing,' the man with the blond hair smiled.

As they spent more and more time in London, it became clear that Jack knew no actors, no theatre people, as he'd once said he did. But now, Evelyn wasn't sure she wanted to be an actress anyway. She wasn't sure she could stand the thought of people staring at her, idolising her, wondering why on earth she had married Jack Lace. All she could stand, for now, was Silenshore. And the more she thought about it, the more certain she became that she shouldn't go anywhere else. Because perhaps if she stayed in Silenshore, she would be closer to finding out where her parents were and if they were ever going to come back.

As the years lingered on, Victoria and Evelyn were inseparable. Evelyn was always by Victoria's side, keeping her away from Jack and away from anything Evelyn thought might have the potential to be dangerous: a label which really could be applied to most things. When Victoria was a little girl, Evelyn would sometimes pluck her from her bed and carry her to her own. Then Evelyn would curl into her sleeping daughter, nuzzling her neck into Victoria's milky skin that smelt of school: of wooden desks and ink and other people's children.

But then Victoria had grown distant somehow. Evelyn had actually been out into Silenshore and bought Victoria a special present for her thirteenth birthday: a handbag with a comb and a silver bracelet with stones the colour of rubies inside. Evelyn had drawn stars on some of the paper from the shop and wrapped the present carefully. Victoria's face on that birthday morning had been a perfect combination of beauty and happiness, and Evelyn had promised herself that even though Victoria was growing up, she would never let them grow apart. She would never leave Victoria, leave her to wonder where Evelyn was and if she even still loved her. At first, it was easy to adhere to her own promise. Even though Victoria was changing before Evelyn's eyes: rounded breasts, widened hips and a slimmer, more knowing, face her character remained much the same. She was intelligent, interesting. Evelyn liked to talk to her, even if Victoria had to come into Evelyn's bedroom and sit on the end of her bed if Evelyn was too tired to get up.

But then Victoria had started to retreat from Evelyn's slow-moving world. It was probably Evelyn's fault somehow. She was always so very tired: tired with the disappointment of everything, the weight of lost hope bearing down upon her each day, exhausting her all the time. It was hard to try to do all the things she wanted to with Victoria with so little energy and hope. And she couldn't pluck Victoria from her bed any more and breathe in her milky skin. She couldn't put Victoria's warm, sticky hand in hers and walk up and down Silenshore's main streets with her. Victoria was her own person now: one who smelt of her own scent of fresh flowers and hairspray; who became frustrated when Evelyn was tired; who was quite obviously too intelligent and full of life to sit in Lace Antiques forever. And so before Evelyn could summon up the energy to understand how she might keep Victoria close to her, Victoria seemed further away than ever, tangled in a mess that Evelyn had no idea how to pull her from without breaking her.

In the end, it was Jack who decided on what was to be done about Victoria and the baby. Although Evelyn supposed it made sense, part of her wanted to pull his callous, brutish fingers away from the leather-covered steering wheel as they motored along the winding roads to Gaspings mother and baby home. She wanted to smash the windows that were trapping her in this horrible, horrible car, grab Victoria and take her somewhere else where they could look after the baby together. But, as always, these days, Evelyn's limbs were heavy and leaden, her mind cobwebbed with fatigue. It was as though her soul was separate from her body, powerless to move it.

And so Evelyn did nothing.

When they'd left their darling Victoria behind, Evelyn twisted her head to watch the red-brick building disappear around the corner, willing for everything to turn out, for May to hurry along, for Victoria to somehow keep her sanity and sense and Harry at the end of all this.

Jack didn't turn his head, didn't move his eyes from the road, but still somehow sensed that Evelyn was leaving a part of herself behind at Gaspings.

'We had no choice. You'd best try and forget the whole business.'

Evelyn rested her head on the hard leather of her seat and closed her eyes against the sharp glare of the sun. Memories floated around in her mind: when her belly had swelled as ripe as a purple plum as she carried Victoria inside her; when her mother had told her that their fortune had gone; when she married Jack and thought that he was the key to Evelyn transforming into who she was meant to be. Image after image, memory after memory, as they juddered along the road away from Gaspings House and back towards Silenshore.

When they reached home, Evelyn's hands wandered to her throat, to pull up her beads over her head, as she always did before she sank into bed. But there were no beads there, no pearls in the golden box on her dressing table, no crystals or diamonds or rubies. When Evelyn and Jack had married, and her parents had vanished, their lights from the castle burned out, Evelyn had been poor for the first time in her life. Her only luxuries had been the Chanel perfume and the lipstick that her mother had sent to her with her other belongings from the castle, and these she used every day, stared at, fingered and remembered. But as Jack's modest wealth began to accumulate, Evelyn's collection of perfumes and dresses and jewellery began to grow, making her feel like she was, underneath the dust of the Lace name, a du Rêve once again. She had started to seek out stones to try and make things right: garnets to bring success to the business, rubies to try and banish the bad dreams and sadness that had cursed Evelyn since the days she met Jack, pearls to fill her life with calm and beauty.

Victoria's place at Gaspings had been paid for by a furious Jack. The money that Evelyn had added of her own accord: notes that were curled and warm from being hidden in Evelyn's shoe, she hoped would make the nurses treat Victoria like the queen that she should be. So now, Evelyn's neck was bare of pearls. The only glittering stones she had not sold were the sapphires that encrusted the mirror. She had slipped it from Victoria's case when she wasn't looking. That, Evelyn would keep here. As long as she kept it away from her, Victoria would surely be safe.

## CHAPTER 17

# *Isobel: 2011*

'Pass those olives, will you please?' Isobel asks Tom.

Tom rolls the closed tub of olives towards Isobel and she catches them. They are sitting on the beach, a tartan blanket spread over the pebble-strewn sand. It's the fourth day of a heat-wave and the sun is raw and burning. Isobel opens the tub, glancing down as she does so. The ruby-red vintage ring that she bought in London glitters in the sun. It's the first time she's worn it since Beatrice was born. She found it the other day in the side pocket of her hospital bag.

'Can I have some falafel, please?' Iris holds her paper plate in the air for Seth to load up.

Isobel rolls up another blanket and then lies down to rest her head on it for a moment, closing her eyes. With her eyes shut, the sounds around her are amplified. She hears Seth's deep laugh, Iris swatting him as he teases her about something. She hears the distant waves crashing against rocks. She hears the cries of gulls that swoop disconcertingly near, drawn by bread and rustling wrappers. She hears Tom make the ridiculous noise with his lips that he always makes to try and get Beatrice to smile, a noise that Isobel not only never thought she'd hear Tom make, but equally never thought she'd enjoy hearing him make.

There's pleasure in today. Isobel can feel it: a bright, smooth, sweet pleasure.

'Oh! Seth, we've forgotten to get out your radio!' Iris says after a while.

Isobel opens her eyes to see Seth brush himself down and then root through one of the numerous bags they brought to the beach. Eventually, he reveals a battered yellow wireless radio.

'Now I know we could listen to music on our phones,' he says, his hands up in anticipatory defense. 'But I love this radio. It's been on so many picnics with me, I just had to bring it to this one.'

Iris beams up at Seth. He wears a pinstriped shirt and black skinny jeans, even though the temperature is rising by the hour. His square glasses sit on the end of his nose and he pushes them up as he tunes the radio.

'It's a great idea,' Tom says. He takes Isobel's hand as a pop song begins to buzz from the speakers, and sways it to the music.

Isobel did an online search the other night, when everyone else, even Beatrice, was asleep. The symptoms she typed in linger in her mind now, at strange odds with the glimpses of contentment that flicker in her body. The website she read in those still, timeless hours are etched in her mind. Blue, rounded words in a simple font that tried to be helpful and kind.

*A feeling of sadness*

*Difficulty sleeping*

*Lack of interest in the baby*

These weren't symptoms, Isobel thought as she stared at the screen. Symptoms were medical and precise. A wild panic had overtaken her then and she'd pressed 'clear history' and climbed upstairs to bed to lie stiffly until Beatrice began shuffling around and grunting with imminent hunger.

*I* am *interested in Beatrice*, she thinks now.

'Has Beatrice got enough sunscreen on?' she asks Tom, who nods assuredly. 'Have you?' he checks.

Isobel fingers her shoulders, tender, pink, just like the day they met.

'Probably not,' she says, thanking Iris as she slides the sand-crusted bottle of Factor 50 towards her.

They spend almost three hours at the beach, until strings of cloud sweep over the sun and turn the sand from yellow to grey. They gather up their belongings, shaking out the blankets so that sand flies away on the breeze, and chasing after stray wrappers, laughing as they nearly get away, other people laughing too as they run past. Today has been the busiest Isobel has seen Silenshore beach for a while. It's as though they've gone back in time, to the days when the beach and the high street were always crowded.

'So, Paris in the morning?' Isobel asks as Iris and Seth say their goodbyes, laden with canvas bags. The yellow radio sticks out of one of them and Isobel feels a pang of sadness that the day is over, tinged with the warm pleasure that it happened at all. She hasn't enjoyed a day this much for what feels like so long, and the enjoyment fizzes around in her blood like sugar.

'Yes! We're so excited. We have all our packing to do, though,' Iris says, glancing up at Seth.

He nods. 'It's true. But we couldn't have missed today. It's been awesome.' He high-fives Tom and Isobel smiles at Iris, their eyes meeting, laughing. Seth and Tom still seem so different from one another. Tom would never initiate a high-five or carry around an old radio. But somehow, they go together well.

Iris bends over Beatrice's pram and peers in. 'She's still asleep,' she whispers as she stands up straight again and moves towards Isobel. The sun has beckoned the freckles of childhood to the bridge of Iris's nose, making her look younger than she is.

Isobel gives her a tight hug. 'Have a wonderful time,' she says as Iris squeezes her.

'I'll take lots of photos for you,' Iris says.

'You don't need to do anything for me. Just have a lovely time with Seth. I'm fine,' she says, motioning to the pram. The hood ripples in the breeze and Tom waits next to it, pushing it gently. He sees Isobel and Iris gaze at him and gives a comical salute.

'You *are* fine,' Iris says, giving Isobel one last squeeze. 'I'll see you in a few weeks.'

Isobel watches as Iris and Seth scramble hand in hand over the bigger rocks that are strewn over the sand towards the promenade. Isobel and Tom will have to go the long way round with the pram. But Isobel doesn't mind. She lets Tom push, and holds onto his arm until they reach the smooth path that leads to the high street, where Tom has parked his car. They bundle everything into the boot.

'I told my dad we'd call in at about four, so we're just on time,' Isobel says. 'We could walk up to his and come back to the car afterwards.'

Tom nods and they continue up the hill to Blythe Finances. They pass Tom's old flat on the way, and as they do, they both glance up at the door. They have just passed when Isobel hears it open, and hears someone shout Tom's name. She turns and looks back to see Lucas, the man who lives below Tom's old flat. He's breathless, jogging to catch up with them.

'Tom, mate!' Lucas says as he reaches them. 'Long time no see. You're a dad now, then?' He peers into the pram at Beatrice and smiles.

'Yeah,' Tom smiles. 'Big changes. All well with you?'

Lucas nods and jogs on the spot. 'Same old with me, really. You should come round one night. We'll have a few beers, catch up. I haven't seen you since the move. I was going to call you, but I thought you might have your hands full.'

Tom laughs. 'Oh, it's not all bad. I can definitely find time for a few drinks.'

They stand for a few more minutes, making small talk, until Tom mentions that they should be getting going. Lucas jogs off across the road, making Isobel wonder if he ever just walks anywhere. They continue up the cobbles, the pram juddering with the uneven ground, until they reach her dad's.

'He might not spend that long talking to us,' Isobel whispers as they open the door. But when they get in, her dad stands from his desk.

'Are you okay in here for a bit, Jon?' he asks his assistant.

Jon smiles. He's a round, pleasant man with a ruddy face and a tendency to tell bad jokes. Isobel's always liked him. 'Course. Have a bit of time with the family.'

'Can you smell the bread I told you about?' Isobel whispers to Tom as they follow Graham up the creaking, narrow staircase.

Tom sniffs gently, not wanting to disturb Beatrice, who he managed to extract from her pram without waking. 'I can, actually. Creepy.'

'I've tidied up today,' Graham says, gesturing grandly at his strangely bare lounge. Isobel wonders where all his junk is and decides quickly that it doesn't matter.

'It's looking lovely, Dad.' She thinks of all the times in the past two years or so that she's tried to get him to clear up his flat. She's tried every tone: firm, sympathetic, despairing, conspiratorial. None have worked. And now, this.

'What about you two? Any closer to getting a place of your own?'

'A little closer every pay day,' Tom smiles.

'I wish I could've had you here,' Graham says as he looks at Beatrice nestled into the crook of Tom's arm. 'I would have loved it. But there's no room here, of course. It's a shame I didn't stay in the house.'

Isobel reddens and her father sees and waves his arm. 'I know you wanted me to move on, Izzie, and I'm glad I did. But I can't help imagining supporting you more than I have done. This flat isn't a family home. That's why my parents got shut,' he explains to Tom. 'They lived here above their bakery until my little brother was about one, then they sold it and moved to a big house on the promenade. I bought this place back when it came on the market, because it made sense to live above my office, with the amount of time I spend there. Izzie's perhaps told you.'

Isobel thinks of her grandparents' huge, elegant house on the edge of Silenshore promenade that her father is talking about. She remembers being there as a small child, remembers white-painted shutters and various cats and dogs slinking about the wide rooms and tired furniture, the taste of salt from the sea in the lemonade she drank in the garden. Over time, lemonade was swapped for water and the white shutters began to peel, and if the dogs and cats became unwell they disappeared rather than going to the vets. Her grandparents died within a year of one another and her parents held whispered adult conversations about money and equity and debt: all words that were out of reach for Isobel. The house on the promenade was sold, and her father began working shifts at the Smuggler's Ship as well as working in his office during the day. As a child, Isobel never questioned it. Now, looking at her father's tired face, she sees somebody who has walked against the wind all his life.

'Let's wake Beatrice up so she can have a play with her granddad,' she says. 'She's had plenty long enough.'

As the car crunches on the gravel of Broadsands' driveway after going to see her dad, Isobel opens her eyes. She must have fallen asleep in the short drive home. It feels as if they've been in the car for hours, even though it has probably only been about five minutes. The glow of the day, already a memory, feels distant and intangible.

'I'll take Beatrice inside, if you like. You get the bags,' Isobel says through a half-yawn. Perhaps she can try and work to get the day's fleeting contentment back.

Tom whistles as he begins to unload the car, and Isobel leans in to unclip Beatrice from her car seat. Beatrice lets out a prompt wail.

'Shhh. Shhh, little Bea,' Isobel sings as she enters the house. She's wearing flip-flops and they click pleasantly on the tiles of the kitchen, sounding like summer and holidays. Beatrice takes a strand of Isobel's hair and weaves it between her chubby, deft fingers. She pulls it tightly, and Isobel lets her, leaning her head in so that Beatrice can get more. The lost feeling of contentment from earlier flutters back down over her lightly, and Isobel sighs with relief. She hums as she puts Isobel in her bouncer, then falls silent as she hears Daphne talking. She had thought Daphne was out.

Daphne's quiet voice is louder than usual, forceful. It's Daphne, and yet not Daphne.

There's no other voice. Daphne is speaking on the phone in the living room.

Isobel moves closer.

'No, you may not speak to him,' she hears Daphne say.

Isobel frowns. Should she interrupt, tell Daphne that Tom is back, and available to talk to whoever it is on the phone? Daphne's voice, sharp as needles, tells her that she shouldn't.

'You shouldn't be calling here for him,' she says next. Isobel leans on the wall for support, unable to stop listening, but unable to bear what she might hear next.

'I know it must be difficult to hear. But you must leave him alone. I don't want you here. He should be focusing on his baby. Not you. You know what was agreed.'

Isobel frowns and touches the wallpaper, faded and softened with age. She brings to mind Tom's face today as he played with Beatrice, and chatted to her father, and swung Isobel's hand in time to the grainy music from the radio. Was it a face that was hiding something?

The beep of the receiver as Daphne ends the call snaps Isobel's thoughts away, and she rushes back out to the kitchen. But Daphne doesn't follow, and Isobel hears the lounge door shut quietly.

Isobel crouches down in front of Beatrice, who bounces and

flails her chubby arms around in pleasure. Her eyes, pinned on Isobel, are turning darker. The baby blue is turning to brown. The irises are almost lost in the dark pools of colour that surround them. Beatrice will have Isobel's eyes. Isobel's mother's eyes. Her hair is the same shade of rich chocolate as Tom's, but downy and soft.

As she stares at Beatrice, something clicks inside of Isobel, and the gnawing in her stomach pulls at her, stronger than before. She thinks back on the day. There's something that bothered her even before she overheard Daphne, but what was it?

'That's all the things in from the car,' Tom says as he shuts the back door neatly. 'Do you want anything to eat? There's quite a bit of that nice olive bread left.'

Isobel stands and notices that she has left grains of sand on the kitchen floor where she crouched in front of Beatrice.

'Lucas said today that he hadn't seen you since Beatrice was born.'

Tom frowns. 'He hadn't, I don't think.'

'But you went round to his when she was about a week old. I remember you going. You said you were picking something up that he was storing for you.'

Tom shakes his head. 'No, I think I just picked something up from the flat, didn't I?'

'No. You definitely said you were going to Lucas's.'

'Well, maybe he wasn't in when I got there.'

'Do you ever speak to Georgia?' Isobel asks. She doesn't know why she has grasped his ex-wife's name from the air. But she watches Tom's face carefully, waits for a twitch or a reddening: something that will reveal everything she needs to know about whether she can trust him or whether she is going to be swept into a tide of pain. But Tom's face, as always, stays the same. His eyes glint ever so slightly, perhaps with a secret, or perhaps with annoyance that Isobel is dragging Georgia into their pleasant day.

'Nope.'

'So she hasn't contacted you recently?'

Tom turns, carves some bread, turns back, tears at it with his teeth. 'Nope.' The word is the same as before: same tone, same enunciation, a duplicate.

Beatrice wails, put out by the lack of attention.

'So who else do you think might phone here for you?' Isobel whispers, in case Daphne is listening. She whispers a lot of words these days. The whispers float around Broadsands, hissing and buzzing around the large, tidy rooms like wasps.

Tom wipes his hands on his trousers, leaving a trail of white flour from the bread on each leg. 'Isobel, I don't know what you're talking about. What's happened? Why are you suddenly wanting to know all of this? Why can't you just trust me?'

Isobel looks at Beatrice, whose face is crumpling, angry and puce with an imminent howl. She doesn't want to pick her up and soothe her. Tom moves over and picks her up instead, and Beatrice is instantly placated. Panic soars through Isobel as she watches Beatrice, red-faced, play with the buttons on Tom's shirt.

*Lack of interest in the baby*

'I heard something. I heard your mother on the phone to somebody just then, when we came in.' More whispered words, wasps in the room.

'About what?'

'I don't know. She was talking to somebody, telling them to leave you alone.'

'It was probably a sales call.'

Tom jiggles Beatrice and walks out of the room with her on his hip, chewing another piece of bread. Isobel looks down at the abandoned bouncer, at the crumbs of grey-gold sand on the floor, at the forlorn bags from their perfect day at the beach. She thinks of Beatrice's eyes and hair and all the things that make her Isobel and Tom's: a painfully sweet mixture of them both. She hears Tom open the lounge door and speak to Daphne, hears him ask her who was on the phone. She listens out for the extended vowels of his ex-wife's name, or for an answer that will make the aching inside her go away.

But she hears nothing except the murmur of calm conversation, the hum of the house around her, the hissing of wasps around her ears.

CHAPTER 18

# *Victoria: 1965*

Victoria's parents were probably about five minutes away from Gaspings House when Victoria was shunted into a room full of chattering women. Matron gave Victoria a tap on the waist to prompt her to enter, and then left her standing in the doorway. A few of the girls looked up, cigarette smoke making their faces grey and distorted. The room was dark, and the girls were seated on mismatched chairs around a long table. The ones who weren't smoking knitted furiously, needles twitching away in time with their mouths as they talked to one another. Victoria could see a few of the items that were taking shape: pale-blue booties, a cream shawl, a yellow hat.

'Are you new?' somebody said over the din of voices and clacking of knitting needles. Victoria stared around the room, trying to find the owner of the voice. Everybody still seemed to be talking. Still, somebody must have asked, and it would be rude not to answer, so Victoria gave a general nod and stepped a little further into the room. It was then that she saw a woman sitting on a straight-backed green sofa in the corner, waiting for Victoria's reply.

The woman was tall and her body stooped even as she sat. She looked older than Victoria, and like everybody around the table, seemed to be quite accepting of where she was, of the predicament she was in. Why weren't they all *crying*? How could they talk and knit booties for babies who they never meant to have, for whom goodness only knew what was going to happen? Victoria's legs went weak at her last thought and she found herself moving towards the sofa and dropping down next to the tall woman.

'I'm Bev,' the woman said, holding out her hand to shake Victoria's. 'Have you just arrived?'

Victoria nodded, 'I'm Victoria.' Then, because she could think of nothing else, 'My parents have just left.'

'You get used to it. Being here isn't so bad. It's not a bad place to live, I mean. It's just the mess we're all in that's the problem. But,' Bev shrugged, 'we'd be in a mess no matter where we were, wouldn't we?'

*No!* Victoria wanted to shout. *No, because if Harry knew about this he'd do something! He wouldn't let this happen! He wouldn't let me be here!*

'So what happened?' Bev asked, standing up and wandering over to the table, where she took a cigarette from an ashtray and sucked on it half-heartedly. She looked down at her own enormous belly and then over at Victoria's. 'I can tell you my story in a couple of words. I thought I was in love.'

'Me too,' said another woman, who had left her half-knitted blanket on the table and now flopped onto the sofa next to Victoria. 'I'm Katherine. I didn't know that mine was married. Turns out none of us here knew much, in the end.' Katherine made a strange sound then, which was somewhere between a hiccup and a cynical laugh.

'Oh, dear,' Victoria said, touching her bump and feeling her baby squirm. It was a girl: she knew it. A girl, just like her, with tufts of almost-black hair and a little button nose. *Henrietta.*

'So, what's your story?' Bev asked, her eyes wide.

Victoria looked down. 'Well. Harry…the father, he is married.

But he did tell me. It's different with Harry and I. We're really very happy together.'

Katherine's gaze moved over Victoria's head to Bev and the two women shared a knowing glance.

'I know what you're thinking. But really, Harry's different,' Victoria said.

Katherine lay a hand on Victoria's shoulder. 'He's not that different, lovey. Otherwise you wouldn't be sitting here with us, would you?'

Victoria sighed and surveyed the room: smoke, ugly furniture, a dark-green stained carpet. It became clear that on one side of the table were the women who lacked the plump, pensive faces of the heavily pregnant. They knitted more slowly, as if trying to delay time. Their smocks were still smoothed over vaguely rounded bellies, but their countenance, their tension, their red-rimmed eyes, set them apart from the others.

Victoria turned to Bev and Kathleen. 'Where are their babies?' she asked in a low voice.

Bev gestured to the back of the house. 'In the nursery. They have set feeding times when the mums go and give them their bottles and change them. Other than that, they don't spend much time in there.'

*The mums.* For a ridiculous moment, Victoria was confused by Bev's words, and wondered why Mrs Lace would be involved in feeding the new baby. After a second, she realised with a jolt that she, Victoria, would be a mum. Her mistake made her face burn, and she thanked the universe that she hadn't stopped Bev and asked her what on earth she'd meant. Bev didn't seem to notice Victoria's puce face and continued talking at full throttle, about bottles and sterilising and feeding times and nappy pins. She was missing the point, it seemed. Bottles and sterilising were all very well, but what about that word she'd just used so fleetingly, so easily? What about all the things that lurked underneath it like corpses under a field?

*Mum.*

'I think,' Victoria said, 'I need to go and have a little lie down.'

'A lie down?' Katherine said, her face contorting slightly and making her seem less attractive than Victoria had initially decided. 'You'll be lucky.' She leant into Victoria. Her breath smelt of smoke and meat. 'They're not too bad here. Apparently there's worse places. But it's not a hotel, love. You can't just do as you please.'

Victoria stared into space, breathing through her mouth to avoid Katherine's unpleasant breath. 'I slept all the time at home.'

Bev yawned. 'I did, actually. At least we're allowed to sit around in here a bit, though. But we have to do our jobs first.'

'Jobs?'

'Yeah. I've got the carpets to clean. Katherine's got the windows. Christine over there's on bottle duty. She makes up the formula. Matron will tell you soon enough what you have to do. You get the same job every day for a week so it gets a bit boring, but you know what's what. Do you have a job at home?'

'My father has an antique shop. I work in there. But it's easy, I suppose. It's never very busy. That's how I met Harry. He came in when it was raining one day and we got along so well. I always think that if it wasn't for the rain that day…' Victoria's smile faded along with her words as she saw the girls' faces droop with anticipatory regret.

'Nasty bloody rain,' Katherine said, pulling a face again. 'If it had stayed fine, you wouldn't be here now, would you?'

'No. But what I was going to say was that I would never have met Harry.'

'You honestly don't regret meeting him in the first place?' Bev asked. Her voice was gentle and had a kind Scottish lilt that made Victoria want to burst into tears.

'No. I really don't. And I know it might sound silly, but I don't regret the baby. I'm scared, obviously. But I want her. I'm going to try and keep my baby.'

Katherine looked incredulous. Bev looked down.

'It's impossible,' Katherine said eventually, shaking her head. Her hair was copper and thick, and bounced rather wildly as she moved. 'You're going to end up going mad with disappointment if you think like that.'

'Oh, I don't know,' Bev sighed quietly. 'What's the harm in dreaming?'

'Dreaming's fine,' Katherine said, with a wave of a freckled hand. 'But the longer you dream for, the harder it is to wake up.'

As it turned out, Bev did sleep in the same room that Victoria had been assigned. The other girls in there were, for the first night at least, a blur of Christines and Jennys and Ruths, a mass of sighs and huge white nightgowns.

As she lay in the hard bed, her blanket sitting over her like a sheet of ice, Victoria stared up at the black ceiling.

'Are you okay?' whispered Bev from the bed next to her.

'I think so.'

'The first night here is definitely the worst. It'll get better.'

Victoria heard Bev's bed creak as she turned over to face Victoria's. 'I can't imagine ever getting to sleep.'

'I know. I felt like that too. But you get so worn out every day,' Bev yawned, 'that you just can't help it as the weeks roll on.'

Victoria was silent, unable to feel reassured. She lay down and listened to Bev's breathing, which soon became deep and rasping. Her eyes adjusted to the pitch black and she saw an outline of her new friend, mouth gaping, belly bulging up from the blankets like a mountain. Bev was in her late twenties, more than ten years older than Victoria. The married father of Bev's baby was young and silly, as Bev had put it. He'd charmed his way into something he probably never really wanted. Bev had told him about the baby and he'd burst into frightened tears, rather like a baby himself. Would Harry have cried? Or would he have been angry, like Katherine's married man, who swore that Katherine had done it on purpose, and refused to have anything more to do with her?

Victoria squeezed her eyes shut and pictured Harry. His face swam before her and Victoria let herself be carried along by the tide of him, towards a sleep where she fell into his arms and told him about Henrietta, their future.

When she woke the next morning, the house's potent smells of eggs, disinfectant and sour formula were thick in the air, clinging to the thin blanket that was tangled around Victoria. She stretched her aching back and then sat up to survey the sleeping girls, the rising and falling bellies, the old, scarred furniture. It was as though it was all haunted by sadness. The sense that other girls in the same unbearable circumstances had come and gone, all worse off for staying here, was as present as the metal-framed beds, the flaking sash windows. Unhappiness was trapped in the room. Victoria pulled her blanket up to her chin and let out a shivering sigh, not really knowing if her body was trembling with cold or fright.

In the bed beside her, Bev stuck out a leg and groaned. 'Feels cold,' she mumbled, her voice heavy with sleep. She hauled herself over to face Victoria's bed. 'Sleep okay?' she whispered.

Victoria sat up, the cold air biting at her neck. 'Not too bad, thanks.'

'It'll be breakfast soon. Let's get to the bathroom before the queue gets too long. I don't fancy standing about in my nightie for ages.' Bev rolled out of bed onto her feet and stretched her back, her belly jutting out into the room. 'Baby doesn't half get in the way when I'm trying to get comfy in that bed. I have to say, I'll be glad to get it out.'

'I know, but then—' Victoria began, but Bev's grimace stopped her mid-sentence. 'Sorry,' Victoria whispered as they crept out into the silent landing. 'I can't help thinking about where my baby might end up after all this.'

'And I can't bear to think of it at all,' Bev admitted as she led Victoria to the bathroom. She looked down at Victoria's feet as they reached it. 'Now, keep your slippers on while you have a wash. If you let your feet touch the floor they'll be so cold you'll scream. I'll hold a towel around you while you get a wash, if you want, and then you do the same for me. People will start barging in soon.'

'Thanks,' Victoria said gratefully as she turned on the stiff tap and slid her bar of soap into the sink. 'There's no mirror in here,' she noticed as she looked around. 'Where do you do your hair?'

'I brought a small mirror with me, so I just use that. There aren't any mirrors anywhere here, apart from the one near the guest entrance, and you can imagine what Matron would do if she caught us beautifying ourselves there.'

Victoria sighed. 'I suppose there's nothing to do your hair *for* here, is there?'

'No. I used to wear a full face of makeup every day. Now, nothing. Matron hates makeup. She told a girl the other week that it was vanity and mirrors that got her into this mess in the first place. The girl said it was more than that, only under her breath, but I'm sure Matron wanted to slap her cheek.'

'I packed a mirror,' Victoria said. 'A beautiful one with sapphires on the back. I found it with some other things in my father's antique shop and I took quite a shine to it. It's one of my favourite belongings. So I brought it to remind me of home. But when I unpacked last night, it had disappeared from my case. Do you think Matron has it?'

Bev nodded, her blond head just visible over the thin towel that she held out for Victoria. 'Wouldn't surprise me. You can borrow mine, if you want. I keep it under my bed with some lipstick for if I'm feeling a bit fed up or if we're all going into the village.'

'You go out? That must be nice,' said Victoria, a little relief washing over her as she pulled on her smock dress and blue cardigan and then held the towel around Bev.

'It's okay. It's good to leave here for a bit. But to be honest, when the villagers see us, a gang of pregnant girls around the corner from Gaspings, they know exactly what our situations are and they can be a bit rude. I bought a magazine the other day and you should have seen the look the girl in the shop gave me.'

'I suppose I should have known. Does it bother you?'

There was a splash as Bev doused herself in water, and no reply from behind the towel.

'Bev? Does it bother you?'

Bev snatched the towel down, revealing her distorted body. Her face was pale with fright. 'Go and get Matron,' she wailed. Victoria followed Bev's gaze down to the floor and saw, with horror, that the water at their feet was tinged pink with blood. She thrust the towel into Bev's hands, and, her head spinning, backed to the door.

'I'm not due yet,' Bev moaned as Victoria turned the doorknob. 'I've got another three weeks to go! Do you think this is it? Do you think that was my waters going?'

Victoria leaned on the door, her hand gripping the cool handle. She didn't know. She didn't know if this was it, or what the blood meant, or what was going to happen. She only knew that she couldn't do this, she couldn't do it without Harry and she couldn't do it knowing that the baby wasn't hers to keep. Fright froze her as she leaned against the door.

'I think I'm starting with contractions,' Bev cried, her face turning from white to a violent red. 'Please, just go and get Matron.'

Victoria stood, frozen to the spot. She watched Bev slide down onto the slimy floor, her naked body wet and shiny, tinged purple with cold.

'Go!' Bev screamed, her face twisting in fright. 'Please! Go and get her! I'm frightened, Victoria! Please!'

Victoria's body, roused back to life by the pleas, began to move again. But Matron must have heard the shouting, because as Victoria stumbled onto the landing, she was standing there with another nurse.

'Let me in,' Matron said calmly, and pushed her way past Victoria.

Further on down the landing, a group of girls stood in their nighties, whispering and pointing to the bathroom.

'Who's in there?' one of the girls, large with buck teeth, asked importantly.

'It's Bev. We were just having a wash and something happened. We think it was her waters going, but we didn't really know. Is there meant to be blood?' Victoria asked, unable to stop herself.

The girls were silent. Some shrugged. They didn't know. For all their apparent acceptance, their quiet sleeping, their calm demeanors, they didn't know. And they all, in their crumpled nighties, their faces pinched by lumpy pillows, their flattened hair, their pale expressions, looked just as frightened as Victoria.

The nurse stepped forward and took Victoria's hand. 'Come on. You can't do anything for her now. You get dressed and then you can go down for breakfast.'

Victoria nodded numbly, grasping the nurse's hand tighter than she knew she should, but unable to loosen her grasp.

By the time they were having their porridge, Bev had been taken off to hospital in an ambulance, and the girls had somehow wiped away their scared expressions, replacing them with calm shrugs and knowing glances.

'Do you think she'll have the baby by now?' Victoria asked.

Katherine shook her head. 'I've heard it takes a while.'

'I don't think she was ready,' Victoria said, staring down at her breakfast. She'd put jam in her porridge and regretted it now, for the pale-pink colour, once she stirred it through, was disconcertingly similar to that of the water that had surrounded Bev in the bathroom.

One of the girls snorted. 'Who *is* ready? I'm certainly not.'

'I held a baby the other week,' Victoria said, pushing her pink porridge away. 'It was the first one I'd ever held.'

It was a few weeks before she'd come to Gaspings House. Mrs Blythe from the bakery across the road, who had a baby and a blue Silver Cross pram, had come into Lace Antiques to look for a present for somebody. Victoria had been staring out of the window and had seen the woman pushing the pram across the road into the shop, a little boy wearing an ugly brown coat at her side. She'd heard the bell jingle and then she'd heard the baby gurgling merrily, the woman singing to him and laughing with delight at his little sounds, the little boy asking his mother questions about what everything in the shop was for, and cost, and meant. Unable to stop herself, Victoria had crept down the stairs to the shop. Her father was in there, talking to the woman about an ugly grandfather clock, and his face, cheerful with the promise of a sale, turned dark when he saw Victoria loitering at the doorway behind the counter. 'Get upstairs,' he'd hissed. But Victoria had ignored him. She'd felt a pull towards the baby who was propped up in his pram, smiling like a little dribbling cherub.

'Please can I hold him?' Victoria had asked the woman.

The woman had beamed and plucked the baby from his chariot. He was squidgy and warm in Victoria's arms and had smelt of soap and warm milk.

'He's heavy, isn't he?' the little boy said, suddenly turning his attention to Victoria. 'I hold him by myself sometimes, though. I'll show you, if you like?'

The boy held his arms out, and Victoria passed the warm, wriggling bundle to him.

'Put him in the pram again, Graham,' Mrs Blythe said, as she leafed through some old magazines.

They left without buying anything, and as they'd manoeuvered the pram out of the shop, Victoria's father called to them to remember about the clock, that they made excellent presents, and that he'd keep it behind the counter for her if she wanted.

'My father went mad that I'd gone downstairs into the shop and made the state that I was in, as he said, obvious. But I couldn't help it,' Victoria told the girls around the breakfast table. 'I've never held a baby, and I thought I'd feel better about it all if I got to hold one. Mrs Blythe didn't even notice I was pregnant when she was in the shop anyway. She was too concerned with her own baby.'

She didn't tell the girls that she'd sneaked out of the back of the shop later on that day and gone into the bakery. The sweet, warm smell of fresh dough had made Victoria's stomach growl as she handed over some coins for a small loaf of white bread. Of course, she hadn't gone in just for bread. She wanted to see the baby again, to somehow settle the flutter of terror that had vibrated in her body since late summer. The pram was behind the wide counter, but the baby wasn't in it any more.

'I liked holding your baby,' Victoria told Mrs Blythe as she pushed the soft loaf into a brown paper bag. 'Where is he now?'

'Oh, he's upstairs having his nap. I've just put him down.'

The little boy had appeared again then and watched Victoria from the corner of the room.

'Hello,' he said. His eyes were a bright green, which reminded Victoria of pixies and elves and fairy-tale endings. 'Are you having a baby too?' He nodded towards Victoria's belly, which had been concealed beneath her coat when she'd left Lace Antiques, but was now poking out. She felt herself redden and gathered her coat around herself again.

'Graham! Have you tidied up your trains? You know how cross your father will be if he treads on one of them again.' She nodded at Victoria, as if to dismiss her. But Victoria couldn't bring herself to turn around and leave. She wanted to answer the boy, to give him a reply that would make him forget about her belly and her wish to hold his baby brother. But the boy had gone already, his question forgotten, his quick steps fading up the narrow staircase that Victoria could see in the room behind the counter.

She stood still and silent, waiting for Mrs Blythe to demand answers, to paw Victoria's hand and ask where her wedding ring was, to tell her to leave Silenshore and stop bringing disgrace to their town, and do all the things she expected people to do if they found out.

But the woman just stared, waiting for Victoria to turn and leave.

And so she did. She turned slowly and clumsily towards the blue door of the bakery, the smell of flour and butter making her feel as sick as she had done at the very start of her pregnancy. As she lumbered across the road to Lace Antiques, sneaked back in and locked herself away in her bedroom again, Victoria wondered if she might have made a terrible mistake. The thought was ugly and dark, and Victoria pushed it to the corner of her mind, wanting it to decompose, to vanish.

The loaf she'd bought sat uneaten, under her bed, blooming with green within two days and making her room smell of mould.

'And so did it?' Katherine asked now, breaking Victoria's reverie. Katherine's eyes narrowed as she bit into a slice of toast and waited for a reply.

'Did it what?'

'Make you feel better? You said you wanted to hold the baby because you thought it might make you feel better. Did it?'

Victoria stood up and brushed herself down, even though she'd eaten nothing. 'No. It didn't. It made me feel worse.'

After Bev's baby was born, Bev migrated over to the mums' table at breakfast and was moved to the mums' bedroom. Her bed next to Victoria's lay stripped, ready for its next victim. Bev's face seemed stripped too, as though a layer of her had been ripped away. Her eyes were vacant and her skin sallow. She didn't talk much to Victoria now.

'I'm going to write to Harry,' Victoria said to Bev a week or so after her baby had been born, to see if her new friend would come to life again. Bev had just been in the nursery to feed her little boy and smelt of milk and talc.

Bev shrugged and looked down at Victoria, who was stooping to scrub the floor of the nursery. The task of cleaning the floors and stairwells had been assigned to Victoria today. It was one of the harder ones: her back felt as though it might snap every time she sat on her heels to wring out her sponge.

'Aren't you going to tell me there's no point?' Victoria said, arching her back and wincing.

Bev shook her head, 'No. I'm sorry. I suppose I'm tired.'

Victoria sighed and knelt back down on the damp floor. It was true: she had thought about writing Harry a letter. She'd even started one.

*My dear Harry,*

*The first thing I want to say is sorry. I'm sorry that I lied to you about where I am. It breaks my heart to think that you might be thinking of me with Sally, or worse, that you might have somehow stumbled across Sally in Silenshore, and found out that I'm not with her and never was.*

*The truth is, I am going to have a baby. Our baby. I did come to tell you, but it was too late, and Sarah wouldn't pass on my message to you. I would have told you sooner, but my father*

It was here that Victoria had stopped writing. Her pen had fallen to the scratchy bedroom carpet with a thump as she let go of it. She shouldn't write, if she could help it. She didn't want Sarah to read it, so she could only post it to Silenshore University. It could quite easily be opened by the wrong person there. And if it was, and it somehow got back to Jack that Harry was the father of Victoria's baby, then Harry would be in danger. Victoria thought of her once-beautiful mother, whose spirit had been beaten out of her. If Jack could do that to his wife, for no reason, what might he do to Harry, for every reason?

Victoria had picked up her pen and put it back on the desk in the corner of the bedroom. And then she tore up the letter into fragments as fine and small as a broken eggshell.

'I don't seem to have much to say any more, do I?' Bev was

still standing in the doorway of the nursery, watching Victoria. She had put her baby back down, and he snuffled quietly, searching for sleep.

Victoria had been so taken with thinking about Harry that she had forgotten Bev might still be there. Guiltily, she lumbered to her feet and put her arms around Bev. 'It'll just take a bit of time to recover, I suppose. But you'll be okay. And so will your little boy.'

'That reminds me,' Bev said, reaching into the pocket of the turquoise smock dress she wore most days. She pulled out a length of red ribbon and handed it to Victoria. 'I bought this in the village just before I had him, because I hoped I'd have a girl. I was going to give it to her, as something to remember me by. But a boy won't want ribbon, will he?'

Victoria reached out and touched the ribbon, which was cool and smooth. 'Bev, I'm sure he'd love to have anything from you. You should still give it to him.'

'No,' Bev said loudly, her voice cracking. 'I don't want to. It's pointless. You have it. I think you're right, you are going to have a girl.'

'Are you sure?'

Bev nodded, trembling, her eyes wide and watery, and Victoria put her arms around her, the ribbon tangled between them.

'Promise you'll put it to good use?' Bev whispered.

As they separated, Victoria nodded and held Bev's hands in hers. As she looked down at the entwined fingers, the sight of Bev's wrists snapped something inside Victoria, made her feel like she needed to sit down, or perhaps be sick.

'Bev? What—' Victoria started to say, but Bev snatched her hands away, her wrists disappearing underneath her cardigan.

Bev shook her head, her chin wobbling furiously and one tear racing down her cheek. 'I've got to get on with my jobs,' she said quietly, before disappearing from the room.

Victoria stared after her, the memory of Bev's torn, burned skin on her wrists already hazy. Had she imagined it? She tried to think of the other girls who had come back from having their babies. None of them had said much about the birth. None of them had spoken about pain or blood, or all of the things that Victoria suspected they had experienced. But then, none of them had spoken much at all, because once they'd had their babies, they moved away from the pregnant girls, separated by a gulf of experience. Victoria shook her head as she felt tears begin to prick at her eyes.

*Not now. Don't think about it all now. Don't think about anything other than Harry.*

*Harry.*

As she moved out of the nursery and towards the stairs in the hallway with her bucket and sponge, Victoria thought again of how she might reach him. As things were at the moment, she would have to rely on a miracle.

'You'll scrub those stairs away if you're not careful,' a voice said from somewhere above Victoria. She looked up and saw Nurse Hammond, the one who had been kind to her when Bev's waters broke. Victoria smiled. The nurse was more like one of the girls than a member of staff; nothing like Matron. It wasn't just that she was younger than the other nurses; she was more friendly, less sneering than the others.

'I'm daydreaming,' Victoria admitted.

'Nothing wrong with that,' Nurse Hammond said. 'Especially when things aren't as you'd like. A bit of daydreaming keeps me going, sometimes.'

Tiny pearlescent bubbles burst as Victoria slopped the sponge onto another step.

'Things aren't as I'd like at all. But that doesn't mean they never will be.'

'Exactly,' Nurse Hammond nodded, her peaked white hat moving up and down. 'You never know what's around the corner. You have to have faith that it's what you've asked for. I know I always do.'

The nurse's cheeks flushed then and Victoria felt a rush of gratitude that she was confiding in her. Victoria lowered her voice to a conspiratorial whisper. 'I'm hoping for my baby's father to come for me any day now. I've left a message for him. I just have to hope that the person I left the message with sees sense.'

She wanted to tell Nurse Hammond that the person she'd left the message with was Sarah, Harry's wife, but that Sarah had trapped him into marriage and that it was Victoria he really wanted. But she didn't say anything, because although Nurse Hammond seemed to be the kind of person who would understand, she didn't want her story of Harry tainted all over again like it had been when she had told the girls here that he loved her, not Sarah. She didn't want someone who seemed as though they could be a friend tarnished by their doubtful reaction and dubious stares. So Victoria simply smiled and stayed quiet. The nurse smiled back. 'Hoping is better than despairing,' she said.

They were simple words, but so very true. Victoria would continue hoping and hoping, and she would never despair. She wrung out the sponge as Nurse Hammond walked away to the kitchen. She imagined Harry arriving at Gaspings House and making everyone swoon and realise how wrong they'd been; making them see how different Victoria was from all of them. He would tell Victoria that Sarah had relented and had told Harry that Victoria needed him more than she did. And then he would come for her.

Any day now, they would be together again.

The letter arrived the day after Victoria's contractions began. Hers weren't sudden and frightening like Bev's had been. They were slow and dragging, like somebody pulling at her insides. They came and went all day.

'The pains need to be closer together,' Nurse Hammond said when Victoria told her. 'You don't need to go anywhere yet. I'll tell Matron that you think you've started, but you just carry on as you are for now.'

By the next day, the pains had gone altogether.

'False alarm,' Katherine said knowingly, even though she hadn't had her baby yet and couldn't possibly know anything for sure.

Victoria shrugged and carried on knitting the shawl she was making. She still wasn't very good at knitting, but it wasn't too bad. She'd chosen a ball of fuzzy peach wool from the shop in the village, and just as Bev had warned when Victoria had first arrived, the woman who sold it to her had scowled as Victoria handed over her money. But Victoria hadn't been as upset as she thought she might. It was wool for her baby with Harry and she felt an elation that compared to nothing else as she wandered back to Gaspings.

The girls had squealed when they'd seen that Victoria had bought peach wool. 'What if you have a boy?' they'd asked all at once, their voices merging into a loud collective caw.

'He'll have to learn to like it. And anyway, it's definitely a girl,' Victoria said.

As she clicked her needles together, Victoria imagined Henrietta swaddled in the shawl, her cocoa hair nestled against the soft wool. A surge of excitement rippled through her abdomen. Harry had better hurry, otherwise he wouldn't get here in time to see his baby on the day she was born.

'Victoria,' Jackie, one of the new girls called as she came into the room. 'You've got a letter here.' She placed the letter on the arm of Victoria's chair, next to the ball of wool.

Victoria put down her needles and took the letter. It was the first she'd received since arriving at Gaspings. She tore into it neatly, Harry's face in her mind all the time. This could be it. This could be the key to her new life with Henrietta and Harry. It was all falling into place. It occurred to her as she unfolded the sheet of paper inside the envelope that it was her father's writing, but perhaps Harry had talked him round, and her father was finally giving his blessing.

She began reading and let out a cry.

'What's the matter?' she heard somebody ask. But she couldn't answer. She could do nothing but read the sloped, uneven writing. As she did, the room around her seemed to collapse in on her. Everything turned black. She felt her knitting needles fall from the chair and her wool spill softly onto her lap. She sensed Henrietta's shawl being pulled away and felt herself being lifted somewhere, and she saw the words from the letter disappearing into the darkness.

When the heavy blackness that had settled around Victoria seemed to begin to lift, she felt warmth on her face, and pulling at her limbs. She strained to try and open her eyes, but her lids fluttered weakly and she couldn't make anything out but a blur of a face, and breath on her skin that smelt of cigarettes and strawberries.

'Victoria! Wake up!'

'Victoria!'

There was more than one voice. She recognised them, but the words floated in her mind, independent of any face or identity. Somebody continued to tug at her arms, to try and lift her up. Slowly, it dawned on her that she wasn't in her chair any more, that she was somehow on the floor now instead, which was cold and unyielding beneath her aching back. She let her arms be pulled, and then felt her body be arranged in a sitting position. She tried to open her eyes again, and this time they gradually focused on a face. It was Katherine's.

'You collapsed, right out of your chair,' Katherine said. She brushed something to the side, so that Victoria wouldn't see it. But Victoria remembered, all at once, what it was.

'My letter,' she whispered. Her voice was thin and strange.

More faces came into view then. One of them belonged to Nurse Hammond. She sat back on her worn black heels and gazed at Victoria. Behind her was the new girl Jackie, perspiring with the dramatic turn of events and hovering to catch a glimpse of Victoria too.

'If the letter is going to upset you, perhaps I should keep hold of it for a while,' Nurse Hammond said, adjusting her hat.

'It's not going to upset me,' Victoria said. 'Because it can't be true.'

She remembered the words now. They burnt every fibre of her body, made the unborn Henrietta rear up in her belly like a frightened horse, made the world fall away underneath her.

*Victoria,*

*Harry is dead. When you return to Silenshore, you must never speak of him. You will tell people that you have been caring for a lady in Lancashire. Do not disobey me.*

*Your father.*

'Have you read it?' Victoria asked. Katherine shook her head, her amber curls bouncing.

'No,' Nurse Hammond said, concern clouding her face. 'We were more worried about trying to get you to come back round. Do you want me to call for Matron? Or I could get you some hot tea?'

'It's absolutely not true.' Victoria stumbled to her feet, her legs trembling with weakness and fright. 'I'm going to our bedroom. If Matron says anything, just tell her that I'm not well.'

She climbed the wide staircase slowly, clutching her chest. Her breaths came sharply and quickly, and acid rose into her mouth. She stopped halfway up the stairs and retched, her throat burning. She had to write to Harry. There was nothing to lose now. Victoria knew her father, knew how he worked. He was full of threats and anger, but he would not kill. Even so, Harry had to be warned, at home or at the university. It didn't matter where she sent it: not now.

She tipped out her drawer when she reached the bedroom and scrambled among her belongings: her hairbrush, cream, socks and the splinter of emerald that her mother had given her, to find her pen. Then, still shivering, she sat on her bed and began to write on the back of a postcard.

*Harry*

*My father says you are no more. This can't be. The world would surely not still be turning.*

*I am going to try to keep our baby. I know that already she has brought out the strongest, best version of me, just as you did. That's what true love should do.*

*Ripping her away from me would kill me.*

*I hope that my father gave me such unthinkable news to make me move on quickly when I return home. But I can't believe it. I cannot give up hope. Instead, I must warn you to stay safe, away from Silenshore and away from my father, until I am back and I can calm him and make him see. Write to me at the address above and tell me where you have gone. As soon as I can, I will follow with our baby.*

*And if you can, my darling Harry, do something for me. Make the best happen for me somehow. I am frightened. Come to me. Be with me.*

*Your loving Queen,*

*Victoria*

She turned over the postcard and stared at the faded, sepia picture of Queen Victoria on the front, remembering the day in London when Harry had given it to her.

*It's to remind you, whenever I'm not there to do it myself, that you, and only you, are my Queen.*

She wouldn't be allowed out now to post it, not after her fainting like that. She'd have to rest for a while first. As she lay back on the cold, overwashed cotton sheets, Victoria felt her belly squeeze together again, as it had the other day. She tensed, waiting for another pain. When none came, she sighed and took her book from the side of the bed.

It was the third time she'd read *The Blue Door*. It was the only book she'd brought with her to Gaspings. She'd read it at home too, twice, since she had met Robert Bell. So she knew what happened on every page. But still, she read every word, because it was Harry's copy that he'd given her on the day of Robert Bell's talk, and because reading every word over and over again somehow made her feel calmer and close to Harry.

As her eyes flickered over the worn pages, she heard the door open softly. Nurse Hammond loitered in the doorway. 'I came to check you were feeling better. What are you reading?'

Victoria closed her book and handed it to the nurse, who turned it over in her hands to inspect it. 'I don't read much. I can never seem to concentrate for long enough.' She flipped it open and stared down at the inscription, and then read it aloud.

*To Miss Lace*

*May your life be filled with dreams come true and blue doors opened.*

*Best wishes,*

*Robert Bell*

'Signed by the author? That's impressive,' Nurse Hammond said, then snapped the book shut, her interest lost as quickly as it was piqued.

'Yes. I want to be a writer, you see. So I went to a talk,' Victoria said, her urge to talk about her life outside of Gaspings, about what she wanted and liked and cared about, spilling from her. 'Robert Bell, who wrote this book, inspired me to write my own mysteries. One day I'm going to write all sorts of things, and keep people guessing about what's going to happen to my characters.'

'Is that what you keep sneaking up here to do? Are you writing a story?' Nurse Hammond asked, nodding towards the letter Victoria had just written to Harry.

Victoria thought of her Queen Victoria postcard, of the curving words on the back that formed her very own romance, her very own mystery that had no ending, as though the very last pages were torn out. 'Yes, I suppose I am.'

## CHAPTER 19

# *Isobel: 2011*

*My poor Victoria,*
*Sally told me everything, all about our secret baby. Did you tell her? She says that you didn't tell her anything, that she heard it from the baker's son at Blythe's, but I don't want to think that you've gone through this all alone, and I don't like to think that news is travelling around the town about you. So I hope that this isn't true, and I hope you did tell Sally and she comforted you and held you like I should have been able to do.*

*The worst of it all is that I confessed to Sarah that I was worried for you, and it turns out she knew about the baby too. She admitted that you visited a month or so ago, and begged her to tell me you'd been. But she didn't, until now. And now I'm worried, so worried, that it's too late.*

*Sally says it's worthless knowing the reason why you've disappeared because we don't know where you've been sent. Your mother daren't tell her, and Sally daren't ask your father. Sarah insists she doesn't know, and even if she did then I doubt she would tell me.*

*I am going to find you somehow. And when I do, I won't tell anybody that I'm coming.*

*The man who is following me…I think it's your father. But it wasn't Sally who told him. She was the one who wrote me the anonymous letter warning me to leave Silenshore. She tells me he's a frightening man. I'm so sorry I didn't protect you from him.*

*I want to be with you. I would leave this town in an instant if I knew where to find you.*

*Times are changing, Victoria. There may be a way around all this. We just have to find it.*

*Wait for me.*

*H.*

As Isobel walks, she feels rain begin to tap onto her shoulders, which are still tingling from the hours on the beach that seemed so *long* ago now. She's almost reached the shore when she sees Daphne in the distance with Hugh.

Isobel came for a walk with Beatrice in the pram to clear her mind, to escape the feeling of being suffocated in a cloud of secrets. She doesn't want to walk with Daphne. She turns around and heads back towards Broadsands. The rain slaps onto the pavements and the scent of hot, damp concrete rises in the air. She takes long strides, her eyes fixed on the house. But before she reaches it, her gaze is interrupted by the figure who loiters in the street. Isobel casts her eyes downwards, looks at Beatrice instead. But as she nears Broadsands, the presence of the old lady from across the road becomes more and more difficult to ignore.

'Isobel?'

The rasping sound of her own name on the woman's cracked lips is startling. Isobel looks up and sees that the woman is standing in her path, gazing down at the pram.

'She's beautiful,' the woman says. She reaches out a crooked finger as if she's going to touch Beatrice, but at the last moment, whips her hand away. 'I won't touch her. She doesn't know me.'

'She wouldn't have minded,' Isobel hears herself say, although *she* would have minded; she minds being there in the rain speaking to the woman, because there's a crawling feeling in her blood and bones that she won't be rid of until she steps inside the house and locks the door behind her.

The woman stares, her pale eyes scoring into Isobel. 'Are you well?'

Isobel has tried not to think about this woman and her strange words about Tom so many months ago. She'd mentioned it to Tom and he'd brushed it off as nonsense. It had been enough for Isobel at the time. She'd thought little of it, only that the old woman had made her feel uncomfortable. But that was before she'd had Beatrice, before everything seemed strange and off-colour. Now that Isobel is breathing the same spring air as the woman, close enough to touch her shrivelled frame, the words haunt her.

*I wouldn't want to share him.*

Why did Isobel ignore it?

Isobel nods, 'I'm fine, thank you.' She's been so stupid. She should have taken notice.

The woman reaches out again, but this time touches Isobel on the shoulder. The smell of her breath lingers as she talks: stale and dry. 'I wanted to say sorry, Isobel.'

How does she know her name? Isobel takes the step back that she wanted to take moments ago, unable to stop her legs from moving.

The woman steps back too, like a frightened animal. 'I know I shouldn't have said anything about Tom that day. I shouldn't have given anything away. It was wrong of me and I'm sorry.'

'I didn't know what you meant,' Isobel says.

'Then think no more of it. Forget it.'

The woman turns to cross the road and go back into her house. Isobel feels a sense of strange relief, until the woman's final words reach her, carried on a breeze that smells of dark rain and damp pavements. 'It's not my secret to tell.'

Isobel doesn't look back at the woman. She yanks the front door open. Even without overhearing Daphne on the phone telling somebody to leave Tom alone, without bumping into Lucas, without Tom being secretive about his phone and his trips out, Isobel would've known. There's something wrong. She tried to stand back by coming out for a walk, to calm herself down instead of doing what she always does and bulldozing into things without thinking them through. She thought she couldn't do that with Tom. She thought there was too much to lose.

But now the urge to know more rattles inside her, threatening to spill out.

Daphne's words that she overheard yesterday echo in her mind as she swings the door shut behind her.

*You must leave him alone.*

Tom's in the house somewhere, but Isobel doesn't know where. He's probably getting ready for his shift at the restaurant. He'll be oblivious, spritzing his neck with his aftershave, running damp fingers through his hair, buttoning his shirt. He won't know what Isobel's doing, he will presume she's changing Beatrice or still out walking or doing something *normal.*

She looks in the cabinet in the hall first. There are a few letters in the mahogany drawers, addressed to Daphne. Isobel pushes them out of the way, to see if there is anything else underneath them. An old wallet, some keys, a torch. Perhaps these belonged to Tom's father. A surge of guilt flies through Isobel, filling her body with nausea. She slams the drawer shut.

The rain clicks on the windowpane of the front door and taps on the letterbox. She glances around, frozen in an instant of panic that Daphne will appear and see Isobel going through her things. But she can't stop. She needs to know.

In the kitchen, the heat spilling out from the Aga combined with the airless warmth of the morning is almost unbearable. Isobel tugs at the neck of her top, feeling stifled and strangled. The drawer of the white dresser is full of old Christmas cards.

Isobel's hopes prickle and dart. It might be in here. Glitter sticks to her hands as she sifts through the greetings cards. Red, gold, green specks twinkle on her palms. She opens each card. None of them are addressed to Tom. She keeps going, searching wildly, until she sees the red envelope that she's been looking for, pushed into the corner.

She tugs it from the drawer, moving her fingers over the smooth red paper. When Tom said on Christmas Day that he didn't know who it was from, she didn't ask again. She believed him then.

It's been opened once, so Tom must have seen it. Isobel imagines him standing by the dresser, tearing open the red envelope and glancing carelessly at the greeting inside before tossing it into the drawer. The image is strong in her mind, but still, she finds her fingers working towards the opening of the envelope, sliding the card from beneath.

It's an old-fashioned card with a Christmas tree and a badly painted fire on the front. Isobel flips it open. The swirling, feminine letters of the writing tangle around each other like ivy. As Isobel stares at them and finally makes them out, a piece of her world falls away.

*Happy Christmas, my darling secret love.*

'Secret love?' Iris repeats. She is folding floral dresses, what seems like hundreds of them, into a polka-dot suitcase. She's leaving for Paris first thing tomorrow, so Isobel should be leaving her to it. But she can't. As soon as she found the card, she scooped Beatrice up from her cot and went to Iris's flat.

'Yes, that's what it said. It had no name on it.'

'But that doesn't necessarily mean Tom is in love with somebody else too.'

'But I saw the envelope at Christmas. It was open, so obviously he has read it and not told me. If he's not involved in this secret love, then why didn't he just tell me? And there's all the other stuff too.' Isobel bites her lip. 'I can't stop thinking about it all.

That old woman across the road even said he has a secret.'

Iris shakes her head and throws a pair of Converse trainers into her suitcase. 'I really think you need to speak to Tom about all of this. Does he even know you're here?'

'Do you think it might be Georgia? I always trusted that Tom never spoke to her, but now I don't even know why I took his word for it.' Isobel's breaths are shallow and fast. 'Should I try and find Georgia on Facebook or something, and message her?'

Iris sighs and snaps her suitcase shut. 'Oh, Isobel. I really don't think you should. That might hurt Tom, going behind his back.'

'But if I ask Tom about any of this, he doesn't give anything away. And there's something I don't know. I'm certain of it.'

'Isobel, you know nothing about Georgia. You have no reason to think this secret even has anything to do her. I don't want you to do something that you'll regret. Tom needs to know how you feel.' She pauses, searching Isobel's face for a clue that she's listening, but Isobel can't meet Iris's eye. 'Normally, you'd say something to Tom straight away. It's not like you to go behind somebody's back trying to find things out about them. Where's the Isobel who just says what she thinks?'

Isobel bites her lip, trying to stop herself from crying. 'I don't know. I'm trying not to lose myself, Iris.' She brushes an irritating tear away from her cheek. She really doesn't want to cry. She's *sick* of crying. She's sick of everything, everything, everything.

Isobel draws her knees up to her chest on the bed next to Iris's suitcase. She's got mascara on her hands where she has wiped her streaming eyes over and over again. Beatrice lies on the floor, kicking merrily, oblivious, grasping at the cluttered items around her: a moisturiser, a lipstick, a nail file, and dropping them again in glee. The lipstick rolls along the wooden floorboards, making a dull, ominous sound as it disappears under the bed. Beatrice begins to whine and Isobel shushes her through her own tears.

Iris picks Beatrice up and lays her on the bed among the rubble of clothes. 'Look, I'm worried about you, Isobel. Tom's probably worried about you too. He loves you, I know he does. We spoke on the phone a few times when Beatrice had just been born, because he wanted to know how he could cheer you up. Why would he ring me and ask for ways to cheer you up, and ask me if I thought you were okay, if he was just going to hurt you anyway?'

Isobel lifts her head. She thinks of Tom hiding his phone, the whispers between him and Iris when Beatrice was born. That's all it was? Him wanting to know how to make things right for Isobel?

'Really?' Relief is near, and Isobel reaches for it, but then it snaps away. 'But what about the card? What about Daphne? The woman across the road? They are all hiding something.'

'Isobel, I know a lot has changed, but I'm worried that you're so anxious. All of these things might have an explanation.'

'Everything has changed,' Isobel cries loudly, her eyes raw and sharp. 'I feel so different.'

Iris puts her arms around Isobel and holds her tightly. Even her scent is different. The lemons have gone and now she smells of Seth and musk and something unfamiliar. 'But things have changed for the better. It just takes a while to see it. You need to talk to Tom properly. Don't accuse him, just talk to him.' Iris stands up. 'Come on. I'll make us some tea.'

Isobel follows Iris to the kitchen. She holds Beatrice and puts her on her knee when she sits at the table. 'I'm so sorry for shouting. I really don't know what's going on with me at the moment. I shouldn't have taken it out on you.'

Iris stirs their tea and clears her throat. 'Isobel, do you think you should go to the doctor?'

Isobel gazes at Iris. She looks just as she did when they lived together, stirring two mismatched floral mugs of tea in the powder-blue kitchen, one leg bent slightly, her bright-red hair hanging straight down her back. But something, everything is different. The notes clamped to the fridge by alphabet magnets are all written by Iris. The fruit in the bowl is the fruit that Iris has chosen. An almost-empty bottle of red wine stands next to the hob, but Isobel isn't the one who shared it.

All the time that Isobel has been at Broadsands, she has missed this flat so much. Now she is here, it doesn't appear to be the place she really wants to be. The place she wants to be, is back with Tom. The weight of tears that has dragged behind her eyes, in her throat, almost constantly since those early, raw days of Beatrice, pulls at her again now. She bounces Beatrice on her knee blindly.

'I felt better before.' She thinks of the picnic, the beach, the sun. 'When we had our picnic? Surely you weren't thinking I was ill then?'

Iris comes over to the table and sets the mugs down. Isobel has the turquoise one with a pink tree on it. Hers every day for over a year at the flat, but forgotten until now.

'I was glad that you seemed a bit happier. But now, since you found that card to Tom, you seem to be unsettled again. Isobel, the doctor might just suggest something to help you feel a bit more like yourself.'

Isobel sips her tea for something to do, but it's too hot. 'But I'm not myself, am I? Like we said, everything has changed now.'

'Since when? Everything is always changing, Isobel. For all of us. You have Beatrice, yes, but she hasn't changed everything, has she? She's just added to it. She's beautiful and healthy. She's not something to have made you this unhappy, and neither is Tom.'

Isobel doesn't answer. Iris and Isobel have always been in the same places at the same time: primary school, high school, sixth-form college, university, disappointing jobs, exciting jobs, flat renters. Now, it's as though they don't live in the same world. Their planets move alongside each other, drifting along, bumping against each other now and again when their universe narrows.

'Are you sleeping?' Iris is asking.

Isobel shrugs, 'Not really.'

Iris takes Isobel's hand. 'Isobel, please. Just think about the doctor. I know you. I know you're aware of what might be wrong. I don't doubt that you were doing well earlier at the beach. But I feel as though going to the doctor and talking to Tom, being more open with him, would be more productive than snooping online at Georgia. Even if she is still in love with him, she's hardly going to post it on Facebook, is she?'

Isobel doesn't say anything. She carries on holding onto Beatrice and drinks her tea from her forgotten mug.

Broadsands is silent when Isobel arrives back from Iris's flat. Tom must have gone to work and Daphne is obviously still out somewhere with Hugh, because the dog, his meaty, leathery smell, his lead and Daphne's long green Hunter boots are all still absent. A brooding quiet fills the house. Isobel puts Beatrice down in her cot and then sits at the kitchen table and thinks about what Iris said.

She sits for a while, thinking. Then she pulls her laptop towards her. But as she types into the internet address bar and loads the page she wants, the page she's been thinking about, she feels a shadow behind her and snaps the laptop shut.

## CHAPTER 20

# *Victoria: 1965*

Jackie, the new girl, was on bottle duty this week with Victoria. She was slow and silent, her whole body seemingly dusted with spilled formula. The milky powder clung to the air.

'The pains have started again,' Victoria said, clutching her enormous bump. 'I think it's going to be soon. Jackie, I'm feeling quite frightened about it all.'

Jackie nodded. Just as Victoria had decided that it was a lost cause talking to this girl, that she wasn't ever going to reply, that she was better off chatting to Katherine when they had finished their jobs, Jackie's mouth fell open, in preparation for her to speak.

'Don't be. You won't remember it.'

'I know that. That's what worries me.'

'Better twilight sleep than unimaginable pain. Katherine said they give you some drugs one minute and the baby's brought to you the next. It's the bit after that which frightens me. The bit where they take it away again and I have to go home to my parents and answer questions about my time in London, working in an office that doesn't even exist.' Jackie plopped some formula into a bottle, red with the effort of so much talking all in one go.

'Have you seen Bev much since she came back from having her baby?'

'Bev? No. I don't know her much. She's going home soon, isn't she?'

'Yes. I suppose she will be.'

Victoria gazed around the windowless room. This dank, odorous kitchen was next to the nursery, and she could hear the wails of babies from their cots. The image of Bev's wrists lingered in her mind: raw, red, stained. She closed her eyes, hoping that the image would go away, but it was replaced by another: of Bev tied down, bloody, writhing and screaming.

'I'm going to find her and ask her exactly what went on,' Victoria said, her eyes flying open. But as she placed down her scoop of formula and took a step towards the kitchen door, a blast of burning pain consumed her body. She doubled over, the floor swinging dangerously near: scrubbed tiles, powdered with fallen milk.

As soon as it arrived, the pain disappeared. Victoria straightened.

'Do you want me to get Matron?' Jackie asked, her eyes wide.

'No. I'll get her,' Victoria said. She swung the door open, the smell of the stale hallway carpet hitting her as she moved slowly along the corridor towards Matron's office. Another contraction, sharp as a knife. Another step. Victoria bit her lip. She needed to stay in control. She needed to act as if the pain was bearable. She needed to stay awake, to tell them that Harry would be coming for her, to watch out for him pull up to the entrance of Gaspings in his red Monza. He must be on his way, because her Queen Victoria postcard would surely have arrived with him by now. As she passed the wide front door, she glanced out towards the expansive driveway, willing him to appear. Another contraction came as she did so, and then another as soon as she had recovered. She banged on Matron's door, a moan escaping her lips as she did.

*Don't,* she told herself, her body. *Don't lose control.* But as the pain engulfed her, and her body began to squeeze with all its force, repelling and straining, her thoughts became fragmented. She saw Harry and the peach shawl she had knitted. She saw an ambulance with pleasant flashing lights. She felt a needle and a gentle pressure on her head, around her mouth. She felt something around her wrists, and the feeling twisted itself around the image of Bev's raw wrists. Nurse Hammond hovered over her, her face long and calm above Victoria's, her brown hair frizzing around her hat. She smelt a salty tang as the nurse opened her mouth to say something, saw something dark flicker in her nut-brown eyes.

*Hope, not despair*, she was perhaps saying. Or perhaps she was telling Victoria to do something. She wanted to ask, but she didn't know how. Talking seemed impossible and foreign.

She heard screaming, although she didn't know if it was her own or not. She heard men, lots of men, none of them Harry. She tried to flip over, flip like a fish away from the pain and voices and warm oozing of blood between her legs.

And then she felt herself being lifted away to another world completely. She heard the voice of Nurse Hammond, and she felt the rush of air as the door swung open. She knew her baby had gone, that she wasn't near her. She saw Harry's face, and Henrietta's face, a perfection that had been lost forever. She saw her curled words on the back of the sepia postcard, her final wish to Harry, and tried to say them out loud.

*I am frightened. Come to me. Be with me.*

She saw stars blinking in the distance and was tugged gently by the promise of dreams: of dancing and champagne and Harry in a world that glittered and shone with hope.

## CHAPTER 21

# *Evelyn: 1965*

It was impossible to tell how long it was until Evelyn received the telephone call. Time often stilled or sped up these days. Evelyn was asleep and the ringing beat its way into her strange, hallucinatory dreams. She had been holding Victoria in her dreams, stroking her shining black hair, holding her hand, wiping fat tears from her daughter's frightened face.

*Poor, poor darling*, she'd been saying to Victoria. And then a ringing had begun, easy to ignore at first, but then louder and louder, pounding into the dream, into Evelyn's head and pulling her from sleep.

She knew, of course. A mother always knows when they have lost their child, whether they are with them or not.

She sobbed on the telephone to Matron, who was cold and crisp as ice as she said the words that turned Evelyn's blood from red to black, from warm to cold. Jack was at an auction in London until tomorrow. He didn't need to know. Not yet. With pale, trembling fingers, Evelyn pulled some money from the safe and then walked in the stiff, mild air to the train station.

When she arrived at Gaspings, she closed her eyes briefly and tried to feel Victoria's presence. She tried to contact her daughter somehow. But there was nothing. Victoria's soul had gone, flown from the creaking windows, far away into another world. The body Evelyn shuddered and wept over was just that: a body, with pale skin and an upturned nose with a scar across the bridge, and gleaming hair, black as a raven's wing. The room smelt of metal and blood, not of her floral, alive Victoria.

'Baby was lost too,' Matron said briskly, as though that was that. A tall nurse handed Evelyn a box.

'Were you kind to her?' Evelyn asked the nurse, unable to hide the desperation in her words.

The nurse nodded, tears in her eyes. 'I collected those things together for you. The other girls here helped me. Victoria was very well-liked. She was special. I'm so very sorry we couldn't save her.'

Evelyn fingered through the contents of the box. A peach shawl, badly knitted. A book called *The Blue Door*. The emerald that Evelyn had pressed into Victoria's cool fingers on the day that they had left her at Gaspings. A smooth red ribbon.

Evelyn twisted her long fingers in and out of the peach shawl on the train home. Her eyes flickered shut, her mind hazy and confused, her limbs aching with grief and shock.

*Oh, my darling,* she thought as the train puffed towards the coast. *If only I could try it all again.*

Only one chance to get things right. It seemed so terribly unfair.

She remembered when she had seen Victoria holding the mirror that had cost them both so much, her precious, pale fingers curled around the intricate handle.

'Victoria!' Evelyn had shouted that day, her own voice surprising her. Her words were never loud. In all Victoria's sixteen years, Evelyn had never really needed to shout. But then, as she saw what was in Victoria's hands, Evelyn felt as though all her breath had been forced out of her, all her blood drawn out from underneath her skin.

That mirror.

The shout was unexpected to Victoria too: so unexpected that she swivelled around in panic, almost dropping the mirror. It slipped slightly from her grasp and she tightened her grip around it, looking up at her mother determinedly, her jaw set firmly against whatever Evelyn was about to say.

'What are you doing with that mirror? Where did you get it from?'

Evelyn had seen a flicker of hesitation dart across Victoria's pretty, rounded face. But Evelyn didn't need an answer anyway: she'd known that the mirror had been locked away in a trunk with other things that she couldn't bear to see, and that Jack had probably dragged the trunk out from somewhere because it was in his way, or because he was planning to root through it greedily to find more stock that would make him rich. But just because the things she had tried to forget were locked away, it didn't mean Evelyn never saw them. She saw them when she was sleeping, drifting across her mind like black clouds. She could not let them haunt her sweet Victoria's dreams too.

'I found it in the suitcase. I like it.' Victoria said after a moment. But Evelyn hadn't processed the words. She'd been moving towards Victoria, trying to peel her daughter's pale fingers from the handle. The rough feel of the gems against her skin made her heart bang in her chest as she remembered her own mother's words, words that Evelyn had dismissed as nonsense when she'd brought the mirror with her from the castle on her wedding day.

*This mirror is a legacy of the castle. If it leaves these walls, whoever has taken it will be cursed.*

It might still be nonsense, Evelyn had tried to reassure herself. But even if it was, the mirror had caused Evelyn pain that she didn't want Victoria to ever feel. It made her remember who she used to be, the dreams she'd had and the nightmare that had instead been her life. She'd never lived in London; she'd never found her parents and she'd never escaped Jack. Victoria *must* have more than Evelyn had ended up with, and if there was any chance that the mirror might somehow ruin things for her, then Evelyn should take no chances.

'You mustn't play with that, darling. It's not safe,' Evelyn had said, but she'd seen that it was no use. Victoria's eyes were somewhere else.

'Victoria!' Evelyn shouted again, desperately. 'You cannot play with that mirror!' The shout made something crumble inside Evelyn and weakness had pulled at her, dragging at her body and mind. Her strength all used up, Evelyn put her hands to her face, the scent of the suitcase – of the mirror and the war and her mother and what could have been – all on her skin.

'Just promise me you will put it away and leave it alone,' she finished quietly, even though she knew that it was too late. She turned and found herself floating from the room, leaving Victoria behind with her bewitched eyes and her flushed cheeks.

Too late, too late.

*Do something else. Do something more*, whispered a voice inside Evelyn's mind.

But what else could have been done? What else, when Evelyn had been so terribly, terribly tired? She floated and floated, until the mirror was far away and she was back underneath her cool, smooth sheets.

Now, on the train from Gaspings, she stopped thinking of the mirror and thought instead of when she had known that Victoria was going to end up in trouble, a day when a purple, angry storm lingered in the air and the flat above the shop smelt of oil and eggs. She knew that Victoria's skirt wasn't fastened properly at the back, that her blouse wasn't quite straight, that her skin was still warm from being so close to Harry's. But she didn't know how to stop it or what to do. She remembered the pull of the new love that Victoria had found and the way she looked at Harry. She remembered the icy day when they'd dropped her off at Gaspings, the Matron's displeasure at yet another unwed mother. She remembered the nurse who had put together the box of Victoria's mismatched things and her sorry face lingered in Evelyn's mind as the train hissed and juddered to a stop.

## CHAPTER 22

# *Isobel: 2011*

*Victoria,*

*Why didn't you just tell me? I knew, you know. When Harry came into Clover's after you'd disappeared and asked if I was Sally, and then asked if my aunt was feeling better, I told him that I didn't have an aunt, and thought he was mistaken. But because he left without even drinking his tea, looking all sad and confused, I just had a feeling. When the Blythe's bakery boy came into the Clover's for a jam tart and asked me where you had gone, and if you'd had your baby yet, everything was suddenly so obvious. I wish you'd told me. I would have helped you.*

*Your mother wouldn't tell me where you went when you disappeared, but she promised me you'd be back home around now, so I'm writing this letter in case you are home already. Anyone who asks, she said, will be told that you've been working for an old lady in Lancashire, and that she sadly died this week so your services aren't needed any more. I can stick to a story. You know I can. A few people have already had their wrists slapped by me for trying to spread gossip about you. I gave the little bakery boy a good shove for telling tales. I haven't uttered your secret to anybody, Victoria. Except, of course, for Harry, because really it's his secret too. I thought it might be best if he laid low for a while, just in case your father found out that your baby was his.*

*I asked Harry to leave me an address to pass onto you if he did leave, but oh, Victoria, he's gone without telling me. I'm worried something has happened to him. I tried to stop the gossip from spreading, and I tried to make it seem like nothing ever happened with you and Harry. But I thought I'd warn you that he seems to have gone very suddenly. Maybe, when you return, he'll come back. There was somebody beaten up at the castle the other night and left in an unbearable state. I haven't prayed since I was five, but since I heard about that poor man I've prayed every second that it wasn't your Harry.*

*I've got so much I want to tell you and there is so much you need to tell me.*

*Cut me a slice of cake, Victoria, and I'll see you soon.*

*Love, your best friend,*

*Sally xxx*

'Why didn't you want me to see what was on your screen?' Tom asks as Isobel slams the lid of her laptop down. He has obviously been in the shower: his hair is sleek with water and he wears a towel around his waist.

'I felt someone behind me. I didn't know it was you. The house was silent, so I thought you'd gone to work. I didn't want your mum to see what I was looking at.'

Isobel opens the lid again, to reveal the website she's looked at so many times since Beatrice was born.

'Iris thinks I should make an appointment with the doctor.'

Tom's face falls as he reads the print on the screen: that blue, kind print that stains Isobel's mind. 'Post-natal depression? I thought you were starting to feel better?'

'I was, a bit. But I don't suppose it's as simple as that.'

Tom had suggested going to the doctors in the early days of

Beatrice, and Isobel had considered it. But in the end she'd decided against it. Going to the doctor meant that you were ill, that you weren't coping, that things were all going horribly wrong. That wasn't what was happening with Isobel. She was just tired, and things had happened so quickly. That was all.

'I should have gone to see the doctor when you said, right at the beginning.'

Tom shrugs. 'You weren't comfortable with going then, which I totally understood. If you are now, then let's make you an appointment. You deserve to be happy, Isobel. Let's get this sorted.'

Isobel stands and hugs him. He smells of male shower gel, a deep, citrusy, clean scent. His damp skin is soft and masculine all at the same time. He squeezes Isobel into him and she buries her head into his chest.

'Iris told me that you spoke to her when Beatrice was first born,' she says, her words smothered.

'I did. We were a bit worried about you. I wanted to know how to cheer you up. Actually, I have something to admit.'

Isobel pulls away so she can see Tom. 'What?' Panic roars through her until she sees the beginnings of a smile on his face.

'Do you remember me saying that I was going to pick up some things at Lucas's flat but then when we bumped into him yesterday he said he hadn't seen me for ages? I realise it must have looked dodgy. But it was just a white lie to keep you off my scent. I didn't go to Lucas's, as you probably gathered, because you asked me about it, but I wasn't quite ready to tell you then.'

'Where did you go?'

Tom presses Isobel gently back down into her chair. 'Wait here.'

She sits, staring at the screen of the laptop, wondering what Tom is rummaging about upstairs for. She hears him open a cupboard and then swing the door shut again. She hears him come back downstairs and into the kitchen. He's holding a square box wrapped in a carrier bag. Daphne has a drawer especially for carrier bags, mostly M&S and Waitrose. Tom takes the box from the creased green plastic and hands it to Isobel. It's a blue, wooden box, hand-painted with white clouds.

'It's beautiful,' Isobel says.

'Open it.'

As Isobel opens the lid, she feels a rush of strange familiarity. She has seen most of the things inside before. She lifts out her map of Vienna that was in the dream box she shared with Iris, her scrapbook of places to visit, a list of the best vintage fairs in the world in her own round handwriting.

'I went to get your things from Iris's that day and ask her what the dream box you had mentioned was all about. I wanted to do something that would make you feel a bit better.'

'You've put new stuff in here, too.' Isobel pulls out a printout of family-friendly restaurants in London and a box of Viennese whirls.

'I thought I'd make you a new dream box. I've been adding things for the past few months. I put in the last couple of things this morning and I think now's the time to give it to you.'

Isobel leans forward and kisses Tom. She hasn't kissed him properly in weeks, and now she can't even think why not. Something stirs in her: longing and contentment all at the same time. When she sits back again, she tugs at the cardboard box of pastries and takes two out. She hands one to Tom and takes a bite of the other.

She leans against the hard wood of the dining chair and the smooth pastry crumbles in her mouth, tasting of butter and sweetness. Isobel watches Tom as he chews and thinks of Iris's words about how he really does love her. But even now there are still flickers of doubt inside her. She wants to ask Tom why things still don't add up. But an instant before the words leave her mouth, something clicks in her mind, a chance that Tom might be telling the only truth he knows, a hope that he's not the one with all the answers.

She closes her eyes and thinks of the opened envelope crammed into a drawer, of the stifling atmosphere of this house, heavy with secrets and lies and doubt.

Daphne.

Tom leaves for work ten minutes later, after sitting with Isobel as she phones Silenshore surgery and makes an appointment for the next day. He hugs her before he goes, but Isobel can see in his face that he is still wondering if she might swing back into a frenzied doubt about him.

But Isobel stays quiet, as Tom unlocks the front door and lets himself out, as he saunters down the driveway, as she hears his footsteps fade into the distance. She stays quiet until the door opens again hours later and Daphne appears in the hallway with Hugh.

'Daphne,' says Isobel, her voice wavering from the start. She clears her throat. She doesn't want to sound weak, or like someone on the verge of postnatal madness and horror.

Daphne bends down to unclip Hugh's lead and avoids Isobel's gaze. 'Yes?'

'Daphne, I feel as though something is happening with Tom.'

Daphne's head shoots up and she drops the lead with a clatter on the wooden floor. 'What do you mean? What's happened?'

Isobel swallows, her throat dry as paper. 'I remember some of the things you said when Beatrice was born. I heard you on the phone the other day, too. I think there's a secret about him. I wondered if you knew what it was. I don't want to lose him.'

'You don't want to lose him?' says Daphne. She is frozen, statuesque.

'Yes. I've tried to ask him about the things I've heard and seen that don't quite add up, but I can't get much out of him. So I thought I'd ask you. I don't want to go digging in your lives, Daphne, but I love Tom, and he's Beatrice's father. So if there's something I should know about, then please, please just tell me.'

Isobel wants to sit down. She's exhausted, her legs are aching, her head pounding. But there is nowhere to sit in the hall and Daphne shows no signs of moving. Hugh stares up at his mistress, his huge brown eyes doleful, before whimpering and trotting off to the kitchen in search of something better than these two strange, tense women.

'Is it Georgia?' Isobel prompts. 'Has Georgia been in touch with you? Does she want to see Tom again?'

Confusion flits over Daphne's face. 'Georgia?'

'Yes. I thought it might be her on the phone the other day.'

'It's not Georgia,' Daphne's voice is barely a whisper. 'Is Tom in?'

'No. He's at work. He's doing a short shift, so he'll be back soon.'

Daphne kneels then, straight onto the floor, her long legs folding beneath her without any warning. She sits on the wood, her head in her hands, her grey hair spilling through her long fingers. Isobel moves towards her and then sits on the floor next to her. Close up, she can see tiny streaks of brown, of the hair that Daphne must have once had.

'Tom's not mine. He never was.' Daphne whispers, her voice barely audible. 'I took him. But I can't lose him, Isobel.'

The words float in Isobel's mind, making no sense.

Daphne looks up, her face white and stricken.

'Let's get you up. I'll make some tea,' says Isobel. She guides Daphne to her feet, feeling the woman's thin arms trembling under her dark-green fleece. When they reach the kitchen, Isobel motions for Daphne to sit down at the table, then puts the kettle on an Aga ring before sitting down.

'I don't know what you meant before,' Isobel starts, as Daphne's words from the hall ring in her ears. 'What did you mean when you said Tom wasn't yours?'

Daphne opens her mouth to speak, but no words come. As the two women sit, Isobel staring at Daphne, they hear the creak of the front door opening. They turn to the doorway of the kitchen, where Tom stands, a brown parcel and a letter in his hands.

He smiles cheerfully and drops the parcel onto the table with a thud.

'This is for you, Mum.'

Isobel and Daphne stare down at it. The handwriting on the brown package is similar to the spindly style on the Christmas card that Isobel found the other day, the handwriting that has been etched into Isobel's exhausted mind, that made her lose all sense of everything.

But instead of Tom's name, it's Daphne's.

## CHAPTER 23

# *Evelyn: 2011*

Victoria's baby hadn't died, of course. It had been a lie. Evelyn had realised that just after leaving Gaspings House.

When the train had stopped at the station after Gaspings and Evelyn had sat, aching all over, her head resting on the seat, her brain clicking through image after image, the face of the tall nurse with brown hair appeared in her mind. She had remembered the nurse's eyes, as Matron said *Baby was lost too*. The nurse's expression had said something different. Her eyes had been wide with fright and excitement and exhilaration and horror. Evelyn hadn't noticed at the time, but she noticed at the precise moment that the train paused in the station.

She had leapt from the train, her body moving faster than it had done in years. She had run back to Gaspings, her heels bleeding, her breath rasping.

The tall nurse had answered the front door and the blood had drained from her face. She wasn't pretty, but her face had a softness to it that compelled Evelyn to take her hands.

'Victoria Lace's baby. I was told that it died?'

'It was a boy,' the nurse said. 'A beautiful boy.' She glanced behind her and bit her lip, put her hand up and brushed it through her dull, brown hair. Evelyn saw the glint of a wedding ring: a plain gold band, a circle of love and commitment.

'Do you have children?' Evelyn breathed, her lungs still struggling for air after running.

The nurse looked down. She shook her head. A headshake of broken dreams, of desperation, of waiting and waiting for something that was already loved, but was never going to come. Evelyn saw it all in an instant.

'Meet me. Tonight. Do you know the castle in Silenshore?'

The nurse stared and stared at Evelyn. Panic fluttered in Evelyn's chest. What if she had it all wrong? What would this woman think of her? But then she remembered the thought she'd had on the train not even an hour earlier as it pulled away from Gaspings, towards Silenshore. *Only one chance to get things right.* She remembered the nurse's face lingering in her mind, telling her that something didn't add up.

Evelyn waited. Eventually, the nurse looked behind her again. Then she nodded so quickly that Evelyn almost missed it.

'Meet me at the gates. Midnight,' Evelyn said.

'Midnight,' the nurse repeated, before swinging the heavy door shut between them.

To anybody else, the castle might have looked eerie at midnight. The moon glowed behind it, broken in two by the turret that used to be Evelyn's bedroom what seemed like hundreds of years ago. As Evelyn waited by the gates she wondered, for the millionth time, what it might be like inside the castle now. She wondered if it might still hold, somehow, the sweet sounds and scents of her mother and father, of the evacuees, of Evelyn's childhood. She wondered if Victoria had ever seen Harry here, if her beautiful, darling girl had been kissed here, if she had felt the thrill of new love with the castle looking down on her.

The castle was the only place at which Evelyn could do what she was about to do. She looked at her watch. It was approaching midnight. A few more strokes and the nurse, if Evelyn had been right about it all, would be here.

Midnight. A black cloud drifted across the moon, casting darkness down on Evelyn.

Silence. The ticking of Evelyn's watch as second after second went by.

And then a figure.

The nurse was stooped, rushing, breathless. She stopped at Evelyn as the cloud passed over the moon, her outline lit by silver.

Evelyn reached out and touched her arm. 'Please, tell me what happened.'

The nurse shook her head, her eyes filling with tears. 'I don't know. I tried to save your daughter. I tried so hard. You must understand, she didn't know what was happening. So she'll be at peace now. I can promise you that.'

Evelyn nodded, her soul ripping in two, her heart stinging and raw. 'And the baby?'

The nurse wept. 'He's so beautiful.'

'He didn't die, did he?'

'No. No, he didn't. I'm so sorry. I wanted to tell you. I…'

'There are some new houses being built here in Silenshore.' Evelyn cut into the nurse's words, pressing her hands against her bony fingers, pushing the notes that she had taken from Jack's hiding place under the floorboards into the nurse's hand. 'Buy one of them. Be nearby to me. I will never tell the baby he isn't yours. I will never take him away from you, as long as you take very good care of him and as long as I know he is near to me.'

There was a strange pause in the black air, as though time had stopped. The nurse looked at Evelyn, her eyes wide and unsure. For a cruel, stretched moment, Evelyn considered taking her by her frizzed brown hair and demanding to know where the baby was right now, to find him, and wrap him in the peach blanket that her darling Victoria had knitted and take him home.

But then she remembered Jack and his brutish strength, and

her own strange weakness that seemed to be tied to him. She remembered Victoria's poor, poor Harry, his death splashed all over the newspapers while Victoria was in that dreadful place all alone. Someone had been waiting for him when he finished work at the university. They'd set upon him, beaten him and left him for dead. He was beaten so badly that it was some time before he was even identified. *Suspicious*, the black print had said. Evelyn had pushed that word to the back of her mind. If Jack knew she had considered telephoning the police and saying that she thought it might have been Jack who had left Harry for dead behind her beautiful castle gates, he would have broken her in two: snapped her like a twig in a second.

No, she certainly couldn't take the baby home to Jack, and she couldn't tell him that the baby was still alive. She would tell him that the baby was dead, so that he wouldn't hunt it down and bruise it and whip it like he did her, or snarl and curse at it like he always had with Victoria, or leave it for dead like he had with Harry. This baby would be the start of a new life with new people and new fortune. He would make a time for change. He would be Victoria's secret, and Evelyn would watch him forever, guarding him with her life.

She stepped away from the nurse, who was still weeping, and turned from the castle. Her legs moved smoothly, carrying her back home.

One chance to do the right thing.

Evelyn was sure that this was it.

The next morning Jack had returned from the auction. Normally, the days after an auction were tight and fraught with anxiety for Evelyn. But at this auction he had won a gilt-lined painting of some snappy-looking hunting dogs and grand horses. He was affable and gentle. He did not even appear to mind that Evelyn wasn't watching the shop. Lace Antiques had been quieter since Victoria had gone to Gaspings anyway. They hadn't told a soul about their daughter's misfortune, but somehow people seemed to know.

Now, none of it mattered anyway.

'Victoria is dead,' she said to Jack as he shuffled a pile of ten-pound notes.

His head shot up from the money and his eyes suddenly appeared to become very bloodshot. His fist curled into a neat ball on the counter, then relaxed as soon as it had tensed. He looked down.

'She's better off dead than in the sorry state she got herself in.'

'Baby was lost too,' Evelyn said next, using Matron's words, Matron's lie.

At this news, Jack shrugged and continued to count the money, though a deadness had appeared behind his grey eyes. Evelyn remembered the first time she had seen those eyes. She had been charmed, seeing his darkness as a symbol of exoticism. Now, she knew different. There was nothing exotic about her husband, nothing charming, only danger.

She swept past him, unable to form words about funerals or death in childbirth or their beautiful lost girl.

Evelyn took to walking up the hill and through the dark, cobbled streets to the new houses that she had told the nurse about. They were almost finished now: lower and wider than any houses Evelyn had seen before. The skeletons of the houses soon became a row of pastel-painted bungalows, spacious and modern.

The sharp, salty air and the daily uphill walk to the houses made Evelyn's limbs ache, made her lungs tight and full, as though they might burst. When she returned home after her walks, she left Lace Antiques closed up and floated upstairs to her soft bed. Every day, she dreamed of Victoria, her poor Victoria, her darling body lying in that horrible place, all alone, silver-white with death.

*I ruined things for you*, she told Victoria in her silent sleep. *I let you ruin things for yourself. I won't let things be ruined for your baby. I won't.*

It was autumn when Evelyn saw them together for the first time. The air sparked with the first electric hints of winter. Copper leaves danced along the streets of Silenshore, and when Evelyn stared up at the castle on her walk to the new houses, it loomed in front of a fluorescent-orange sky. So taken was she with staring up into the turret that used to be her bedroom so long ago that she almost missed them.

He was in a navy-blue Silver Cross pram, his face only just visible in a twist of pale-blue blankets. The nurse from Gaspings was pushing him along, her tall figure stooped over the curling white handle. She didn't see Evelyn silently observing her from the corner of West Street. She stopped for a moment, reached a slim hand into the pram, perhaps to stroke his cheek, or cover him more securely, or wipe a tear. Her line of vision did not move from the pram. If the world had crumbled around her, the nurse wouldn't have noticed, as long as the pram and the baby within it remained.

Once Evelyn knew that the baby was living in Silenshore, she walked across the road every day, through the lane to West Street and up and down, her heart dull with a heavy ache, in the hope that she would see one more glimpse of Victoria's darling baby. As the season changed to winter and the air became sharp with a hostile iciness, Evelyn wondered if there was any point in walking up and down West Street now. Surely the nurse wouldn't take him out until the spring.

Just one attempt and then Evelyn would stop herself from trying to see him again.

It was on the one attempt, though, that Evelyn saw the nurse pushing the pram towards the beach. Evelyn walked behind her, far away enough not to be seen, her body tight with the chill of the air and the thrill of seeing her grandchild. He was growing now: even at a distance, Evelyn could see his cherubic face staring from the pram as he sat up. The nurse was thin, rather drably dressed in a shapeless beige coat. Evelyn walked a little further, blind to the sea beyond, the declining cobbles beneath her, the wide row of new houses beside her.

*Turn around now*, she told herself. *Go back home and leave them*. The wind bit into her cheeks and salt settled on her lips. She paused, let the nurse retreat an instant further towards the promenade and tried to gather the strength to turn her back to them. But she found herself unable to move and so instead she watched until the figure of the nurse and the blue pram turned into a blur, an indistinguishable dot, and then nothing.

The year swept by, coming to a close as Evelyn lay alone in bed listening to the sound of the crashing black waves, isolated cheers on the streets, the clanking of bottles as people left The Smuggler's Ship, the clanging of the various clocks in the shop downstairs as they struck midnight. Jack was out somewhere and would be back in the early hours, angry about something or other and reeking of stale cigarette ash and sloshed, warm bitter.

The new year brought with it angry storms from Jack as Lace Antiques stood forlorn and empty of custom.

'They don't want to know us now. Nobody wants to know us because of what happened,' Jack yelled, banging his ugly fist down on the counter.

Evelyn sighed. It was probably more to do with changing tastes and times, but she wouldn't say that to Jack. He liked to blame her and Victoria for things that went wrong: he always had. Lost shoes, broken clocks, lost fortunes at auctions, were all somehow twisted into the endless fault of Evelyn and poor Victoria. Now, even though Victoria lay still in the ground in a churchyard near Gaspings House (with what Evelyn presumed was an empty coffin at her feet), she was still being blamed for things that had gone wrong.

'I don't know why we bother,' Jack was ranting. 'I might as well close the bloody place.'

Evelyn closed her eyes and took a deep breath.

'Let's close it. Let's sell it. I've seen a house for sale on West Street. It's cheap. You'd like it.'

Jack stared at her, his dull, brown eyes burning into hers. Evelyn shifted, leaned on the counter, thought of her bed. She could mumble an apology for speaking out of turn, for presuming that she should offer ideas, and then she could sink into her soft bed and close her eyes, and dream of Victoria and the baby and another life altogether.

She'd seen the house that morning when she'd been out walking around West Street. It was directly opposite the one that she had seen the nurse emerge from with the baby.

She gripped the counter so that the bones of her knuckles protruded from her papery skin. No. She could not give up on this. She would never take the baby. She couldn't; she'd done such a terrible job with Victoria. But if she could persuade Jack to buy that house, then she would be able to watch him, to make sure that he was safe in her own way, to perhaps see him sometimes and transmit, somehow, that he was special, rich and royal.

It wasn't clear why Jack listened to Evelyn. Perhaps, for all these years, she'd been wrong. Perhaps if she'd spoken to him more, told him her ideas, he would have nodded along, and they would have sailed along more peacefully, without purple bruises and a heavy feeling of sorrow and days when the only thing to do was sleep.

But then again, perhaps they wouldn't have.

The house was narrow and dark; not much different from the upstairs of Lace Antiques that Evelyn had spent the last seventeen years in. It smelled of damp and the paint on the walls cracked in spidery lines.

Jack managed to sell Lace Antiques at a high price. But the man who bought it turned his nose up at the stock.

'It's a holiday town,' the man said, without expanding. Jack was furious. But Evelyn felt like she knew what that meant.

On their first night in the new house they lay in their bed, surrounded by the boxes of unwanted antiques. The ticking of old clocks and the scent of the past lingered in the air.

As the years rolled by, Jack and Evelyn led separate lives. Evelyn watched the family across the road grow and shape themselves into a unit. She saw the nurse's husband knock a house sign that said *Broadsands* into the brick next to the front door, and thought what a nice name for a family home that was. She listened carefully to snatches of conversations as the family pushed their bicycles into the garage, as they left the house and piled into their car, as they shouted to one another in the back garden and walked to the beach and over the road to Castle Street. She watched as the baby changed into a toddler then a schoolboy then a tall, sophisticated man who wore woollen coats and striped scarves, who once helped her when one of her shopping bags split in two so that her tins of peaches rolled along the cobbles, who drove a rather intimidating black car. She gazed at him from the narrow, smeared windows of her cottage and wondered at how different he was to Jack, who was short and aggressively opposed to men like her grandson: tall men who dressed well and were gentle and subtle.

She watched and listened and waited. She found out their names.

Daphne.

Philip.

Tom.

She waited when Tom disappeared for years and then watched again as he came back to Silenshore with someone who appeared to be his new wife. She held her breath when the wife appeared to stop visiting Broadsands with Tom, when his left ring finger became suddenly bare, his face drawn and tired. She stood at her window and sobbed as she saw a hearse slide against the kerb of

Broadsands, as the man who had accepted the role of Tom's father so graciously for over thirty years was carried out. She watched the nurse who had become a mother and the baby who had become a man weep as they climbed into the car, shrouded in neat, black clothes.

And then more time rolled by, season by season, month by month, day by day. Evelyn became weaker and Jack became slower, his breaths rasping whenever he climbed the stairs or got up from his chair too quickly. He was finally weaker than her. He barked commands from his chair, twisted his face into bitter smirks, made the whole house smell of unwashed skin and misery.

And then came the blue-black autumn evening when Evelyn was standing in her usual place at the window, absently rubbing her chest. A woman, no older than thirty, in a bright-blue coat and glittering beret that caught the streetlights and twinkled with movement, arrived at Broadsands with Tom. The woman gripped Tom's hand and they looked at one another as they walked up the drive. This was a big occasion, Evelyn saw. She saw it in the way Tom inclined his head towards the woman slightly, the way he placed his hand on the small of her back. He'd never been like that with the wife who disappeared. She saw the woman's hair flying out in the wind from beneath her beret: a beautiful burnt copper. She saw them disappear into the hall and shut the door softly behind them. It was a few weeks after that, a night of driving, angry rain that Evelyn saw the same woman swinging a yellow car onto Daphne's driveway. As the woman got out of the car, her auburn hair whipping around her delicate face, Evelyn found herself running to her door, flying out into the rain. Her muscles ached and moaned in pain: she never moved very far these days. As the woman hammered on the front door of Broadsands, Evelyn stopped.

She could not tell them now. She would wait. She needed to wait until Jack was gone. He could barely move and Evelyn could sense that death was near to him. But after Harry, poor Harry all those years ago, she could take no risks.

She allowed herself to watch the scene for a little longer, the rain stinging her eyes and drumming through her clothes onto her frozen skin. The woman turned around and met her eyes, and for a moment Evelyn was unable to move. She stared into the woman's round, dark eyes until the door of Broadsands opened and the woman was ushered in by Daphne. Daphne's word of greeting was carried on the wind, across the wide, flooded road.

*Isobel.*

As another silver Christmas fell softly down on Silenshore, Evelyn tried hard to avoid Isobel, tried not to stare as she and Tom wandered to and from the house, sometimes holding hands, sometimes not. But on Christmas Eve, Evelyn had been unable to stop herself from speaking to Isobel. Evelyn had been asleep for days on end and had emerged from her bedroom thick with dreams and sadness. Isobel had been on her way home, her chin nuzzled deep into her scarf, her mind obviously elsewhere, and Evelyn had found herself floating towards her, heard herself rambling about Tom and his other wife. She shouldn't be talking, she thought, but she just wanted to say something nice, to see Isobel up close: her bright hair and her feathery, mascara-ed lashes and the pale freckles on her cheeks. She wasn't going to tell Isobel anything, or even mention Tom, but then she heard her own voice, old and shaky and unrecognisable: words that made Evelyn's worst fears dance in the air, words about sharing Tom and wanting to be his number one, because that's what Evelyn dreamt of, and in those dreams, Tom mixed with Harry and Harry mixed with the man that she first thought Jack was on the day she met him. The words and dreams tumbled from Evelyn's cracked, thinned lips, making Isobel stare at her in fright and rush away.

And as Evelyn tried and tried to keep away from Isobel and Tom, and mouthed sorry when she saw them, and made herself stay indoors, away from trouble, Jack faded and faded in his chair. He slept silently, until sleep became death and eventually Evelyn was free of him. On the day of Jack's sad, empty funeral, Evelyn saw Daphne at the window of Broadsands, staring down at the hearse. As the slow black car glided down the street, she gazed up at Daphne. Evelyn's body was failing now. The lump on her chest was becoming bigger. She hadn't told the doctor and she had no plans to. She, like Jack, was running out of time. Her body became more frail with each day, her bones as brittle as hair. But her eyesight was still bright and clear. She could see the golden castle, her old home from so many years ago, rising up over Silenshore. She could see the outline of wispy clouds, the gleam of spring sunlight, the motes of dust in the hearse. She could see the pain etched on Daphne's face, the realisation that Jack was dead, that the obvious reason for Evelyn keeping their secret was gone. She could see the fright scored on Daphne's features, the same fright that she'd seen a glimpse of on Isobel's face that day she'd spoken to her: horror that her time with Tom might now be up.

Two days after Jack's funeral, Tom and Isobel brought home their baby. Evelyn heard yowls and murmurs as they carried the bulky, ugly car seat into the house. She wondered if she might be able to go over and speak to them, act like a neighbour who wanted to see a baby for no reason other than being neighbourly, but then she remembered her garbled words when she'd tried to speak to Isobel, the look of panic on Isobel's pale face. Perhaps she would telephone them instead.

After a few months of considering it, dreaming about it every time she slept, Evelyn pulled her telephone directory from its place under her book-laden coffee table and coughed as dust flew from under the table and scratched its way down her throat. She found the surname she had seen on a letter some time ago and underlined the number in sharp blue ink.

Daphne was angry, or perhaps she was just frightened. Her words hissed down the telephone.

*No, you may not speak to him.*

*You must leave him alone.*

*You know what was agreed.*

Evelyn remembered that night at the castle when Daphne stood before her and told her that the baby had lived. She remembered what she had promised Daphne. And she had kept her word. She'd sent Tom a Christmas card for the first time a few months ago: had risked walking across the wide, grey road and along the crunching drive of Broadsands to slip a red envelope through the heavy brass letterbox. She'd written the card years before, when her hand was still steady, when the future was still wide and held a chink of hope. Years passed and the light of the future diminished, until last Christmas, when she knew there would be no more chances. But she asked for nothing in her words; she had never tried to take Tom back, had never intended to, not even when her heart felt as though it might be implode, because she knew that Tom had a better chance at life with Daphne, away from Evelyn, because everything Evelyn touched fell apart.

Now, time is slipping away and Evelyn is becoming weaker with each day. She is fading away and her connection to Tom is crumbling, disintegrating by the minute. Just one more letter, that's all she needs to write now. And then the rest, once she is gone, will be taken care of.

*Dear Daphne,*

*I must thank you for being such a good mother to Tom for all this time. I can see that the years have been blighted with fright that you should lose him. I would never take him from you, for he is not mine. He is not yours either. He used to be Victoria's, but now he belongs to Isobel and their baby. It should stay that way, whatever you decide to tell him. I am fading now, going into another world where I might see Jack and Victoria, or I might see nothing but black.*

*I don't have much to leave Tom when I go. Jack spent most of our money. I have this house, which Tom is welcome to. I have left everything I have to him. I know you mustn't have given him my card this Christmas, or told him that it was from me, because he has never so much as glanced at me. I sent it because I knew it would be my last chance to send him a Christmas card, to let him know somebody was thinking of him and how special he is.*

*If you tell him now what you have been keeping from him, you might lose him. But if you don't he will lose his connection to me, to his real history.*

*You have made choices that have shaped Tom's life, as parents are meant to, as I never did for Victoria. This last choice also lies with you.*

*Think carefully.*

*My thanks are with you forever.*

*Evelyn*

When she has pressed the lid back onto her best fountain pen, the scent of fresh blue ink floating up from the paper, she opens the box that she has kept for so many years. Memories fly out, clawing at her, trying to pull her under, and she turns her head slightly so that she can't see the things she's packing into the parcel for Tom. A small case. A peach shawl, badly knitted. A book called *The Blue Door*. The emerald that Evelyn had pressed into Victoria's cool fingers on the day that they had left her at Gaspings. A smooth red ribbon, which Evelyn ties around a neat pile of unopened letters: those that Harry and Sally sent to Victoria at Lace Antiques, and Evelyn kept for when Victoria came home from Gaspings, hidden inside her pillowcase and under a loose floorboard and behind the books that Jack never read. To look at these things that were all from so long ago, to really see them properly, would break Evelyn forever, and it's too soon for that because there's something she needs to do first.

She smiles into the mirror encrusted with sapphires that has brought and cost so very much, and her lips crack and sting. She thinks of her mother warning her off the mirror. How different life might have been if Evelyn had never found it, never taken it from the castle. Would she never have met Jack? Would she have walked past his shop that day, past a future of misery and on to a different one in London? Would she not have lost her parents? She knew now that it was Jack who had frightened them away. The day he died, Evelyn had dragged his chair out of the house, wanting to be rid of his every fibre. Underneath the chair a floorboard was loose. There had probably been all sorts of things kept in there by Jack, Evelyn realised as she stared down at the space where a faded letter lay, things that she didn't even want to know about. She had pulled the letter free, the handwriting making her heart sink and sing all at once.

*Evelyn*

*We have come to France sooner than planned. As I told you, we owed money to different people in Silenshore. We were hoping that word hadn't got out that we were in trouble, that we could sneak away from some of the people we owed the least to and get their money to them in the future somehow. But oh, Evelyn, we received a letter the morning after your wedding telling us that everyone knew we had lost everything, and that if we didn't pay back every penny then our lives, and yours, would be at risk. It threatened to tell the newspapers what we'd done, that we'd squandered away our fortune on parties that we couldn't afford. I couldn't bear it for you, and for Jack, our new son. Of course, it wasn't clear if the letter was to be believed, but to be safe we decided to come to your father's family earlier than planned. Please, write to me at the address above and we can arrange to see each other again.*

*Your loving,*

*Mother and Father*

Jack, Evelyn had thought. It had been Jack who had written to them, his fury at the loss of what he saw as his fortune spilling out into a cruel letter. And they had fled to try and protect him.

How little they had known him.

She stared at the address at the top of the page: the address that she had searched for, for so many years. Jack must have known that Evelyn had been looking. He must have moved it around the house so that Evelyn had chased it endlessly. There must have been others, thrown on the fire perhaps, or torn into senseless pieces. But this one, he had kept. Perhaps he'd thought that finding it when it was too late would be more painful for Evelyn than never seeing it at all. And in some ways, it was. Grief pulled at Evelyn as the address blurred with her tears. But like all the other pain she now bore, it was a softer pain than she used to feel. Time and old age had weakened her senses, and now it was too late to feel anything other than a dull ache where a roaring pain should have been. But along with the ache came a sense of calm. Evelyn's parents hadn't abandoned her. She had been right for all these years. They hadn't simply disappeared without telling her where they were or how to reach them.

They would be gone now, to another world with no secrets and no curses. And soon, Evelyn would be returned to them.

Now, thinking about her parents, Evelyn looks down into the mirror again. Her hair is silver where it was once golden. Her eyes are still blue, but now they are pale, and sit in a sagging face, the skin weighted down by time. Her collarbone juts from beneath the cool-blue blouse that she wears. She sees shards of herself glittering in the air as she throws the mirror across the room. It shatters into a thousand pieces and she sweeps them up, light-headed with relief.

The sun bakes the world as Evelyn steps out of her house onto the bright white street. She stares across at Broadsands, as she has done so many times in her life. The house stares back, unwavering, hostile. There is nothing to indicate anything is any different today. The front door is shut. The hanging basket creaks backwards and forwards slowly in the summer breeze. The curtains are open, the blinds half drawn as always. It's a normal summer's day with nothing to suggest a time for change.

And yet.

Evelyn crosses the road. Her steps are small, weak. If a car was to come careering around the corner from the promenade, she would be gone, her delicate bones crushed, her body catapulted into the summer air like a doll. The letter and the package she has kept safe for so long would fly from her hands into the breeze and back down into the debris of her death.

But no car comes.

The door remains closed, even when she taps her long, yellowed nails against the oak. She's just about to leave the package on the door when Tom arrives. Evelyn stares at him, at his easy, open features that show his charm and innate goodness, his greying hair that betrays the years that have passed, his smile that is a replica of the original, a carbon copy of the smile that cost Victoria so very much: his left canine slightly crooked, the rest of the teeth in perfect white rows.

'Can I help you?' he asks, his voice similar in tone to Harry's, his words dusted with the same easy charm.

'I need you to give this to your mother, please,' she says, handing over the package and the letter. Their hands touch and something crackles in her blood.

'Of course,' he says.

Then the door swings shut and he is gone.

# *Epilogue 2015*

Isobel glances in the mirror as she brushes through Beatrice's hair and their eyes meet. Their faces match: they are starting to merge into a clear pair. Mother and daughter. The sight of them together in the mirror gives Isobel a thrill.

'Plaits or ponytail?' she asks.

Beatrice wrinkles her nose in thought and then grimaces as Isobel pulls a brush through her hair.

'Plaits,' she says eventually, her bright voice high and clear.

As Isobel weaves Beatrice's hair into thick, dark plaits, she looks away from the mirror. The soft-yellow light of spring, of daffodils and sunlight and honey, leaks through her bedroom window. The light and the warmth in the air remind Isobel of another time, of a walk on the beach and the first days of Beatrice. She shakes her head slightly, freeing herself of the discomfort from the memories, and strokes the brush through Beatrice's hair again.

'Are you excited?' she asks and Beatrice nods. Her nod is decisive, sure. Everything about it is like Tom.

At the thought of Tom, Isobel's mind wanders to the last few years. They've been years of change: decay and grief for what was, but of blossoming and ripeness too.

The day that Isobel confronted Daphne about what she had been hiding, the day that Tom brought in a brown parcel with Daphne's name on the front in swirling writing, was a day of fleshed-out, splintered secrets. Daphne had tried to take the parcel away, but her trembling hands, the tears escaping from her in sorrowful gulps, made Tom rip open the thin brown paper himself.

Inside was a small pale-blue suitcase, with the letters V.L. inexpertly embroidered on the silk inside, so shakily that the initials bled together on the cream satin lining. A stack of unopened letters was bundled together with a piece of red ribbon, and a small green gem was covered in a fine layer of dust. An old mystery novel filled the kitchen with the scent of damp pages as Tom leafed through it. On the inside cover was an inscription to somebody called Miss Lace. Tom's eyes flicked over it for meaning, and Daphne sobbed and sobbed. He put the book to one side and pushed the suitcase away, towards where Isobel was sitting.

'What's the matter?' he asked Daphne. 'Who's sent you all these things?'

Daphne's face melted in agony, 'I can't lose you, Tom,' she said.

The words hung in the room. They were Isobel's words too, the words she had wanted to say all year, dressed up now in Daphne's hoarse voice.

Tom had pulled the truth from Daphne, and when it came, cloaked in fright, he had pushed the suitcase slightly, so that it skated across the table and thudded onto the kitchen floor, the letters releasing themselves from the ribbon and floating through the air like ghosts. He had turned from Daphne and left Broadsands. Isobel had followed him, running after him towards the beach, the salty summer wind snatching at her hair and face.

'She's a fake,' Tom had said, his words shaken, his voice not his own.

Isobel had pushed the image this conjured of Daphne from her mind: capes and furtive glances and evil plans.

'She's not. She loves you, Tom. I don't know what happened, but you need to find out. She brought you up. She's still your mother.'

Tom shook his head.

'Tom! She is. She was there all the way through your childhood. She must have wanted you badly to hide this from you.' Isobel held out her hand and took his. 'Come on. I don't know what she'll tell you, but you can't turn your back on her.'

In the end, after walking back to Broadsands with Isobel, and listening to Daphne's trembling words, after reading the unopened letters, sifting through what was left of his real mother and father's lives and deaths, Tom had reacted in the way Isobel has come to know is uniquely his: calm, steady, logical. Now, words and glances sometimes betray a lingering sadness. But as soon as Isobel feels the tip of sadness, it disappears like a minnow darting beneath the water and she can't tell if it's from Daphne, or Tom, or both of them. Gone are the wasps of secrecy buzzing in the air around them, the taut string of tension between them all.

Isobel looks around her bedroom. From her window, she can see Broadsands. Daphne will be out walking with Hugh, who is slower now than he used to be, bony and laden with age, but faithful to the end. His strides will be shorter than Daphne's: hers will be purposeful and wide as always. Sometimes, Isobel sees Daphne as Evelyn must have done from this window, her willowy body stooped against rain, or wilting in dry summer heat as she walks towards the narrow promenade.

Evelyn disappeared after giving the parcel to Tom. He tried to visit her a few times after Daphne had told him that she lived opposite Broadsands, but her door was bolted shut, a colourful fountain of junk mail visible behind the glass pane in the front door. A few weeks after, Tom had received a letter saying that Evelyn had passed away, and that the house Isobel stands in now had been left to him, along with the few possessions in it:

framed photographs of Victoria, her hair dark like his and Beatrice's, her smile secretive and romantic; a collection of clocks that clicked with each second and a trunk of old stock from what Daphne says was an antique shop. Tom spent the first few months of living in the house sanding down walls, pulling away its crumbling paper and wood and making it into a brighter, happier place to be. He worked quietly, showing Isobel items that he'd found now and again in cupboards and underneath tired furniture: a photograph of a child in front of Silenshore Castle, perhaps Evelyn; a browned piece of paper with Evelyn du Rêve written in swirling letters; a fragment of broken sapphire, sharp and glittering.

'Are you excited?' Beatrice asks Isobel, breaking into her thoughts.

'I'm so excited,' Isobel says. 'I've wanted to go on this holiday for a very long time.'

'Why are we only just going now, then?' Beatrice asks, ever curious. Her eyes are round and bright, constantly questioning everything around her, then drinking up the answers.

Isobel sighs. 'Oh, because although I wanted to go, there didn't seem to be a right time. I wasn't very well, and then as soon as I was better your daddy was opening his restaurant.'

'I helped paint the walls,' Beatrice says, swinging her lilac legs forwards and backwards.

'I know,' Isobel thinks of du Rêve's, the restaurant that Tom opened a few years after they had inherited Evelyn's house. The money that they were going to save for a house deposit no longer needed, they put their savings into a small but perfectly formed place near the castle and transformed it into Tom's restaurant. The day that they all painted the walls a pale gold seems to be one of the first fully formed of Beatrice's memories: paint in their hair, snatches of French bread and apples whenever they got hungry, a tiny roller for Beatrice's miniature hands, Iris and Seth breezing in every now and again to comment on the colours and sing made-up rhymes about painting to Beatrice. 'That was a good day, wasn't it?'

Beatrice nods. 'It was my favourite day.' She lifts up her hand to feel her plaits. 'I'm going to keep them neat.' She grins as she says this. It's a standing joke: her plaits always fall out way before the end of the day.

'There's a first time for everything,' Isobel says. 'Come on, let's go downstairs and watch out for Grandpa.'

Graham arrives the moment he says he would, his suitcase a small navy-blue one that makes Isobel remember holidays from another life: caravans and hot chips doused in vinegar and ketchup and walks around tiny shops full of candles and sweets and things made from shells and glass.

'All ready, Bea?' he asks.

'I'm ready, Grandpa!' Beatrice points at her frog-shaped suitcase that stands in the corner of the lounge, and has done for over a week.

'We're just waiting for Tom and then we'll set off. He's just handing over a few things at the restaurant,' Isobel says to her dad.

Tom arrives home minutes later, smelling of fresh mint and spilled red wine and warm, potent garlic. He pulls all the suitcases into the hallway and Isobel sees him glance through the window of the front door, towards Broadsands.

'She could still come, you know,' Isobel says. There's a tug of something in her voice that even she can't identify: more complicated than sadness, but softer than guilt.

Tom shakes his head. 'I think she'll be okay. She doesn't like leaving Hugh or the house. I did ask her a few times. And it's only a couple of days. She'll be quite happy as long as we come back.'

Isobel looks up at him. 'If you're sure.'

'I'm sure.'

'Then let's go. Vienna beckons.'

They step outside into the pale-gold light and Isobel stands back and watches her family: Tom loading up the car methodically, her father telling Beatrice something about Viennese music, Beatrice looking up at him searchingly, insatiable questions forming on her small pink lips more quickly than she can ask them. The daylight rises behind the castle and the sea glitters in the distance like a thousand pieces of glass.

Today is the day they will be able to tick Vienna from their list.

Today, as every day, is a day for change.

Acknowledgements

Special thanks go to Charlotte Ledger, who always understands my writing so perfectly. I also want to thank everyone else at Harper*Impulse*, and especially Cherie Chapman for designing such a beautiful cover. Finally, thank you to my amazing family, for everything.